MacCallister
The Eagles Legacy
Dry Gulch Ambush

MacCallister
The Eagles Legacy
Dry Gulch Ambush

William W. Johnstone
with J. A. Johnstone

PINNACLE BOOKS
Kensington Publishing Corp.
www.kensingtonbooks.com

PINNACLE BOOKS are published by

Kensington Publishing Corp.
119 West 40th Street
New York, NY 10018

PUBLISHER'S NOTE
Following the death of William W. Johnstone, the Johnstone family is working with a carefully selected writer to organize and complete Mr. Johnstone's outlines and many unfinished manuscripts to create additional novels in all of his series like The Last Gunfighter, Mountain Man, and Eagles, among others. This novel was inspired by Mr. Johnstone's superb storytelling.

ISBN-13: 978-0-7860-2482-7
ISBN-10: 0-7860-2482-8

First printing: April 2013

10 9 8 7 6 5 4 3 2 1

Printed in the United States of America

Prologue

Argonne Forest, October 3, 1918

The American attack had begun at 5:30 a.m. on September 26, but the results were less than hoped. The Fifth and Third Corps were successful, but the 79th Division failed to capture the town of Montfaucon, and the 28th Division was stopped cold by formidable German resistance. The 91st Division was forced out of the village of Épinonville, and the 37th Division failed in its attempt to advance at d'Argonne. The result was an attack that ground to a halt, and for the next two days the American troops dug in, and waited for orders for the next move.

The entrenched infantrymen became passive participants as the Allied and German artillery continued to exchange fire. As they passed overhead, the shells from the French 75's, and the American 155 heavy guns would make a sound similar to that of an unattached railroad car rolling down a track.

That made it easy to tell the outgoing fire from the incoming fire, because the arming bands on the German 105 howitzer shells would emit a high-pitched, bansheelike whistle.

"Incoming!" someone yelled, though the warning wasn't necessary as everyone could hear the shell come screaming in. The intensity of the whistle would also give some indication as to how far away the shell would be, and Duff Tavish MacCallister, Jr., who had his Springfield '03 rifle disassembled and spread on a sheet of canvas before him, didn't even bother to duck.

The impact was some two hundred yards away, and Tavish, as he was called, heard the heavy thump of the explosion, then a whirring sound of the shrapnel that spread out within the hundred-foot bursting radius of the shell. He was cleaning his rifle, and he picked up the barrel and looked down inside. That was when his platoon leader, Lieutenant Fillion, arrived in an olive drab, open body, Dodge touring car.

Tavish stood up and smiled, saluting the lieutenant when he stepped out of the car.

"Well now, Lieutenant, when did you get so highfalutin' that you rated a car like that?"

"It's not me, Sergeant. It's you. General Pershing wants to speak with you, and he sent his car."

"Wait a minute. The general wants to talk to me?"

"He wants to speak with Sergeant Duff Tavish

MacCallister, Jr., personally, and he emphasized junior. I'm to take you to him."

"All right, sir," Tavish said. "Give me a moment to put my rifle together."

It took but a moment to reassemble the rifle, and then Tavish followed the lieutenant back to the car.

"Sergeant MacCallister, do you know the general?" Lieutenant Fillion asked.

"No, sir. Oh, I mean I recognize him when I see him, but you sure couldn't say that I know him. Do you know why he wants to see me?"

"I don't have the slightest idea," Fillion said. "I thought perhaps you would know."

"I'm afraid not, Lieutenant."

When the car arrived at the Château de Chaumont, Tavish was taken up to the castle. A guard saluted Lieutenant Fillion, who returned the salute.

"Sergeant, would you clear your weapon please?" the guard asked.

Tavish operated the bolt several times until the five .30-caliber rounds had been ejected. He left the bolt open, and the guard nodded, indicating that he could go in.

Inside the castle was a great room that was filled with tables manned by soldiers. In one corner of the room was a field telephone switchboard, and the operator was busily pulling and connecting cords. Attached to the back wall was a large map, marked with pins, and pieces of paper. There were at least four staff officers studying the map, one of whom was General John J. Pershing.

"Wait here, Sergeant," Lieutenant Fillion ordered.

"Yes, sir," Tavish said.

Fillion spoke to a major, who approached a colonel, who was one of the staff officers. The colonel looked back at Tavish, nodded, and then spoke to General Pershing. Pershing nodded, and then approached Sergeant MacCallister and Lieutenant Fillion, with a broad smile spread across his face.

Both Tavish and Lieutenant Fillion came to attention and saluted him.

"At ease, at ease," Pershing said easily, returning the salute, and then offering his hand to Tavish. "Sergeant, would your father be a big, ugly Scotsman who owns a ranch just outside Chugwater, Wyoming, called Sky Meadow?"

Tavish smiled. "I wouldn't call him ugly, General. But he is a big Scotsman who owns Sky Meadow."

"I thought so. The name, Duff Tavish MacCallister, Jr. gave me a hint. Then, when I checked your service file and saw that you had fired the maximum score on the KD range for rifle, I knew it had to be you. I'm a pretty good shot myself. Did you know that?"

"No, sir, though, as a general, I would expect you to be good at just about anything you attempted."

Pershing laughed out loud. "Spoken like a true diplomat. But I'm talking about when I was a lieutenant. I was rated second in pistol, and fifth in rifle, out of all soldiers in the entire U.S. Army. That's pretty good, wouldn't you say?"

"Yes, sir, I would say that's damn g . . . that is, I mean, very good, sir."

Pershing laughed again. "Damn good describes it, I would say."

"Yes, sir."

"I see you brought your rifle with you."

"Yes, sir, but it's cleared, sir," MacCallister said.

"Yes, your bolt is open and I can see that. Come out back with me. Major Purcell, the little demonstration I asked you to arrange a bit earlier. Did you take care of setting things up?"

"Yes, General, I did."

"Good. Gentlemen, I invite you all out back. Sergeant MacCallister is going to put on a display of marksmanship, the likes of which none of you have ever seen. Sergeant MacCallister, are you ready?"

"I beg your pardon, sir, but I'm not sure what this is all about," Tavish said with a puzzled expression on his face.

"I'll tell you what I'm talking about, Sergeant. I'm setting you up," General Pershing said. "I'm going to have you attempt a very difficult shot. And I'm putting pressure on you, by having as big an audience as I can arrange. You see, it is important that you have pressure, even if it is simulated pressure. Because if you miss this shot now, you will have embarrassed yourself, me, your company, and your father."

"My dad?"

"I'll get to that later. In the meantime, if you can make this shot, and Sergeant MacCallister, I sincerely hope that you can make it, then I'm going to have a very special assignment for you—an assignment that could well be the means of ending this war. Are you game to try?"

"Yes, sir," Tavish said.

"I never doubted for a minute. Gentlemen," he said to the officers who were still gathered around. "Let's go out back."

Tavish followed General Pershing and half a dozen of his staff officers outside to the walled-in grounds behind the castle. He looked around once they were there, and saw a table some distance away. Sitting on the table was a wine bottle, and sticking out the top of the wine bottle was a candle. A tiny flame was perched, motionless, on top of the candle.

"I imagine you are wondering about the candle," General Pershing said.

"Yes, sir, I am," Tavish admitted.

"How far away is that candle, Major Purcell?"

"It is exactly two hundred and eighty-seven yards, General," the major replied.

"There's your range, Sergeant. Two hundred and eighty-seven yards. And, because we are inside the walled grounds of the castle, you have no wind to worry about. It should be an easy shot."

"You want me to shoot the bottle from here, General?"

"Heavens no, Sergeant. I want you to extinguish the flame, without harm to the candle or the bottle."

"What the hell?" someone in the group said. "Nobody can do that."

"I don't know, I bet a really good shot could," another said.

"Gentlemen, I am betting that the sergeant can do it," General Pershing said. "And I will personally cover up to twenty-five bets, as long as none of them are over a dollar."

"You've got yourself a bet, General," a colonel said.

"I want some of that, too," another officer said.

"Major Purcell, will you hold the bets, please?" General Pershing asked.

"Yes, sir, General," Purcell answered.

Pershing looked up at Tavish and smiled.

"There you go, Sergeant. There's a little more pressure on you now. If you don't make the shot, you are going to cost me twenty-five dollars. And I don't like losing money."

A few of the officers laughed.

"Are you getting nervous, Sergeant?" General Pershing asked.

"No, sir," Tavish said.

"No? Why not?"

"Because I'll make the shot, General," Tavish said easily, confidently.

"Well, Sergeant, that's a little arrogant, don't you think?" a captain asked, with a derisive tone in his voice.

General Pershing held out his hand. "It isn't arrogance at all, Captain, it's confidence," he said. Then, stepping back, he held his hand out in a sweeping motion. "Sergeant MacCallister, the stage is yours."

"Thank you, General," Tavish said. He took a single round from the ammunition pouch on his web belt, rubbed the point of it against the side of his nose, then put it into the chamber of the rifle, and closed the bolt.

"Don't get nervous now, Sergeant," one of the officers said.

Tavish paid no attention to the kibitzer. Instead, he raised the rifle to his shoulder, leaned his head down against the stock, and set up his sight-picture between the rear and front sights. He rested the nonflickering flame just on top of the front sight, took in a breath, let half of it out, then held it, and slowly began squeezing the trigger.

The rifle boomed, and the recoil rocked the end of the barrel up, but nobody was looking at the rifle. They were looking at the candle flame, which was instantly snuffed.

The crowd cheered and applauded, even those who had bet and lost a dollar.

General Pershing collected the money, and then gave all of it to Lieutenant Fillion. "Lieutenant, you and Sergeant MacCallister are in the same company, are you not?"

"Yes, sir, A company, 1st Battalion, 38th Regiment of the Third Infantry Division."

"I believe the commanding officer of that company is Captain Royal?" Pershing asked.

"Yes, sir."

"Give him this money and tell him to use it to throw a party for his company the next time they are off the line."

"Yes, sir!" Fillion said with a broad smile.

"Sergeant, come with me."

Not only Tavish, but Lieutenant Fillion and Major Purcell, who was General Pershing's adjutant, started with him as well.

"No, gentlemen," Pershing said, holding out his hand to stop them. "I want to speak to the sergeant alone."

Tavish went back into the castle with Pershing, through the great room, and to a smaller room off the great room. There, Pershing poured two glasses of wine and handed one glass to Tavish. "To fallen comrades," he said, holding his glass out, inviting a toast.

"To fallen comrades," Tavish repeated.

"Before I tell you what task I have in mind, I want to talk to you a bit about your father . . . about my personal encounter with him, and also what I learned about him from Colonel Gibbon, who was once my commanding officer. It might be a rather long story, if you have the patience to hear me out."

"General, I'll stay here as long as it takes, and feel honored to do so," Tavish replied.

Pershing opened a silver cigarette case, offered one to Tavish, and when he declined, lit one for himself before he continued.

"It all began in Chugwater, Wyoming, in 1888."

Chapter One

Chugwater, Wyoming, July 4, 1888

There was a banner that stretched all the way across First Street from Bob Guthrie's Lumber Supply to Fred Matthews' Warehouse. The banner read:

HAPPY 112TH BIRTHDAY
TO THE UNITED STATES OF AMERICA
FROM THE PEOPLE OF CHUGWATER, WYOMING

The entire town was turned out for the Independence Day celebration, with First Street turned into a midway of sorts. On each side of the street, the ladies from town and from the surrounding farms and ranches were manning booths where they sold everything from home-canned tomatoes, to baked goods, to quilts. A traveling medicine man had set up his operation at the far end of the street and the barker was doing a brisk business.

The most important event of the day, however,

was the big shooting contest, and after two hours of participation, the field had been narrowed down to four people: Elmer Gleason, Biff Johnson, a visiting U.S. Army lieutenant named John Pershing, and Duff MacCallister.

Elmer Gleason was Duff's ranch foreman. Biff Johnson, who was one of Duff's closest friends, owned Fiddler's Green Saloon. Biff, who had served with Lieutenant Pershing during the Apache campaigns in New Mexico and Arizona, was well aware of the young officer's marksmanship, and had invited him to participate in the shooting match. The competition among the four men, though spirited, was friendly.

For several minutes, as bets were made and covered, the four shooters matched each other shot for shot, with no apparent separation between them.

Rarely had such shooting been seen anywhere, and as word spread through the town of the amazing accuracy shown by the four shooters, the ladies who were manning the booths, and then even the medicine show barker, closed down their own operations so they could witness the magnificent marksmanship that was on display here today.

Each of the shooters had their own supporters, and Duff's biggest supporter was Meagan Parker, owner of the Ladies' Emporium, a dress shop which was next door to Fiddler's Green.

Finally the judges conferred, and then decided to move the target farther away. They did that, and the four men stayed neck and neck until they were shooting from two hundred yards. At the two hundred yard mark, Biff Johnson fell out of the contest, one of his bullets striking three-fourths of the way in, and one-fourth of the way out of the bull's-eye.

There were no other dropouts until the three hundred yard range, when Elmer dropped out. Now, only Duff and Lieutenant Pershing remained.

"We're out of targets. What are we going to do now?"

"Light a candle," Duff suggested. "We'll use that as the target." A candle was lit, and Lieutenant Pershing fired first. The flame flickered at the pass of the bullet, but didn't go out.

"Hit," one of the judges said, observing the candle through a pair of field glasses.

"T'was nae a hit," Duff said.

"Sure it was," the judge said. "I saw the flame flicker."

"T'was but the wind of the passing bullet, t'was nae a hit. If it had been a hit, the candle would have gone out."

Pershing laughed. "There is no way you are going to snuff a candle from three hundred yards. Not unless you hit the candle. And we aren't shooting at the candle, we're shooting at the flame."

"I can do it," Duff said, matter-of-factly.

"If you can put the flame out from here, Mr. MacCallister, I'll hold that you're a better man than I am," Pershing said.

"I tell you what," Duff said. "If I can nae snuff the

candle with this shot, I'll be declarin' you the winner. If I snuff it, I'm the winner."

"You don't have to that, Mr. MacCallister," Pershing said. "You're putting it all on the line with one shot."

"Aye, but there's other things to do today than stand here shooting until nightfall. And as good as you are, 'tis likely to come down to that."

"I'll say there's other things to do, today," Meagan said. "You'll not be forgetting there's a dance tonight, Duff MacCallister."

"Sure 'n how would I be forgettin' the dance, now, when I'll be takin' the prettiest lady in Laramie County, aye, and in the whole territory of Wyoming."

Shortly after Duff MacCallister had arrived in Chugwater, eight men had come to kill him, and before it was over, all eight were lying dead in the street. Duff hadn't done it without help.

A man, who was on the roof of the Ladies' Emporium with a bead on Duff, was shot by Biff Johnson. Fred Matthews had tossed Duff a loaded revolver just in time, and Meagan Parker risked her own life to hold up a mirror that showed Duff where two men were lying in wait for him.

Meagan and Duff had maintained a "special" relationship ever since.

"Now, you're saying you are going to snuff the flame, without hitting the candle, is that right?" Pershing asked.

"Aye."

"All right, Mr. MacCallister," Pershing agreed. "If you can do that, you sure as hell deserve to win."

A buzz of excitement passed through the crowd as news of the arrangement moved quickly from mouth to mouth. The contest was to end, right here and right now, on one all-or-nothing shot.

All the contestants had been using the same rifle to ensure fairness. That rifle, a 45- caliber Whitworth, was furnished by the marksmanship committee. The Whitworth had a long, heavy, octagon-shaped barrel of the type favored by Berdan's Sharpshooters during the Civil War. It was especially designed for accuracy.

Preparing for the shot, Duff poured in the powder, and then tapped a paper wad down to seal in the powder. Next, he used a bullet starter, which was a pistonlike arrangement that helped to seat the bullet, which was slightly larger than the diameter of the lands, but not quite as large as the diameter of the grooves. The end of the piston was shaped to fit the nose of the bullet. With a smart blow from the palm of his hand, Duff drove the bullet down into the barrel, engaging it in the rifling. He then used a ramrod to push the bullet down until it was properly seated.

With the loading ritual completed, Duff picked up a little dirt from the street and dropped it, watching the drift of the dust. Next, he rubbed a little dust on the site bead at the end of the rifle barrel. Then, using the sling to help him hold the rifle steady, he aimed at the tiny, flickering flame three hundred yards away.

"Now, don't be getting all nervous," Pershing teased, just as Duff started to aim. A few laughed.

"'Tis thankin' you I am for that kind word of encouragement," Duff replied with a smile.

Duff aimed again. He took a deep breath, let half of it out, and slowly began to squeeze the trigger.

The rifle boomed and rocked back against his shoulder. A great billow of gun smoke obscured his vision of the target for a moment, but he didn't have to see it. The reaction of the crowd told him what had happened, as they cheered and applauded his shot. When the smoke drifted away he saw that the candle was still standing, but the flame had been extinguished.

The crowd rushed toward Duff to congratulate him, Lieutenant Pershing being the first one to do so.

"Folks," Biff said. "I can't afford a beer for ever' one, but I will stand a free beer to all the lads who took part in this shootin' contest. Come on over to Fiddler's Green."

"Good man, Biff," one of the shooters who had dropped out much earlier said.

"Tell me, why do you call this place Fiddler's Green?" someone asked Biff, as all the shooters stood at the bar drinking their free beer.

"I call it Fiddler's Green because I'm a retired

first sergeant. I served with the lieutenant here down in Arizona, when we were chasing Apache."

"He did more than serve with me," Lieutenant Pershing said. "Every young officer needs a noncommissioned officer who'll take him under the wing and teach him things he didn't learn at the Point. Sergeant Johnson did that for me."

"It was my pleasure, Lieutenant. Before I was with General Cook, I was with General Custer and the Seventh Cavalry," Biff replied.

"How lucky you are to have left before his fateful battle," one of the shooters who had dropped out earlier said.

"Oh, but I didn't leave. I went on that last scout with him."

"I don't understand. How is it, then, that you weren't killed?"

"I wasn't killed because I was in D troop with Benteen. We came up to save Reno, but we were too late to help Custer."

"Now you can see why he calls this place Fiddler's Green," Lieutenant Pershing said.

"No, I don't see at all."

"You want to tell this young man who wouldn't know 'Stable Call' from 'Mess Call,' Lieutenant?" Biff invited.

"I would be glad to," Pershing said. "It's something all cavalrymen believe. We believe that anyone who has ever heard the bugle call "Boots and Saddles" will, when they die, go to a cool, shady place by a stream of sweet water. There, they will see all the other cavalrymen who have gone before them, and they will greet those who come after them as they await the final judgment. That place is called Fiddler's Green."

"Do you really believe that?"

"Why not?" Pershing replied. "If heaven is whatever you want it to be, who is to say that cavalrymen wouldn't want to be with their own kind?"

"Biff," Duff said. "Would ye be for settin' up all these gentleman shooters with another round on me?"

"With pleasure," Biff replied as the shooters responded in gratitude.

Next door to the saloon, in her apartment over the Ladies' Emporium, Meagan Parker was getting ready for the dance that evening. Meagan not only owned the Ladies' Emporium, she actually designed and made many of the dresses that she sold there, and she had designed and made the dress she would be wearing tonight. It had a very low neckline, no sleeves, and a tight, uplifting bodice. It was a dress that would show off her figure to perfection. She picked it up, and then held it in front of her as she looked in the mirror. She smiled at the image.

"Mr. Duff Tavish MacCallister, are you ready for Meagan?—because she's ready for you," she said. Laying the dress down, she went back to fill the tub for her bath.

* * *

The dance was being held in the ballroom of the Dunn Hotel. The hotel was on the corner of Bowie Avenue and First Street. The Ladies Garden Club had turned the ballroom into a showplace of patriotism, stringing red, white, and blue bunting all about, and displaying lithographs of Washington, Adams, Jefferson, and Lincoln on the walls.

All was in readiness for the dance.

Chapter Two

Meagan arrived before Duff and, after receiving compliments from the other women about her dress, as well as admiring glances from the men, she walked over to one side to keep an eye open for Duff. She didn't have to wait long.

Duff arrived within a few minutes after Meagan and he was in his kilt. For most men, in fact, for just about any other man Meagan knew, wearing such a get-up would have elicited a great deal of derisive laughter. But Duff towered over every other man there, not only in his height, but in his raw power, broad shoulders, powerful arms, and muscular legs, shown off by what he was wearing.

While in Scotland, Duff had been a captain of the Black Watch Regiment. Because of that he had a complete Black Watch uniform, which consisted of a Glengarry hat, with the cap-badge of the Black Watch, Saltire, the Lion Rampant and the Crown with the motto *Nemo Me Impune Lacessit* (No one provokes me with impunity), a kilt of blue-and-green tartan, black waistcoat, an embossed leather sporran which he wore around his waist, knee-high stockings, and the *sgian dubh*, or ceremonial knife, which he wore tucked into the right kilt stocking, with only the pommel visible. During his time with the Black Watch Regiment, he had been awarded the Victoria Cross, Great Britain's highest award for bravery, which was awarded him for his intrepidity, above and beyond the call of duty during the battle of Tel-el-Kebir in Egypt.

Duff was also carrying his bagpipes, having been asked by Biff Johnson to bring them. Biff's wife was Scottish, and she had a fondness for the pipes.

Duff and Meagan saw each other at about the same time and, with a big smile, Duff came toward her.

"Sure m'girl, an 'tis a vision of loveliness ye be, like the beauty of a field that is arrayed in the rainbow colors of sparkling dew."

Meagan laughed. "I swear, Duff, if ever the needle breaks on my sewing machine, I'll call upon your tongue, for it can weave magic with your words."

Lieutenant Pershing, who was in his full dress uniform, came up to Duff and Meagan.

"I'm glad to see that I'm not the only one in uniform, though I must say, Duff, yours is a bit more grand than my own." Pershing pointed toward the Victoria Cross. "And with a most impressive decoration," he added.

"Thank you."

Pershing smiled at Meagan. "And I do hope, Miss, that you will take pity on a lonely soldier, far from home, and save at least one place on your hop card for me tonight."

"Hop card?" Meagan asked with a puzzled expression on her face.

"Forgive me, that is how we referred to them at the Academy. I mean, of course, your dance card."

Meagan looked at Duff and smiled. "Of course, I will save a dance for you," she said.

Pershing made a slight bow with his head, then walked away.

"I must say, lass, it seemed to me as if you were quick to oblige the leftenant's request."

"Why not?" Meagan replied. "It can't do harm to let you know that you aren't the only rooster in the chicken house."

Duff laughed out loud.

"Ladies and gents!" someone shouted, and looking toward the sound, they saw R.W. Guthrie. Guthrie was mayor of Chugwater, and the master of ceremonies for the ball.

Conversations ended as everyone looked toward the mayor.

"I want to say a few words," Guthrie began.

"Oh, for heaven's sake, Mayor, you was just elected last year. You got three more years yet, don't go politickin' on us now," someone shouted, and the others laughed.

"No politicking," Guthrie replied with a good natured smile. "All I want to say is welcome to our Fourth of July dance. Now, grab your partners, and let the dancin' commence!"

The music began then and the caller started to shout. The floor became a swirl of color as the dancers responded to the caller's commands, the brightly colored dresses with the skirts whirling out, the jewels in the women's hair, at their necks, or on their bodices, sparkling in the light.

In between the calls, the fiddler worked the bow up and down the fiddle, bending over, kicking out one leg, then the other as he played, his movements as entertaining as the music itself. Then, when his riff was over, the caller would step up again.

After a few more dances, Guthrie came over to ask Duff if he would play the pipes.

"You're sure 'tis not against the wishes of the band?"

Guthrie smiled. "There ain't none of 'em ever heard the pipes and they're curious about it."

Duff chuckled. "I've found that love of the pipes is an acquired taste. There are some, even my friend Elmer, that find no joy in the pipes."

"But there's them that do," Elmer said, having overheard the conversation. "So don't you go deprivin' them none because of me."

"You did bring your pipes," Guthrie said. "I assume that means you are willing to play them."

"Ha!" Meagan said. "I'd like to see someone try to stop him."

Duff smiled. "Ye've talked me into it. I'll play."

"What are you going to play? I'll let the folks know."

"Duff, please," Meagan said. She put her hand on his arm. "'The Skye Boat Song.'"

Meagan knew what nobody else at the dance knew. The woman Duff was to have married back in Scotland was named after this song. Her name was Skye McGregor. It was because Duff had killed the men who killed Skye, that he was forced to leave Scotland.

Duff nodded, and then picking up his pipes got ready as Guthrie made the announcement to all who were present.

"Ladies and gents, Mr. Duff MacCallister has agreed to play a tune for us on his bagpipes."

"The song Mr. MacCallister has chosen, is a song of Scotland, called 'The Skye Boat Song.' Duff, the platform is yours," Fred said.

There was a scattering of applause as Duff moved up onto the platform. He inflated his bag, and there was a tone from the drone and chanter as Duff began to play.

After he finished, several came up to thank him for playing. Meagan, especially, was moved.

"Thank you for playing that song, Duff," Meagan said. "I know it is difficult for you, but you play so beautifully, and with such feeling. I know that you think about her when you play it."

"Meagan, I'm sorry if . . ." Duff started.

"Don't apologize for still being in love with Skye," she said. "It is one of the things that make you so wonderful in my eyes," Meagan said.

"Ladies and gents, form your squares!" the caller shouted, and once again the ballroom was filled with happy dancers.

When the dance broke up just after midnight, Duff, leading his horse, walked Meagan back up First Street to her home, which was located on the second floor above her business.

"I have a bottle of Scotch in my apartment, if you would like a drink before your long ride out to your ranch," Meagan invited.

Meagan led the way up the outside stairs, and then unlocked the door to her apartment. Just inside the door was a lantern and she lit it, filling the room with a golden bubble of light. She poured a glass of Scotch for Duff, and a glass of wine for herself.

Duff held out the glass. "Here's tae the heath, the hill and the heather, the bonnet, the plaid, the kilt and the feather."

Meagan touched the wineglass to his whiskey. "To the copper penny: May it soon grow into a dime and then swell into many."

"Ah, I'll make a Scotsman out of you yet," Duff said as they drank to their toasts.

"How are my cattle doing?" Meagan asked.

She had recently invested some money in the ranch, so was now half owner of the outstanding herd of Black Angus cattle that populated the fields of Sky Meadow.

"My cattle are growing fat, while yours are growing thin," Duff replied.

"How do you know which cattle are mine and which are yours?"

"Because mine are fat and yours are thin," Duff said, laughing.

"You may be Scottish instead of Irish, but you do have a bit of the blarney in you," Meagan said.

"I've recently made a deal with the United States Army to furnish them with two thousand head of cattle for beef. We'll be getting forty dollars a head, so you're about to make forty thousand dollars," Duff said.

"Oh, my!" Meagan said. "Why am I wasting time making dresses? I should be a full-time rancher."

"And where, I ask you, would you be for getting a frock as lovely as the one you are wearing tonight? And 'tis nae just you; think of the foine ladies of this town who would have no place to go to buy dresses for to please their husbands."

"Ha! Do you think ladies dress only to please their husbands?" Meagan asked.

"And others," Duff added, the expression on his face giving indication of how pleased he was with what Meagan was wearing.

They talked awhile longer, speaking of cattle and

business, sharing stories from their past. Then Duff put down his glass.

"I suppose I'd best get back to the ranch," he said, starting toward the door. She went with him, and just before he left, he put his finger to her chin then turned her face toward his so that they were but a breath apart. "Take care, Meagan, that ye dinnae put yourself in danger. I dinnae ken what I would do if something should happen to ye."

"I am always careful," she said.

Still holding his finger under her chin, Duff leaned forward, closing the distance between them. He kissed her, not hard and demanding, but as soft as the brush of a butterfly's wing.

When the kiss ended, Meagan reached up to touch her own lips, and she held her fingers there for a long moment. She knew that the kiss had sealed no bargain, nor by it, had he made any promise to her. It was what it was—a light, meaningless kiss.

No, it wasn't meaningless. She had very strong feelings for Duff, and she knew that he had strong feelings for her. She knew, too, that it wasn't because his heart was too full of Skye. He told her that he had accepted her death, was ready to get on with his life, and she believed him. But what he wasn't ready to do was love another woman, then lose her as he had lost Skye. Meagan knew that was what he meant when he said, "*Take care, Meagan, that ye dinnae put yourself in danger. I dinnae ken what I would do if something should happen to ye.*"

With a smile and a nod, Duff walked down the steps, mounted his horse, and rode away. Meagan stayed on her balcony watching him until he disappeared in the dark. Overhead a meteor streaked through the night sky.

Chapter Three

Wind River Indian Reservation, Wyoming

Yellow Hawk, a Shoshone, began thinking of the ceremony seven days before he went into the *sintkala waksu,* the sweat lodge, paying attention to his surroundings, his feelings, and dreams. Early in the morning of the day he was to enter, he blackened his face with charcoal in preparation and then selected the sacred rocks that would be used.

Because he wanted the sweat lodge to be very hot—the better to bring about the vision he was seeking—he used many rocks. Once all the rocks were gathered and the fire roaring, it was time for the ceremony to begin. Stepping inside, Yellow Hawk dropped the flap over the lodge opening, and then sprinkled medicines on the rocks. The lodge was very dark and quiet, and Yellow Hawk could see only the glowing red-orange stones within the circle.

This was the "First Endurance," and Yellow Hawk faced to the east.

"I call upon the *Huntka*, the god of the east, to give me a vision," he said aloud, though he was the only one in the sweat lodge.

For the "Second Endurance," Yellow Hawk, who was now sweating profusely, faced south. "I call upon the *wanagi yata*, the place of souls, to give me a vision."

For the "Third Endurance," Yellow Hawk faced west and began smoking his pipe, as he gazed into the red glow of the rocks. "I call upon the *wakina*, the thunder, to give me a vision."

For the "Fourth Endurance," Yellow Hawk faced north. "I call upon *katiyimo*, the enchanted mesa, and *ptesan-wi*, White Buffalo Woman, to give me the vision I seek," he said aloud, his voice sounding strange to him inside the dark, steam-filled lodge.

Then the vision came, and when Yellow Hawk stepped out of the sweat lodge, his body, mind, and spirit cleansed, he knew what he would do.

Yellow Hawk informed the elders that he would speak at the council fire that night, and the elders gave him permission. Because Yellow Hawk was young, curiosity as to what he might say was high, and nearly every young man of the village gathered around the council fire that night to hear what he would say.

After the pipe was smoked, Standing Bear, who

was the chief of the elders, rose to speak to those who had gathered.

"When we hold a council fire, all are invited to attend, but most do not come," Standing Bear said. "Tonight I see many here, and I see many of our young men. I think this is because we, the elders, have told Yellow Hawk that he may speak and I think that has filled the young people with interest to see what he will say."

Standing Bear turned to Yellow Hawk. "You may speak," he invited.

Yellow Hawk stood, and then addressed the assembled people of the village.

"I do not need the permission of Standing Bear to speak," he said. "I did not ask the elders for permission to speak. I told them that I was going to speak. I can do this, because I am Yellow Hawk."

There was a murmuring reaction from those who had come to the council, for the young did not speak to the old in such a manner. But his insolence did get the attention of all.

"In the sweat lodge I was there for all four endurances. At the end of the Fourth Endurance, White Buffalo Woman appeared before me."

There were gasps from those who were gathered around the fire, for White Buffalo Woman was the most sacred of all their totems, and if Yellow Hawk received a vision from her, they wanted to hear.

"And what did White Buffalo Woman tell you?" one of the elders asked.

"She said I should call upon those who are brave,

and those who want to win honor for themselves to follow me on a path of war."

"War?" one of the elders asked. "There is no war now! And that is as it should be, for war causes our wickiups to be empty and our women to cry."

"You are old and frightened," Yellow Hawk said with a tone of derision. He turned to others. "I am leaving this reservation. Those who are brave of heart, come to me tomorrow at the place of the Weeping Rocks." Weeping Rocks referred to a nearby waterfall.

"Do not do this, Yellow Hawk!" the chief of the elders shouted as Yellow Hawk left the council. "You will do nothing but bring sorrow on the rest of us."

"All who are cowards and who have fear in their hearts can stay here and hide behind the skirts of this woman," Yellow Hawk said pointing derisively toward the elder who had called out to him. "All who are not cowards, but who have courage, follow me, for I will lead you to glory!"

Mounting his horse, he rode away.

Sky Meadow Ranch

Though the first structure Duff had built was little more than a cabin, he now occupied a house that was as fine as any that could be found anywhere on the Wyoming range. Made of debarked logs fitted together, then chinked with mortar, it was sixty feet wide and forty feet deep, with a porch that stretched all the way across the front.

Sky Meadow was situated between Bear and

Little Bear creeks, both streams year-round sources of good water, and in an area where good water was scarce, the creeks were worth as much as the gold mine that was on the extreme western end of his property. The view from Duff's front porch displayed the rich green of gently rolling pastureland down to Bear Creek, which was a meandering ribbon of silver, sparkling in the mid-afternoon sun.

Beyond the creek stood a range of mountains which not only made for beautiful scenery, but also tempered the winter winds, and throughout the spring and summer, sent down streams of water to make the grass grow green.

Since Duff MacCallister had immigrated to America from Scotland, he had built Sky Meadow into one of the most productive ranches in all of Wyoming by taking a chance on introducing Black Angus cattle, the first rancher in the West to do so.

Duff wasn't new to cattle ranching; he had owned a Black Angus cattle ranch in Scotland. There, however, it wasn't called a ranch, it was called a farm. And whereas Sky Meadow was now some 40,000 acres, his operation in Scotland was only 300 acres. Duff was a Highlander, meaning that he was from the Highlands of Scotland, but compared to the magnificent mountains in the American West, the Highlands were but hills.

At the moment Duff was standing on his front porch enjoying the view. His foreman, Elmer Gleason, was sitting on the top level of the steps that led up to the porch. Elmer was wiry and raw boned with a full head of white hair and neatly trimmed beard. He leaned over to expectorate a quid of tobacco before he spoke.

"I reckon you seen me with Vi, last night," Elmer said. Vi was Violet Winslow, the attractive widow who owned a business establishment called Vi's Pies.

"Aye, I saw you. T'was a foine-looking pair, you made."

"I reckon so," Elmer said. "But I'm a' feared she's expectin' more of me than I'm wantin' to give. Much like Miss Meagan is with you, I'd wager."

"Meagan and I are just very good friends," Duff said.

"Yeah, that's just what I was thinkin'," Elmer said as he carved off a little more tobacco and stuck it in his mouth. "So, tell me, Duff, when is it we're goin' to be a'takin' them beeves to the Yankee soldier boys."

Elmer, who had fought for the South during the Civil War, continued to call the Civil War, the "War of Yankee Aggression," and to this day referred to the army as "Yankee soldiers."

"About a week, I would say. As quickly as we can get two thousand head of cattle rounded up and ready to drive," Duff said. "Two thousand head at forty dollars a head. I tell you the truth, Elmer, if I don't sell another cow, this contract alone will make for a very profitable year."

"I reckon it will at that. Have you figured out our route, yet?"

"Yes, we'll follow the Chugwater to the Laramie

River, then the Laramie River to the Platte. I figure we will be on the trail for six, maybe seven days."

"Good idea following the rivers like that," Elmer said. "Cows that have plenty to eat and drink don't get too discombobulated. And cows that don't get discombobulated is a lot easier to handle."

Duff chuckled. "Aye, we'll nae be wantin' to deal with discombobulated cows now, will we?"

When Duff came to take possession of his land the first time, he was told stories of a ghost that inhabited the old abandoned and played-out mine that was on his property. When he examined his mine, he found that the ghost who had kept others frightened away wasn't a ghost, and he also found that the mine was anything but played out. The ghost was Elmer, who was "protecting" his stake in the mine. At the time, Elmer was more wild than civilized, and he had been living on bugs and rabbits when he could catch them, and such wild plants as could be eaten.

By rights and deed, the mine belonged to Duff, but he wound up taking Elmer in as a full partner in the operation of the mine, and that move was immediately vindicated when shortly thereafter, Elmer saved Duff's life.

Duff had returned home to find an Angus Somerled waiting for him with a loaded pistol. Somerled, an old enemy, had come all the way from Scotland to kill him.

"Somerled," Duff said.

"Ye've been a hard man to put down, Duff Tavish MacCallister, but the job is done now."

Duff said nothing.

"Here now, lad, and has the cat got your tongue?"

"I didn't expect to see you," Duff said.

"Nae, I dinnae think you would. Would you be tellin' me where I might find my deputy?"

"Malcolm is dead."

"Aye, I thought as much. Killed him, did ye?"

"Aye—it seemed to be the thing to do."

"There is an old adage, if you want something done right, do it yourself. I should have come after you a long time ago, instead of getting my sons and my deputies killed."

"That night on Donuum Road, I was coming to give myself up," Duff said. "None of this need have happened. Your sons would still be alive, Skye would still be alive. But you were too blinded by hate."

He cocked the pistol and Duff steeled himself.

Suddenly the room filled with the roar of a gunshot—but it wasn't Somerled's pistol. It was a shotgun in the hands of Elmer Gleason. Gleason had shot him through the window, and the double load of twelve-gauge shot knocked Somerled half way across the room.

"Are you all right, Mr. MacCallister?" Gleason shouted through the open window. Smoke was still curling up from the two barrels.

"Aye, I'm fine," Duff said. "My gratitude to ye, Mr. Gleason."

Gleason came around to the front of the cabin and stepped in through the front door.

"Seein' as how I saved your life, don't you think me 'n' you might start callin' each other by our Christian names?"

"Aye, Elmer. Your point is well taken."

"Sorry 'bout tellin' you he was your friend. But that's what he told me, and I believed him."

"And yet, you were waiting outside the window with a loaded shotgun."

"Yes, sir. Well, considerin' that the fella you went to meet in Chugwater was from Scotland, and wasn't your friend, I just got to figurin' maybe I ought to stand by, just in case."

"Aye. I'm glad you did."

Gleason leaned the shotgun against the wall and looked at the blood that was on the floor of the cabin.

"I reckon I'd better get this mess cleaned up for you," he said.

"Elmer, I'm sure you don't realize it, but you just did," Duff said.[1]

The two men became friends after that, and, over the few years that Duff had been in America, he was given occasional glimpses into Elmer's mysterious past. Elmer had ridden with Quantrill during the war, and even let it slip that he had once followed the outlaw trail with Jesse and Frank James.

---

1. *MacCallister, the Eagles Legacy*

Although Elmer had never told him the full story of his life, and seldom released more than a bit of information at one telling, over time Duff was able to learn a great deal about him. He knew that Elmer had been to China as a crewman on a clipper ship, and in that, they shared somewhat of a kinship, for Duff had worked his way to America as an able-bodied sailor aboard the sailing ship *Hiawatha.*

Elmer had lived for two years with the Indians, married to a Shoshone woman who died while giving birth to their son. Elmer didn't know where his son, who would be nineteen years old, was now. He had left him with his wife's sister, and hadn't seen the boy since the day he was born. He had blamed the baby for killing his mother, though he knew that wasn't fair. He had left the child unnamed, and uncared for. That was something that Elmer regretted having done.

Because of the gold mine, Elmer had money now, more money than he had ever had in his life. He could leave Wyoming and go to San Francisco to live out the rest of his life in ease and comfort, but he had no desire to do so.

"I got a roof over my head, a good friend, and all the terbaccy I can chew," Elmer said. "Why would I be a' wantin' to go anywhere else?"

"Why indeed?" Duff had responded.

Chapter Four

Fort Laramie

First Lieutenant Clayton Scott of the Fifth Cavalry, United States Army, stood at the mirror as he worked up lather in his shaving cup before using the brush to apply it to his face. He was wearing blue trousers with a yellow stripe that was intersected by the yellow galluses that hung in a loop by each side. Scott's wife, Sue, was in the bedroom behind him, getting dressed for an evening at the commanding officer's quarters. There, they would socialize with the other post officers and their wives.

"Have you heard anything back from your father?" Scott asked. "Has he answered my request?"

"No, I've not heard," Sue said.

"Did you write to him, like I asked?"

"Yes."

"I don't understand," Scott said. "Your father is a general. He could help me if he wanted to. There is no reason why he can't bring us to Washington and put me on his personal staff."

"We've talked about this before, Clayton," Sue said. "You know Daddy doesn't want to do that. It would look as if he were playing favorites to have his son-in-law on his staff."

Scott shaved away the lather, leaving a small moustache in place.

"He wouldn't have to put me on his staff. All he would have to do is bring me to Washington. I'll never get promoted as long as I'm out here in this godforsaken wilderness. The days of real military opportunity, when we were fighting Indians, is over. We serve no purpose here now, and an officer without purpose is an officer without hope of promotion."

"Daddy says you're getting good experience out here," Sue said. "You are getting experience that the officers back in Washington aren't getting. He says that if we get into another war, there will be a need for line officers."

"What war? It'll be a hundred years before we get into another war."

Scott put on his tunic, then turned and primped in front of the mirror until he was certain everything was just right.

"Are you ready?" he asked. "I hate arriving last, where everyone stares at you."

"I'm ready," Sue said.

"You're wearing that dress?" Scott asked.

"Yes, why not? It's a beautiful dress. My sister gave it to me for my birthday, don't you remember?"

"Why aren't you wearing the dress I bought for you?"

"I told you, I will wear it as soon as some alterations are made."

"Alterations? What kind of alterations?"

"It's—a little low cut for my tastes. It shows too much of my bosom."

"Nonsense. It doesn't hurt if you show a little of your titties to the right people. Colonel Gibbon for example."

"What?" Sue gasped. "For heaven's sake, Clay, Colonel Gibbon is a happily married man! And Kathleen Gibbon is my friend!"

"A lieutenant's wife can be friendly with a colonel's wife, but she can't be friends. On the other hand, you can put the colonel in a good mood, if you know what I mean, and it might pay off for me when the colonel does his Officer Efficiency Reports."

"Clay, I can't believe what I'm hearing. You actually want me to flirt with Colonel Gibbon?"

"Come on, Sue, it's not like you don't know how to do it. You think I haven't seen the way you flaunt yourself in front of Jason Holbrook?"

"You are just being silly. You know Lieutenant Holbrook has eyes only for Mary Meacham. Why on earth would he be interested in a married woman?"

"Why indeed? Now put on the other dress like I

told you, and make certain that Colonel Gibbon gets an eyeful tonight."

"Clay, please . . ."

Scott pulled his hand back as if to hit her, but he withheld the blow.

"Do it!" he demanded.

Fifteen minutes later, now in a very low-cut dress which made her feel uncomfortable, Sue walked with her husband the hundred yards that separated their quarters from a large white building, called by everyone "Old Bedlam." Old Bedlam was not only the post headquarters, it was also the home of Colonel John Gibbon. A private who was walking guard, halted, and brought his rifle up to present arms in salute.

Scott waited until he was even with the sentinel before he returned the salute, and by so doing required the young soldier to hold the weapon in an uncomfortable position longer than necessary. Scott giggled as they passed him by.

"Why did you do that?" Sue asked.

"Why did I do what?"

"Why did you wait so long before returning the salute? You made that poor soldier stand in an uncomfortable position for longer than was necessary."

"He is an enlisted man, Sue. Enlisted men are the lowest form of life on the planet. Why should I care whether or not he is uncomfortable? I do such things to remind the enlisted men of the differences in our station."

"Daddy would never do such a thing to an enlisted man."

"No, your father does such things with junior officers," Scott replied. "Even to his own son-in-law."

Colonel Gibbon's wife greeted them as they came into the house.

"Sue," Kathleen Gibbon said. "You look absolutely beautiful, tonight."

"As do you, Mrs. Gibbon."

"Please, come in. The post singers will be here shortly, to entertain us. Then we'll enjoy a good dinner."

As they went on into the house, they were greeted by some of the other officers, and by Colonel Gibbon.

"Lieutenant Scott, I believe you know Lieutenant Pershing," Gibbon said. "He is on temporary duty with us, down from Fort Assiniboine."

"Yes, we were classmates at the Academy," Scott said. "Hello, John."

"Clay," Pershing replied. He smiled at Sue. "And, Mrs. Scott, please give your father my kindest regards next time you write to him."

"I certainly shall, Lieutenant," Sue replied.

"I understand that you are serving with the colored soldiers," Scott said with a smirk.

"The Tenth Cavalry, yes, they are called buffalo soldiers," Pershing replied.

"It is my understanding that an officer can refuse

an assignment to serve with colored soldiers, if they want to."

"Why would I want to? The buffalo soldiers are very good soldiers, as fine as any I've ever served with."

"Yes, I'm sure they are," Scott said sarcastically, lifting an eyebrow, and tilting his head. "But I think you made a big, big mistake, and your career is at a dead end because of that assignment. Mark my words, no one will ever hear of John J. Pershing."

"I'm serving for the honor of serving my country, Clay, not for any hope of glory or fame."

Scott applauded slowly and quietly in a deliberately false fashion. "How very—noble—of you, John. Or, shall I call you Black Jack?"

"Clay, must you be so cynical?" Sue asked.

Scott broke into an easy smile, and then stuck his hand out toward Pershing. "I'm just teasing. Why, Pershing and I are old friends. We even did a couple of punishment walks together, right, John?"

"Just because one day we replaced the sugar with salt in all the sugar bowls in the faculty mess," Pershing replied. "Clearly, the faculty had no sense of humor."

Scott and Pershing laughed, and the earlier, strained, conversation was forgotten.

"Mrs. Scott, what do you hear from General Winfield? He is getting along well, I take it?" Colonel Gibbon asked.

"Yes, thank you. Both he and my mother are doing well," Sue answered.

"He is a fine man, as fine an officer as I ever had the privilege of serving under," Gibbon said.

"You served with General Winfield, sir?" a newly minted second lieutenant asked.

"I did indeed. Gentlemen, let me tell you about General Winfield," Gibbon said to the other officers. "When I was a fresh out of West Point shavetail lieutenant, this young lady's father, Major General Nathan Austin Winfield, was then Lieutenant Colonel Winfield. He was my commanding officer when we fought the battle of Sailor's Creek.

"General Winfield was brilliant. He succeeded in collapsing the Confederate line, capturing around 3,400 men and routing the rest. Among the prisoners were 6 Confederate generals including their commander, General Richard Ewell.

"But we didn't stop there. No, sir, we continued on, and trapping the Confederates as they were trying to cross the bridge, we attacked at dusk, steadily driving the Confederates back until we took the bridge. Within a month, Lee surrendered at Appomattox, and there are historians who said the battle of Sailor's Creek was the one that finally broke the back of the Confederacy."

"I believe Tom Custer was awarded one of his two Medals of Honor there, was he not?" Pershing asked.

"Yes. I saw the action that merited the award. It was during a charge made by our brigade at Sailor's Creek, Virginia, against General Ewell's Corps. Having crossed the line of temporary works in the flank road, we were confronted by a supporting line. It was from the second line that Tom Custer single-handedly grabbed the enemy's colors. As he approached the colors, he received a shot in the face which knocked him back on his horse, but in a moment he was upright in his saddle. He shot the enemy color bearer, and as he was falling, Captain Custer wrenched the standard from his grasp and bore it away in triumph."

"And you saw that, sir?" Pershing asked, impressed by the story.

"I did, indeed. And now the noble captain, who fell with his brother at Little Big Horn, lies buried at Fort Leavenworth," Gibbon said.

There was a moment of silence, then the colonel's orderly spoke up. "Colonel, the post singers are here, sir."

"Oh then, by all means, show them in," Gibbon said.

Four soldiers with great voices sang a medley, ending with "I'll Take You Home Again, Kathleen."

Because that was Kathleen's name, and because she had come to America from Ireland when she was young, the song was particularly moving to her, and Sue noticed her wipe a tear away.

After the music, the officers and their wives gathered around the table for a dinner of ham and fried potatoes.

"Gentlemen, I'm sorry I can't offer you steak," Gibbon said, "But at the moment the army inventory is very short of beef. That situation is about to change, however. The army has recently purchased two thousand head of Black Angus cattle, and they are to be delivered here where they will be processed and shipped on to other army posts throughout the West."

"Oh, Colonel Gibbon, have you ever eaten Black Angus beef?" Major Allison asked.

"No, I can't say as I have," Gibbon replied. "But I suppose beef is beef, is it not?"

"No, sir," Allison replied. He smiled. "Compared to Black Angus beef, eating longhorn is like eating shoe leather."

"Really? Well then, I shall certainly look forward to the beef."

"Where is it coming from?" Kirby asked.

"The deal was made with a man by the name of MacCallister. Duff MacCallister," Gibbon said. "He will be delivering the herd here within the week."

"Duff MacCallister, you say?" Pershing asked, perking up at the name.

"Yes. Do you know him, Lieutenant Pershing?"

"I met him on Independence Day. I must say he is a fine, imposing gentleman. And speaking of Medals of Honor as we were, I might point out that Mr. MacCallister, while serving as a captain in the Black Watch, was awarded the Victoria Cross. That is certainly the equal to our Medal of Honor."

"Well, then, I shall look forward to meeting him," Colonel Gibbon said.

"Colonel, I have a proposal, if you are interested," Major Allison suggested.

"What would that be, Phil?"

"As soon as Mr. MacCallister arrives with his herd, I think we should have an outdoor cookout, perhaps an entire side of beef, for all the men on the post," Major Allison suggested.

"Good idea!" Gibbon agreed. He chuckled. "And since it was your idea, I shall place you in charge of seeing that it is done."

"Gladly, Colonel," Major Allison replied. "I'll turn the task over to Sergeant Beck. He fancies himself, and rightly so, quite the master at barbeque."

"I'm looking forward to seeing Mr. MacCallister again," Pershing said. Then he smiled. "Almost as much as I'm looking forward to eating the beef that Sergeant Beck will prepare."

"Do you think Jason Holbrook got enough of a look tonight?" Lieutenant Scott asked after he and Sue returned to their quarters that night. His voice was dripping with sarcasm

"Clayton, you are not being fair!" Sue said. "I didn't want to wear this dress. You are the one who insisted that I wear it."

"Yes, but it was meant as a tactical move to pique Colonel Gibbon's interest, not to seduce Lieutenant Holbrook. Or was it John Pershing you were interested in?"

"Clayton, please," Sue said as tears welled in her eyes.

"Oh, so now you are going to start crying again.

That seems to be your most accomplished talent. You can turn the tears on and off at will."

"Only when you say things that are hurtful," Sue said.

"Don't be such a baby," Scott said in a scoffing tone of voice. Then, abruptly, he smiled.

"On the other hand, if it was your husband you were trying to seduce, you succeeded. Come to bed now."

"Clay, you can't be so cruel to me one moment, then the very next moment think that I might want to lie with you."

The smile on Scott's face was replaced by a sneer. "Maybe you don't understand," he said. "It makes no matter whether you want to lie with me or not. I am your husband, and I have the right to demand it."

Martin Farm

Yellow Hawk, and six young men who called themselves warriors, approached the ranch just before dawn. With their horses staked out behind them, they moved down to the edge of a tree line which afforded them an excellent view of the house and grounds. The farm was small enough to be worked by Carl Martin and his fourteen-year-old son.

Yellow Hawk had chosen it as his target for several reasons. Because it was small there would be no resistance, and it would be an easy and quick victory for him. It also had a smokehouse filled with meat that Yellow Hawk would be able to take as rations for his men.

"Look, there is the man," Spotted Eagle said, pointing.

Carl Martin came from the back of the house and started toward the very small house behind. This, Yellow Hawk knew, was the toilet.

Spotted Eagle raised his rifle and took aim.

"No," Yellow Hawk said. "The rifle will make noise."

Yellow Hawk had a Winchester rifle, but he also had a bow and quiver of arrows. Fitting an arrow into the bow, he raised it, took aim, then let the arrow fly.

The arrow sped silently across the distance, and then buried itself in Martin's neck.

Without a sound, Martin put his hand up to his neck, totally shocked and surprised, pulled at the arrow, then collapsed and lay perfectly still.

"Papa!" a voice shouted and a young boy ran out of the house to see to his father, who was now lying on the ground.

"Now!" Yellow Hawk shouted, and he and those with him swept down upon the house.

A mile away from the Martin farm, Martha Dumey was feeding chickens when she saw a column of smoke rising into the air.

"Chris?" she called to her husband. "Chris, come out here!"

Chris Dumey stepped out onto the back porch, holding his cup of coffee. "What is it?"

"Look!" Martha said, pointing. "Do you think that's the Martin house?"

"I'll be damned!" Chris said. "It looks like it might be on fire."

"Maybe we'd better go see what we can do to help."

"I'll hitch up the buckboard," Chris said.

Half an hour later, Chris, Martha, and their sixteen-year-old daughter, Jenny, arrived at the Martin House. Though in reality, it could no longer be described as a house. What it was now, was a pile of blackened, and still smoking, lumber.

"Where are the Martins?" Martha asked.

"Maybe they left already," Chris said. "It could be that . . ." Chris paused in mid-sentence. "Oh, my God," he said. "Martha, look over there."

Chris pointed to two bodies lying on the ground.

"Is that Carl and Jimmy?" Martha asked.

"You and Jenny stay in the buckboard. I'll take a look."

Chris walked over to look down at the two bodies, and then gasped. Both had been scalped.

"What the hell?" he said aloud. "Scalped?"

Chris walked over for a look at the smoldering pile of lumber and as he got closer, he got a whiff of the smell of burnt flesh. Taking his handkerchief from his pocket, he held it over his nose as he moved in for a more thorough examination.

That was when he saw them, two blackened lumps. They were burned beyond recognition, but he knew that it was Rosemary and her ten-year-old daughter, Anna Jane.

Looking back toward the buckboard, he saw that Martha had climbed down.

"No!" he shouted, waving her back. "Get back in the buckboard! There ain't nothin' here for you to see!"

"Rosemary?" Martha asked.

Chris walked slowly back to the buckboard. "Like I said," he said. "There ain't nothin' here for you to see."

Chapter Five

Sky Meadow

Most of Meagan's sewing over the last few weeks had been to get ready for the Fourth of July dance, and all those jobs had been fulfilled. At the moment, she had no outstanding projects so, long before daylight on the morning that the drive was to take place, she hung a sign in the door saying that the store would be closed for at least two weeks. That done, she rode through the early morning darkness down to Sky Meadow, where she intended to join in the drive to Fort Laramie. She had not informed Duff of her intention to do this, so she wasn't sure how he would take it when he saw her this morning. But short of an actual breach in their relationship, she intended to make the drive.

By the time she arrived at Sky Meadow, it was still very early in the morning, so early that the just risen sun was still bloodred, and the mist upon the valley had not yet burned away. There was dew on the grass, and it was sparkling with all the colors of the rainbow.

Meagan smiled as she looked out over the dew, recalling the words Duff had spoken to her on the night of the dance.

"Sure m'girl, an 'tis a vision of loveliness ye be, like the beauty of a field that is arrayed in the rainbow colors of sparkling dew."

The air was permeated with the rich smell of coffee brewing, bacon frying, and biscuits baking. That was because Elmer, who had risen quite early, was preparing breakfast for the drovers so that they would "start out on a full stomach."

"Why, Miss Parker," Elmer said. "Come to see us off, did you? I didn't expect to see you here."

Meagan chuckled. "I'm pretty sure Duff isn't expecting it either," Meagan said. "And I'm not just here to see you off."

"Really? You mean you are plannin' on askin' him if you can go with us?" Elmer asked.

Meagan shook her head. "I don't plan on asking him anything. I plan on telling him. Half the cows that are making this drive are mine. If he won't let me go with his cows, I'll just go with my own."

Elmer laughed out loud. "Whoowee, you are a keg of gunpowder you are," he said. "I'd love to see Duff's face when you tell him that you ain't askin'."

"You'll see it," Meagan said, easily. "I plan to tell him as soon as he shows up this morning."

"Well, how about a cup of coffee while you're waiting for him?" Elmer said.

"Best offer I've had all day," Meagan answered.

"Ha! Seein' as how the day ain't even begun, I reckon that ain't hard to do," Elmer said as he poured coffee into a cup, and then handed it to her.

Meagan blew on the coffee, then slurped a swallow through extended lips because it was too hot to drink normally.

"Here's your chance," Elmer said. "Duff's a' comin'."

"Meagan!" Duff said with a broad smile. "You didn't have to come see us off. That's awfully nice of you, but I hate to think that you had to get up so early."

"I'm not here to see you off, Duff," Meagan said.

"Oh? What do you mean? Why are you here?"

Meagan took another swallow of her coffee before she answered.

"I'm going with you," she said, matter-of-factly.

Duff looked as if he was about to argue with her, then he smiled and nodded.

"Why not?" he asked. "After all, half the cows are yours."

"I'll be damned," Elmer said.

The hardest part of the drive was to get the cows moving. They were used to the area; they knew every blade of grass and they knew the water. In addition, they knew every tree and overhanging bluff that could provide some respite from the sun. That made them reluctant to leave, and this morning they showed every intention of staying right where they were.

The drovers shouted, probed the animals with sticks, and swung their ropes to get the herd underway. Eventually, their efforts paid off, and the herd began to move. Then, once the herd was underway, it changed from two thousand individual creatures into a single entity with a single purpose. The inertia they needed to overcome to get the herd moving in the first place now worked in their favor as the cows would plod along all day long at a steady clip, showing no inclination to stop, the cacophony of bawls and snorts a song that was as much a part of a cowboy's life and as comforting as his own mother's words.

Duff liked trailing cattle; he liked the sounds of the shuffling hooves and the whistling and shouts of the cowboys as they kept the herd moving. He liked the sight of a sea of black moving slowly but steadily across the plains, with mountains beside and behind them. There was a distinctive smell to a herd this size. The smells came from sun on the hides, dust in the air, and especially from the animals' droppings and urine. The odor was pungent and perhaps, to many, unpleasant. To Duff, however, it was an aroma that was both familiar and agreeable.

They reached Box Elder Creek after only a few hours on the trail. The lead animals bawled and refused the ford at first, but the drovers forced them in. Then, once the herd was started across the water, it again became one entity, with all the trailing cows following without protest.

With his leg hooked across the pommel of his saddle, Duff sat astride his horse on the south bank and watched as the stream of animals moved down into the water. Their hooves made clacking sounds on the rocky bank of the stream as the cows, like a black, moving stream, flowed across in an unbroken line.

Late in the afternoon of the first day of the drive, Meagan couldn't recall when she had been so tired. It was a bone-aching, backbreaking tired, and yet there was an exhilaration that transcended the tiredness. The exhilaration came from the excitement of the drive and from meeting the challenge. Even though she had made a big thing about participating in this drive, she was not really sure she would be able to. She had told herself this morning that if the drive became too grueling she would go back to Chugwater. But, as it grew later and later in the day, she began to have more confidence that perhaps she could do this. At least, she was willing to give it another day, and if she got through the next day, another beyond that.

The yellow glare of the sun-filled sky mellowed into the steel blue of late afternoon by the time the herd reached the place where they would be halted for the night. The sun was low in the western sky, and behind the setting sun, great bands of color spread out along the rim of the Laramie Mountains. Those few clouds that dared to intrude on this perfect day were under-lit by the sun and they glowed orange in the darkening sky.

After supper that evening, when most of the others had bedded down for the night, Meagan saddled a horse and rode away from the camp. Swallowed up by the blue velvet of darkness, she could feel the night air caressing her skin like fine silk, while overhead the stars glistened like diamonds. Meagan was aware of the quiet herd, with the cows lying down, but just as many standing motionlessly at rest. An owl landed nearby and his wings made a soft whirr as he flew by.

Meagan came to a small grass-covered knoll, and, on the other side, she could hear the splashing, bubbling sound of the Chugwater. She dismounted and climbed to the top of the small hill so she could look down at the water. Here, the creek was fairly swift, and it tumbled over the rocks, causing white eddies that were luminescent in the moonlight. The contrast between the dark water, and the white swirls made the stream even more beautiful at night than it was by day.

Meagan sat down in the grass and pulled her

knees up under her chin. The constant chatter of the brook soothed her, and she was enjoying the contemplative silence—a silence that was soon interrupted.

"Would you like some company?" a voice asked.

"I would love some company," Meagan said, smiling back at Duff, who was walking down the knoll. He sat down on the grass beside her.

"Shouldn't one of us be watching the herd?" Meagan asked.

"And would ye be thinking now that they'll take wing and fly away?" Duff teased.

"Aye, and t'would be a big surprise now if cows suddenly took wing, wouldn't it?" Meagan replied.

"Och . . . and now 'tis mocking my accent you're doing," Duff said. "The Lord does not love a mocker."

Meagan laughed. "I'm sorry," she said. "It's just that you are so easy to mock."

"What are you doin' out here so late? Didn't Elmer tell me he was making a bed for you in the chuck wagon?"

"Yes, and a fine bed it is, too," Meagan replied. "But I couldn't sleep."

"It has been a long day for you, Meagan, and you got up very early this morning so to make this drive with us. I cannae imagine ye having trouble sleeping."

"Sometimes my mind is filled with thought," Meagan said. "And I can't turn it off."

"What is it you are thinking of?"

Meagan wanted to tell him that she was thinking of them, wondering where their relationship was heading, but she didn't.

"I was thinking about you, Duff Tavish MacCallister. What was your life like in Scotland? What were you like as a boy?"

"Oh, t'was a good bairn, I was," Duff teased. "I worked hard on m' fither's farm till I was of the age to go into the army. Then I was lucky enough to be selected for Sandhurst."

"Sandhurst?"

"Aye, 'tis like your West Point."

"You've never told me what that medal is that you wear on your kilts," Meagan said.

Duff laughed, "I dinnae wear it on my kilts, lass. I wear it on my tunic. 'Tis the Victoria Cross."

"How did you get it?"

"T'was a bit of a skirmish at a place called Tel-el-Kebir, in Egypt. T'was a poem written about it, if you'd care to hear."

"I'd love to hear it," Meagan said.

Duff cleared his throat, then placed his right hand across his heart, and extended his left.

Meagan chuckled. "What are you doing?"

"Getting ready for a bit of elocution in the way I was taught by my teacher in fifth year."

"Just say the poem, Duff. There is no need to make a speech."

"Aye," Duff said. He began to recite.

"Ye sons of Great Britain, come join with me,
And sing in praise of Sir Garnet Wolseley;
Sound drums and trumpets cheerfully,
For he has acted most heroically.

"Therefore loudly his praises sing
Until the hills their echoes back doth ring;
For he is a noble hero bold,
And an honour to his Queen and country, be it told."

"That's a wonderful poem," Meagan said. "Even without the elocution"

"Aye, well Field Marshal Wolseley is a foine soldier and a great man," Duff said.

North Laramie County

Three freight wagons were making a trip from the river port at Hartville to the settlement of Raw Hide Butte with two men on each wagon. John English was driving the first wagon, and he was having a spirited discussion with his backup driver, Dan Owen.

"Have you ever heard of the pygmy people?" English asked.

"No, what's that?" Owen asked.

"It's little bitty people that live in Africa. They're so little you can just hold one in your hand."

"I ain't never heard of such a thing, and you ain't neither. You're just makin' that up."

"No, I ain't. I seen a picture once. He wasn't this

high." English measured a distance between his thumb and forefinger.

"That was the picture, that wasn't real."

"I don't know, it looked pretty real to . . ." English stopped in mid-sentence and pointed. "Dan, lookie there. Ain't them Injuns?"

"Yeah," Owen said. "What the hell are they doin'? Looks like they're comin' this way."

"We ain't got trouble with Injuns, do we?"

"John, what'll we do?" Kingsley shouted. Kingsley was the driver of the second wagon.

"Let's get out of the wagons and see what this is about," English said. "Get your rifles out."

English no sooner got the words out before he heard the bark of rifles from the Indians. Owen was hit, and he handed his pistol to English.

"I am killed—I won't live ten minutes. You'll need this."

The other four drivers jumped down from their wagons and came to join English. All five took cover behind English's wagon and began returning fire. Kingsley was hit, and went down with a bullet in his chest. By now the Indians had come up on them, and they were riding in circles around the three wagons, firing at the defenders. A man named Burleson was hit, then Daughtery, then Bell.

Now only English and Bill Williams were left alive.

They were both killed on the next pass.

As the others scalped and mutilated the six

drivers, Yellow Hawk climbed into the wagons to see what, of the freight, might be used. Breaking open one crate, he saw twenty Winchester rifles.

"*Woo, woo, woo, ya, ya, hey!*" he shouted loudly, holding one of the rifles aloft.

Chapter Six

With the cattle drive

Duff slapped his legs against the side of his horse and urged it into a gallop, dashing alongside the slowly moving herd, then up the side of a small hill where he stopped. Dismounting, he looked back down on the cattle company. It made an impressive sight, a little over two thousand head of Black Angus, three or four abreast and over half a mile long, moving slowly but inexorably alongside Chugwater Creek.

From this position Duff could see the entire herd. Meagan was the flank rider on the left side, near the front, and Jory Bates was on the same side, riding in the swing position, or near the rear. Jimmy Sherman was riding swing on the right and Jeff Ford was riding drag, bringing up the rear. The wagon was already a mile ahead of the herd, with Elmer sitting straight in the driver's seat, having gone out ahead of the herd to find their stopping place for tonight, and to set up his chuck wagon so as to have a hot dinner ready for the riders when they brought the herd up. Everyone would be eating lunch in the saddle, lunch being a couple biscuits and some bacon left over from breakfast.

As the herd moved north, they traveled not in one large mass, but in a long plodding column. This was because there simply wasn't that much flat ground adjacent to the creek to allow the cows to spread out. That gave the men a big advantage, because it was less likely that the herd would be stampeded that way. Also, with a steady supply of grass and water, and a slow, unhurried walk, there was little incentive to stampede.

An average day was ten to twelve miles. While on the move, one of the cowboys would be riding as point man ahead of the herd scouting for anything that might represent trouble. Flankers rode on either side of the herd, keeping them moving, while one man rode drag, meaning the rear. This was the least desirable position because the cowboy who rode drag had to swallow all the dust.

Duff didn't ride in any specific position, but moved around the herd several times during the day in order to make certain that the cows were proceeding as they should. Often, he would ride for several minutes alongside Meagan. At first, he told himself that he was doing that just to be there on hand if she needed anything. After all, she was a seamstress, not a drover.

To Duff's surprised satisfaction, Meagan, who

learned quickly, was handling her position superbly. But he found himself riding with her quite a bit, not because she needed him to help . . . but because he was genuinely enjoying her company.

They spoke for a few minutes, then Duff slapped his legs against the side of his horse and rode on ahead. He had gone about five miles ahead, when he saw the chuck wagon stopped. There was a small detachment of soldiers around the wagon.

"This here is Mr. Duff MacCallister. He owns the cows," Elmer said. "Duff, these here Yankee soldiers want to talk to you."

"Aye, gentlemen, what can I do for you?" Duff asked.

"I'm Sergeant O'Riley, in command of this scouting party. And would you be for tellin' this old fool that we ain't Yankee soldiers?" Sergeant O'Riley said.

"You're wearin' blue, ain't you?" Elmer asked.

Duff chuckled. "I guess some things die hard. Are you here from Fort Laramie to meet us?"

"No, sir, I wouldn't be knowin' nothin' about that. 'Tis from Fort Fetterman my lads and me are, out tryin' to find a band of renegade Injuns."

"Indians, you say? Och, I thought all the Indian troubles were over some time ago."

"Yes, sir, well, I reckon as far as your Injun wars is concerned, where you got maybe hundreds, or maybe thousands of Injuns on the warpath, that has all done passed. But these here heathens are a bunch of Shoshone that went off the Wind River Reservation."

"I know lots of Shoshone," Elmer said. He didn't add that he had once been married to a Shoshone woman, and that he had a Shoshone son. "They ain't took to the warpath since just after the Custer battle."

"These here ain't your regular Shoshone. Their regular ones is stayin' on the reservation like good Injuns. These here is a bunch of renegades, and 'tis near a dozen people these black-heart heathens have kilt. The one that's leadin' 'em is a wild young buck named Yellow Hawk. Would you be for knowin' him, now?"

"No," Elmer said, shaking his head. "I don't know nobody named Yellow Hawk."

"And would you be tellin' me, Mr. MacCallister, if you've seen any Injuns since you started your drive?"

Duff shook his head. "We've seen nae Indians."

"How many are in your company?"

"There are five of us, six, counting the woman that's with us."

"A woman, you say?"

"Aye."

The sergeant shook his head. "That's just about the size outfit Yellow Hawk is likely to go after. And I don't have to be for tellin' you, that they've no respect for women. So, you keep an eye open for 'em."

"I thank ye for the fair warnin' ye've given me, Sergeant O'Riley."

"Scotsman, ye be?" O'Riley asked.

Duff chuckled. "An' what gave me away?"

"T'was your Scottish brogue. Havin' come here from Ireland, I picked it up right away," O'Riley said.

"*Sláinte chugat,* Sergeant."

Sergeant O'Riley smiled. "And *saol fada chugat,*" he replied. "Oh, and one more thing. I was wonderin' if maybe you could see your way to sell us one of your beeves. We could take it back to the post, and it would make a good meal for us."

"I'll nae sell you a cow," Duff said.

"Aye, I figured you might have 'em all counted out."

"I'll give you one," Duff said.

"Really?" A huge smile spread across the sergeant's face.

"'Tis my thinking that you'll be getting some of them anyway. My contract is with the army. Fort Laramie is just where I'm to deliver them."

"'Tis a fine man, you be, sir," the sergeant said. "Even if you are a Scotsman," he added with a smile.

"If you'll send one of your men with me, he and I will bring a cow back," Duff offered. "But I'd be for takin' it kindly if the rest of ye would stay here with Mr. Gleason until I return. I dinnae ken of any Indians, but I've nae wish to leave the wagon exposed like this."

"I don't need any Yankee soldiers to be lookin' out for me," Elmer complained.

"Elmer, maybe 'tis nae worry ye have about your own hide, but 'tis my wagon you're drivin', and I've nae wish to see it fall into the hands of savage Indians. So I'll thank ye to wait here with the sergeant and his—Yankee soldiers till I get back."

"Don't ye be worryin' none now, Reb," the sergeant said with a chuckle. "M' lads and I will be lookin' out for you."

"Hrmmph," Elmer grunted.

Duff rode off with one of the soldiers, and Elmer pulled a plug of tobacco from his pocket, and then glanced up at Sergeant O'Riley. "Do you chaw, Sergeant?" he asked.

"I've been known to," O'Riley replied.

Elmer offered the stick of tobacco to him, and Sergeant O'Riley carved off a piece.

"Tell me what you 'n' Duff was a' sayin' to one another a moment ago. What language was that, anyhow? I thought Scotts and Irish talked English."

"Aye, we do," O'Riley replied. "But we also speak Gaelic."

"What was that you said to each other?"

"He wished me good health, and I wished him a long life."

"Well, I don't reckon you can be all bad, for all that you are a Yankee," Elmer said.

* * *

A few minutes later, Duff and the soldier who had gone with him returned with one of the beeves.

"*Go raimh maith agat,*" Sergeant O'Riley said. Then to Elmer, "I told him thanks."

"*Tá failte romhat,*" Duff replied.

"You don't have to explain that to me, I'm pretty sure you told him he was welcome," Elmer said.

"Elmer, m' lad, sure 'n' 'tis be Gaelic ye will be speaking before you age another year," Duff teased.

Elmer looked toward Sergeant O'Riley, then held his hand up, palm out. "*Toksha ake wacinyuank-tin ktelo le mita cola,*" he said.

Duff chuckled. "Now you'll have to tell us what you said."

"That was Shoshone. I said, 'I'll see you later, my friend,'" Elmer translated.

"'Tis good to see that I've gone from Yankee soldier to friend," Sergeant O'Riley said. "Take care."

Sergeant O'Riley ordered his men into a column of twos. He saluted Duff.

"Be sure 'n' keep an eye out for Injuns there, Mr. MacCallister. Sure 'n' I'm not wantin' to come back and find you done in by the heathens."

"We'll be alert, Sergeant. Thank you for your concern."

"And thanks again for the beef." Sergeant O'Riley stood in his stirrups. "Forward, ho!"

The detachment left at a trot.

"Elmer, given the situation I think it might be best if you kept the wagon back with the cattle drive," Duff said.

"All right, Duff, if you think so."

Duff waited until Elmer turned the wagon around, then rode with him until they rejoined the herd.

Meagan was the first to see them coming back, and she rode out to meet them.

"Anything wrong?" she asked.

Duff hesitated a moment before he answered, not wanting to frighten her. Then, because he knew that Meagan had enough spirit not to be unduly frightened, he decided to tell her.

"Apparently, there are some renegade Indians bent on causing a bit of trouble," he said.

"Indians? I thought that was all over."

"Aye, I think for the most part it is. But 'tis a gang of hoodlums I'm told, not regular law-abiding Indians. I think it might be best if we stay together."

Meagan nodded. "Probably a good idea," she agreed.

The Wind River Reservation

In the village of Standing Bear on the banks of the Wind River, a ring of campfires burned brightly around the outer ring of the circle of the camp. A circle was very important to the Shoshone, as they believed that the power of the world worked in a circle. Long before the Europeans had accepted the concept of the earth being round, the Shoshone already knew it to be so. They reasoned that if the sky was round, the moon is round, and the sun is round, then the earth, too, must be round. This universal circle, they believed, was not without purpose.

The seasons also formed a circle: summer, fall, winter, spring, then summer coming back again. The nests of the birds are round, tepees are round and always set in a circle, and all meeting and ceremonies took place in the center of that circle. Ska Luta, who had passed seventeen summers, knew this, because it had been taught him since he was a very young boy.

Everyone in the village knew what Yellow Hawk was doing. When he attacked the Martin farm and killed Martin, his wife, and two children, the Shoshone learned of it before the white men learned of it. And when he attacked and killed the men who were driving the freight wagons, the Shoshone learned of that, too.

It was for this reason the ring of council fires had been lit, and the elders were meeting. The subject being discussed was what should be done about Yellow Hawk. Some had suggested that the Shoshone should send warriors out to join Yellow Hawk, as he was bringing honor back to his people.

There were others, though, who believed that what Yellow Hawk was doing was dishonorable, and they suggested that the Shoshone should send warriors, not to join Yellow Hawk, but to capture him and give him to the soldiers.

Ska Luta listened to the discussion with a great deal of interest, because he knew that whatever was decided, it would have a direct effect on everyone in the village. Ska Luta was so named because in his veins ran the blood of the Shoshone and the blood of the white man. Ska Luta meant Red White.

Ska Luta had never seen either his mother or his father. His Shoshone mother died as she was giving birth to him. His white father abandoned him, and he was raised by Elk Woman, who had no children and was glad to have a child of her own.

Life had not been that easy for Ska Luta. Elk Woman had been older when she took him in. Because of that, and because he was half white, he had a difficult time fitting in with the others, who often teased him. Now Elk Woman was very old, and the relationship had changed. She was no longer taking care of Ska Luta; he was taking care of her.

As word of Yellow Hawk's raids came back to the reservation, it was the youth of Ska Luta's age group who were most impressed. Yellow Hawk became a hero in their eyes, and many spoke openly of leaving the village to join him.

Ska Luta did not share the hero worship of Yellow Hawk, believing that what he was doing could only bring trouble to the rest of them. But, he didn't share his opinion with the others.

"Ska Luta, if there is to be war between the red man and the white, which of your two bloods would guide you? Would you fight for the red man, or the white man?" Brave Elk asked.

"I am Shoshone," Ska Luta said resolutely. "Never have I seen the man whose white blood runs in my veins. I was born here. I was raised here. Here are my people. Why would you ask such a thing?"

"I ask because you are of two bloods, and it is not known which blood is the stronger."

"Do you think red blood is so weak, that the white blood will win?" Ska Luta asked, and the others laughed.

"Brave Elk thinks red blood is weak," Beaver Tail said.

"I do not think this!" Brave Elk said, defensively.

"Then, if you know that red blood is stronger than white blood, you know where my heart will be if war comes. But I think there will be no war."

Chapter Seven

From the *Central Wyoming News:*

Indian Depredations

> Reports from other Wyoming newspapers bring the disturbing news that Yellow Hawk has left the Wind River Reservation with a band of no less than twenty Shoshone. Although the Indian wars are all but over, there have been, from time to time, disturbing incidents such as this, where young firebrands, seeking to emulate acts of derring-do as told around campfires by the elders, go off on their own adventure.
>
> With no wars to fight, these young ne'er-do-wells create their own adventures to the detriment, not only of the White citizens, but to their own fellow Indians. Yellow Hawk and his band have raided some isolated farms and ranches with indiscriminate murders and robberies.
>
> Their most recent atrocity was the

> murder of six men, teamsters all, driving wagons for the McKnight–Keaton freight line. The six men were killed, scalped, and the wagons looted. It is said that there were twenty rifles and one thousand rounds of ammunition being transported in the wagons, and those weapons fell into the hands of the marauding Indians.

Fort Laramie

"Have you seen this newspaper article, Sue?" Lieutenant Scott asked, thumping the article with his hand. "The one about the Indian raids?"

"Oh, yes," Sue said. "How awful."

"Awful? What do you mean, awful? Why, it's fantastic! It's wonderful," Scott said enthusiastically.

"What do you mean, it's wonderful?" Sue asked. "All those people they've killed? Why, they murdered an entire family, a husband and his wife, and their two children, a young boy and a young girl."

"Yes, well, it's too bad they were killed, but you just aren't looking at this the right way," Scott said. "But then, why would I expect you to understand? I see this as opportunity! I'm going to see Colonel Gibbon and ask him to let me take out a troop of cavalry in pursuit of those Indians."

"Wouldn't it be better if he sent out Captain Kirby? After all, Captain Kirby has some experience in fighting Indians."

"He has had his moment of glory," Scott said. "Now it's my time. If I pull this off, your father is sure to notice me, and he's sure to bring me back to Washington to serve on his staff. Then I'll not only have line experience, I'll have battle experience."

"I wish you wouldn't go. I would worry about you," Sue said.

"Ha! I'll have an entire troop of the Fifth Cavalry with me. We'll be going after a bunch of half-naked, untrained savages. The only worry would be if we don't catch up with them."

"All right, Lieutenant," Colonel Gibbon said. "I know you have been chomping at the bit to prove yourself. And Captain Kirby is a bit under the weather now, so you can take twenty men from A Troop. Go twenty miles north and make a sweep toward the west, maintaining a distance of twenty miles from the post. Stay out no longer than two days, return tomorrow and give me a report. In the meantime, I will have been in telegraph contact with Fort Fetterman, so we can coördinate before you go out on your next scout."

"Thank you, sir!" Scott said, coming to attention and snapping a sharp salute.

Ten minutes later, Scott was standing in A Troop's orderly room, talking to First Sergeant Miner Cobb.

"How soon can you have twenty men ready to go?" Scott asked.

"We can be ready within the hour, Lieutenant," Cobb replied.

"Not good enough, First Sergeant. The sloppy way this troop has been run is going to change. You will have twenty men ready within thirty minutes. Do I make myself clear?"

"Yes, sir. Thirty minutes."

As soon as Scott left the orderly room, First Sergeant Cobb called his clerk over.

"Go find Sergeant Caviness," Cobb said. "Bring him to me."

"Yes, Sergeant."

After the clerk left, Cobb began making a list of twenty names. He was to number eighteen when the clerk returned with Sergeant Caviness.

"What's up, Mr. Cobb?" Caviness asked.

"Have you heard of the band of Indians that have gone out on the prowl?" Cobb asked.

"Yeah, I read about it in the paper," Caviness said.

"Somehow, Lieutenant Scott has convinced Colonel Gibbon to send out a scout after them, with Scott in charge."

"I feel sorry for the men who will make up that scout."

"Then you're feeling sorry for yourself, because I want you to be the noncom."

Caviness smiled, and nodded. "Yeah, I sort of

thought you might be thinking of something like that."

"Sam, you've had battle experience with Indians. The lieutenant hasn't. I figure that having you along might improve the odds somewhat."

"First, you are forgetting one thing," Caviness said.

"What's that?"

"Lieutenant Scott isn't going to listen to a thing I say."

"Do what you can. Here, I've come up with seventeen names. You can come up with three more. Scott wants to be ready to leave in"—Cobb looked over at the wall clock—"twenty minutes from now."

Caviness checked over the list Cobb had drawn up for him. "Good list," he said. "All good men."

Lieutenant Pershing walked out onto the parade ground where Scott was standing alongside his saddled horse.

"I'm told you're going out after a renegade band of Indians," Pershing said.

"That's right."

"I wish I could go with you."

"I just bet you do. But, being as you are a part of the Tenth Cavalry, and not part of the Fifth, there's no way."

"So Colonel Gibbon said," Pershing replied. He patted the face of Scott's horse.

"Clay, I'm also told that this will be your first encounter with Indians."

"What does that matter?"

"No matter, really," Pershing said. "But, as you know, I have had a few encounters with them, so, if you don't mind, I'd like to give you just a quick word of advice. Friend to friend."

"All right," Scott said. "Friend to friend. What is your advice?"

"If you see the Indians . . ." Pershing started, but before he could finish his comment, Scott interrupted him.

"It's not a matter of if I see the Indians. I will see them."

"Not before they see you," Pershing replied.

"I beg your pardon?"

"That's the point I'm trying to make. Anytime you see Indians, they will have seen you first. There's very little you can do to avoid that, but you do need to be aware of it."

"Thank you, John, I'll keep that in mind," Scott said.

"Good luck," Pershing said and, turning away from him, he started back toward the headquarters building.

"Bugler," Scott ordered. "Sound 'Boots and Saddles.'"

The stirring notes of the call, "Boots and Saddles," rolled across the parade ground and sounded throughout the post. The rest of the men were coming out onto the quadrangle then, leading their horses. Soldiers and civilians stopped what they were doing long enough to step out in front of the various occupied buildings to watch the departure.

Colonel Gibbon strolled out onto the parade ground.

"Mr. Scott, are you ready to depart?" Gibbon asked.

"I am, sir," Scott replied, as he saluted.

Gibbon returned the salute. "Proceed, Lieutenant."

"Yes, sir," Scott replied. "Troops, to horse. Colors and noncommissioned officer, post," he ordered.

Sergeant Caviness "posted," by taking his place at the head of the formation, facing Scott. The soldier, who was carrying a swallow pennant version of the American flag, came up beside Caviness.

"Prepare to mount," Scott said. Then, "Mount."

As one, the men mounted.

"Right, by column of twos. Forward, ho!"

At his command, the mounted soldiers began moving out at a swift trot, following Lieutenant Scott. Sergeant Caviness and the color bearer were just behind Scott.

A couple of the post guards opened the gate to allow the riders to exit the fort. One hundred yards later, the horsemen were on the banks of the wide, shallow Platte River, riding quietly, with the only sound being the dull thud and brush of hooves in the dirt and dry grass, the twist and creak of leather, and the subdued clink of bit chains.

Lieutenant Pershing was standing alongside Colonel Gibbon as the two men watched the troops depart the post.

"Tell me, John, what do you think of Scott?" Colonel Gibbon asked.

"He was a classmate, sir."

"That doesn't answer my question. What do you think of him as an officer?"

"Colonel, I'm really not in position to answer that question, having never served in the field with him."

"I understand, and forgive me for asking the question. I have no right to put you on the spot like that. And, he may turn out to be a fine officer. He is the son-in-law of General Winfield, you know."

"Yes, sir, Lieutenant Scott and Miss Winfield had a chapel wedding on the very day of graduation."

"General Winfield is a fine man. Maybe Scott will turn out all right. How are you and Lieutenant Holbrook coming with the writing of the TO&E?"

"The lieutenant and I are making very good progress I believe, sir," Pershing said. "We should be finished by the end of the month."

"It's about time the table of organization and equipment was updated," Gibbon said. "The way it is now, you can go from the Fifth to the Sixth, to the Seventh Infantry and it's almost like going from one army to another."

"Yes, sir, well, you should try in the Ninth and Tenth Cavalry. We are last in line for everything. But I think a standard TO&E will take care of that."

"I'm sure it will. By the way, if you don't have anything else planned, Mrs. Gibbon and I would love to have you as our guest for dinner this evening," Colonel Gibbon said.

"Thank you, sir. It would be a great honor to attend."

With Scott's detachment

It was midway through the afternoon, and the column was moving slowly but steadily, a symphony of sound with jangling equipment, squeaking leather, and the dull thud of hoofbeats. As the horses proceeded through the dry grass, they stirred up grasshoppers to whir ahead of them in long, wing-augmented hops. The dusty grass gave up a pungent but not unpleasant smell.

"Lieutenant," Sergeant Caviness called. "With your permission, sir, Trooper Jones and I will go up on the ridgeline there and have a look."

"Very well. We'll take a short break here to give the horses a blow," Scott said. "You may give the order."

"Troop, halt! Dismount, take ten!" Caviness ordered. "Trooper Jones, with me."

Jones didn't dismount, but rode up to be with Caviness. There, he dismounted, and leaving their horses behind, Caviness and Jones started up the hill. Below and behind the two men, the other soldiers took advantage of the break, some of them stretching out to rest on the ground, while others walked around to stretch out the kinks of saddle weariness.

Caviness and Jones climbed the hill to have a look around. When he got there, Caviness saw only dusty rocks, shimmering dry grass, and more ranges of hills. He started to drop the glasses when he noticed something that looked a little different. He examined it more closely, then dropped the glasses. "God in heaven," he breathed.

"What is it, Sam?" Trooper Jones asked. Like Sergeant Caviness, Jones had been with Crook in Arizona, where he was awarded the Medal of Honor. He had been a sergeant several times, but a penchant for alcohol prevented him from keeping his rank. Jones was just a private now, but there had been times during his career when he had actually outranked Caviness. As a result, the two men were close friends, and on a first-name basis.

Caviness handed his field glasses to Jones. "Take a look," he said. "If I'm not mistaken, that's a burned-out wagon."

"Yeah, it is," Jones said. "Oh, damn. Damn, damn, damn," he exclaimed. He was still looking through the glasses. "Damn!"

"What is it, J.C.? What do you see?" Caviness asked.

"Bodies, Sam. I see bodies."

"We'd better tell the lieutenant," Caviness said.

Caviness and Jones hurried down the side of the hill.

"Lieutenant, we seen somethin' you should know about," Caviness said.

"What did you see?"

"We seen a burnt-out wagon, and I'm pretty sure there's some bodies lyin' around it."

"Where?"

"Just over the next rise. About another mile."

"Mount up!" Scott called. When all were mounted, he gave the command, "Forward at a trot!"

As the column lurched forward, sabers, canteens, mess kits, and rifles jangled under the irregular rhythm of the trotting horses, and dust boiled up behind them. Scott held the trot until they were within one hundred yards of the burned-out wagon.

"At a gallop!" he called, and he stood in his stirrups and drew his saber, pointing it forward. The saber wasn't drawn as a weapon, but rather as a signaling device, for a drawn saber meant that carbines should be pulled from the saddle scabbard and held at the ready.

Every nerve in Scott's body was tingling as the group of soldiers swept down on the wagon. He was alert to every blade of grass, every rock and stone, every hill and gully. They reached the wagon, and Scott held up his hand, calling the men to a halt.

"Line of skirmishers, front and rear!" he ordered, and the squads of horse soldiers moved into position.

"Sergeant, take a look," Scott ordered.

Caviness walked toward two clumps on the ground. As he approached, he could hear a buzzing sound as flies swarmed around the bodies of a man and woman, lying side by side in the grass. Both had been stripped naked. The man had been scalped, and arrows had been shot into his penis.

"Let's get out of here, Sergeant," Scott ordered.

"Lieutenant, ain't we goin' to bury 'em?" Sergeant Caviness asked.

"Yeah, all right, you can bury 'em, but make it fast."

"Yes, sir," Caviness said. He called for half a dozen men and the men, moved by morbid curiosity, didn't even protest the order as they took shovels and began to dig the graves.

"Sergeant!" one of the men called. "We found another body. A young girl."

Caviness went over to investigate and saw the body of a young girl, who couldn't have been over fourteen. She was holding a pistol in her hand, and there was a bullet hole in her temple.

"She must 'a shot herself," one of the soldiers said.

"Yeah, well, who can blame her. Look what happened to her ma and pa," another said.

"How come she ain't all butchered up like they are?"

"Accordin' to what the Injuns believe, there's no honor in butchering up someone if you wasn't the one that kilt 'em," Jones said.

"Honor? What's the honor in butcherin' up somebody, whether you kilt 'em or not?" a soldier asked.

"You have to think like an Injun," Jones said.

"Sergeant Caviness, we found somethin'," another soldier said, and he came from the back of the wagon carrying a small, leather-bound notebook.

"What is it?"

"Looks like maybe one of 'em was keepin' a diary," the soldier said.

Caviness opened the book and began to read.

MY DIARY
by Wanda Cassidy

Ma and Pa said we were going to move from Castle Butte to Theresa, because he bought some farmland there. I didn't want to move, because I have made many friends in Castle Butte, but Ma said I will make new friends in Theresa. I guess I will make new friends in Theresa, but Billy LeGrand lives in Castle Butte, and on the night before we left, I let him kiss me. I haven't told Ma and Pa that I let him kiss me because Pa might . . .

Caviness slammed the book shut, then looked back toward the little girl.

"Bless your heart, darlin'," he said quietly. "Billy will never know what he lost."

"What's it say, Sarge?" one of the soldiers asked.

"Nothin'," Caviness said. "It don't say nothin'. When you bury the little girl, bury this with her."

Chapter Eight

Fort Laramie

The dining table at Old Bedlam was set with enough silver, crystal, and china to do credit to any formal dinner anywhere. Adorning the menu were delicacies recently received by the sutler: Champagne, German chocolates, and tinned brandied peaches. The meat was elk, supplied by a recent hunting party.

"I'll be glad when we can have beef again," Kathleen said. "John, how much longer do you think it will be before the herd arrives?"

"I imagine it will be here within the week," Gibbon said.

"Good, I am so tired of wild game," Kathleen said. "I mean, don't get me wrong, I'm appreciative of the soldiers who have managed to keep meat on the tables. But how much I would love to have a pot roast beef with potatoes and onions."

"Tell me, Lieutenant, are your quarters agreeable?" Colonel Gibbon asked as he carved his meat.

"Quite agreeable, sir," Pershing replied.

"You live in the BOQ up at Fort Assiniboine, I take it?"

"Yes, sir."

"How do you like duty . . . up there?" Gibbon asked, pausing briefly before finishing the question.

Pershing smiled. "Sir, are you asking me how I like serving with the colored troops?"

Gibbon chuckled, self-consciously. "I suppose I am."

"I was serious when I told Clay Scott that I was very much enjoying my assignment. The buffalo soldiers make exceptionally good troops."

"Why are they called buffalo soldiers?" Kathleen asked.

"It's a name the Indians have given them, and there are several different explanations given. I suppose you can accept the one that suits you best. Some say it's because the hair of the colored soldiers remind the Indians of the fur of the buffalo. Some say it's the color of their skin, and some say it's because the Indians respect the fighting ability of the soldiers, and are honoring them with the name, because the Indians have such respect for the buffalo."

"How do the soldiers feel about the name?"

"They take great pride in it, sir," Pershing said. "I'm also proud to be a buffalo soldier."

"What do you mean, Lieutenant Pershing?"

Kathleen asked. "How can you be a buffalo soldier if you aren't colored?"

"No, I'm not colored, but I am a member of the Tenth Cavalry, and that means I am a buffalo soldier," Pershing said proudly. "I must confess, though, that I have a personal reason for feeling such a strong attachment to the buffalo soldiers.

"A couple of months ago some renegade Sioux attacked a ranch near Fort Assiniboine. I led a patrol of seven men out to the ranch, where we found the body of Tom Pryor, who was visiting the ranch owner, burned in the ruins of the smoldering house. We were just getting him out of the house when the Indians returned. We had left our mounts with one of the troopers, and the Indians started after them.

"I asked Sergeant Kendall to cover me, and I started across an open area to try and get back to the horses. The Indians started shooting at me, and I went down. Sergeant Kendall and the others thought I had been hit, so they came out to rescue me and, with accurate fire, killed three of the Indians and drove the others away."

"Had you been hit?"

Pershing chuckled. "No, I had just tripped over the rough ground. But the fact that those men risked their lives to save me when they thought I had been hit is all the incentive I need to be proud of the Tenth Cavalry, and the men in it."

"I don't blame you, John," Colonel Gibbon said. "I don't blame you one bit."

Pershing and Gibbon talked for a bit longer, exchanging stories, and laughs about their days at West Point. Then Pershing excused himself, and started back to the BOQ. A gentle breeze was blowing from the south and it carried upon its breath the smell of lye soap from Soapsuds Row. From one of the married NCO houses, Pershing could hear the sound of a crying baby. From the nearest barracks, he could hear a group of soldiers singing.

Halfway across the parade ground, a soldier appeared, carrying a trumpet. The bugler raised the instrument to his lips, and blew air through it a couple of times as if clearing it out. Then he pursed his lips to play, and Pershing stopped to listen to the clear melodious notes of the call.

"Taps" was the official signal that it was time for everyone to be in bed, and the mournful notes filled the air. Sweeter in sound from the cavalry's trumpet than they ever could be from the infantry's bugle, the music rolled across the flat, open quadrangle, hitting the hills beyond the walls of the fort, then bouncing back a second later as an even more haunting echo.

Of all the military rituals, the playing of "Taps" was the one that most affected Pershing. He never heard it without feeling a slight chill.

Day is done.
Gone the sun
From the lake

From the hill
From the sky.
Rest in peace
Soldier brave,
God is nigh.

The last note hung in the air for a long, sorrowful moment, and Pershing thought of the things about the army he liked: the loyalty of men to their country and their officers, the responsibility the officers felt toward their men, the feeling of belonging . . . and he knew there would never be another thing in his life that he could love more than he loved being a member of this elite band of men.

"Corporal of the guard! Post number six, and all is well!"

The plaintive call from the furthermost guard came drifting across the post.

"Corporal of the guard! Post number five and all is well!"

The second call was a little closer. They continued down the line until post number two's call, and his call was so close that Pershing felt a moment of embarrassment, as if he had intruded upon the quiet, lonely moments that were part of a sentry's privilege and duty.

Pershing stepped into the BOQ, then into his room. As "Taps" was officially the call for lights out, he lit neither candle nor lantern, but undressed in the moonlight that spilled in through the window.

With the Scott detachment

The night creatures raised their songs to the stars as Lieutenant Scott's detail made their night encampment. A cloud passed over the moon, then moved away, bathing the prairie in silver before them. The soft hoot of owls, the trilling songs of frogs, and the distant howl of coyotes created nature's concert.

Scott was sitting on a rock in front of the Sibley tent that a couple of the privates had pitched for him. He was sole occupant of the tent, whereas the other tents were small, two-man pup tents.

"Sergeant Caviness, do you think we'll run into the Indians?" Scott asked.

"Yes, sir, but it's more 'n likely that they'll run into us," Caviness responded.

"You have fought Indians before, haven't you?"

"Yes, sir, me 'n' Sergeant . . . that is, Private," he corrected, "Jones. We was with Crook durin' the war with the Apache."

"The Apache," Scott said with a dismissive grunt. "Rabble. You can hardly call skirmishes with Apache warfare."

"Yes, sir, maybe that's so. But Geronimo and just a handful of bucks held off the United States Army for quite a while. And they had their women and children with 'em, too."

"Nevertheless, they are hardly the equal of the Sioux, Cheyenne, and Shoshone. And we, should we be fortunate enough to encounter them, will be engaging Shoshone."

"Lieutenant, these here Injuns we're goin' after ain't exactly like the Injuns Custer and the boys of the Seventh run into. From what I've heard, these ain't nothin' but a bunch of renegades that have left the reservation on their own. They ain't even got their own tribe behind 'em."

"Nevertheless, Sergeant, I intend to make my mark with this very scout. It may not be much of a war, but it's the only war we've got. And once General Winfield gets wind of what I've done, I expect good things to happen."

"Yes, sir. Well, I do hope it all works out for you."

Bordeaux, Wyoming

Although Bordeaux was on the map, it could scarcely be considered a town. It consisted of exactly eight buildings, and four of them were outhouses. The other four buildings were two private homes, a general store, and a saloon.

Despite the modest size of the town, the saloon was surprisingly busy, filled as it was with nearly two dozen men: cowboys, trappers, and some who were just passing through. Inside the saloon, Muley Harris stood at the bar nursing a beer. He had come in with just enough money for a beer and a plate of beans. He wished he had enough money to go into the back room with one of the two women who were working the bar, but he didn't. He didn't even have enough money for a second beer. If everything worked out though, that would soon change. He was here to meet a man to plan a job.

After that, his pockets would be full again. He looked over at the wall clock.

"Is your clock right?" he asked the bartender.

The bartender, who was busy polishing glasses, set the towel down and pulled out his watch. He flipped open the case and looked at it, then glanced back at the clock.

"Yeah, it's right," he said. "It is lacking five minutes of nine o'clock."

"Thanks," Harris grunted.

"You 'bout ready for another beer?"

"No, I ain't finished this here beer, yet," Harris said.

"I was just thinkin', you been nursin' it so long, it's prob'ly gone flat by now."

"Yeah? Well, I'm the one that's a' drinkin' it, not you," Harris said.

"Very good, sir." The bartender went back to wiping glasses and Harris raised his nearly-empty beer mug, just enough to wet his lips.

Harris was supposed to meet someone at exactly nine o'clock. He wished he hadn't come so early, as he was getting tired standing here for so long.

Harris took another swallow of beer, and then made a face. The bartender was right. He had been nursing the beer so long now that it had gone flat on him. He looked back toward the clock and saw the minute hand move to the twelve. It was now nine o'clock. Nine o'clock and the man he was to meet wasn't here.

Damn it, where the hell was he? He stared into his glass.

"Mister, you think if you just stare at the mug long enough, it'll fill itself back up with beer?" someone asked.

Harris smiled at the question, because he recognized the voice. The speaker was Ira Adams, and Harris turned to greet him.

"Adams, you ugly old polecat, how come you ain't been shot yet? Wait, don't answer. There ain't nobody shot you, 'cause you ain't worth the price of a bullet."

The two men shook hands.

"What do you mean, I ain't worth the price of a bullet? Why, I'm a genuine Injun fightin' hero."

"What do you mean you're a Injun fightin' hero?"

"Both of us is. We was both at the battle of Sand Creek, wasn't we?"

"Hell, they's some folks don't think that was much of a battle. Chivington ain't exactly a hero."

"What the hell? We kilt us a bunch of Injuns, didn't we? And as far as I'm concerned, a dead Injun is a good Injun," Adams said.

Harris laughed. "You want to call us heroes, who am I to fight it?" He lifted his glass. "Here's to us Injun fightin' heroes."

"To us," Adams replied, taking a drink from his own glass.

Harris finished the rest of his beer, then wiped his mouth with the back of his hand. "So, you said meet you here, I'm here. What you got in mind?"

"I got two thousand dollars in mind," Adams said.

"Damn! A thousand dollars apiece? That sounds good. That sounds damn good."

"Oh, hell, it's better 'n that," Adams said. "What I'm actually talkin' about is four thousand dollars. Two thousand dollars apiece. Are you interested?"

"Damn right I'm interested. Who do we have to kill?"

"Nobody. All we got to do is run off a few head of cows."

"How many head are you talkin' about for four thousand dollars?"

"A hunnert head," Harris said. He smiled. "And I've already got 'em sold. All we have to do is deliver the cows."

"All right, sounds interesting enough to me. Where do we go to find these cows?" Adams asked.

"That's the beauty of it," Harris said. "We don't have to go nowhere. All we have to do is wait for a couple of days, and they'll be brought to us."

"What do you mean, they'll be brought to us?" Adams asked.

"There's a rancher deliverin' two thousand head to the army at Fort Laramie, and he ain't got nothin' but a handful of drovers with 'im. He's comin' up the Chugwater. I've got it figured out that he'll be at North Laramie two nights from now. We'll just wait, then when they make camp, we'll sneak in and pull a hunnert head out of the herd, more 'n likely without them even a' knowin' about it. Are you with me?"

Adams took another swallow of his beer before he replied. Then he flashed a broad smile. "Yeah," he said. "Yeah, I'm with you."

"We need to go over the store and get us some vittles for campin', then get on out there. I don't want to take a chance on them gettin' by us without even knowin' they was there."

"Uh, I ain't got no money for vittles. Truth is, I ain't even got enough money to buy myself another beer," Harris said.

Adams smiled. "The fella that I'm sellin' the cows to has done give me forty dollars. Here's twenty for you. That'll do us till we get us some real money."

Chapter Nine

It was mid-morning of the next day and the horses were being watered and the men were dismounted for a break. Again, Sergeant Caviness and Trooper Jones climbed to the top of the highest knoll, looking toward the east.

"There they are," Jones said. "Do you see 'em?"

"Yeah, I see 'em," Caviness said. "We'd better tell Lieutenant Scott."

The two men half walked, and half slid down the steep incline, then hurried over to Lieutenant Scott. Looking toward them, Scott could tell by the expressions on their faces that they had something to report.

"Have you seen anything?" Scott asked, hopefully.

"Yes, sir. We seen the Injuns from the top of the rise there," Jones said.

"Come back up with me. I want to see them, too."

"Yes, sir, the hill's kind of a steep climb, Lieutenant. But we'll go up with you if you want to."

The three men went back up the hill, which was so steep that it couldn't be walked up, but had to be climbed. After about five minutes, they were once again on top.

"Now, where are they?" Scott asked. He was gasping for air, out of breath from the climb.

"They're a couple of miles over that way," Jones said, pointing.

Scott raised his binoculars to look, but a moment later, he lowered them with a frustrated sigh.

"I don't see a damn thing," he said.

"No, sir, more'n likely they've gone behind that long ridgeline there, but if you look close, you can see the dust still hangin' in the air," Jones said.

"Dust? You brought me up here to look at dust? Anything could have caused the dust, Private," Scott said angrily.

"Yes, sir, anything could, only this wasn't just anything. It wasn't just dust that me 'n' Sam seen. We seen actual Injuns."

"Sam?" Scott said, challengingly.

"No, sir, what I mean to say is that me 'n' Sergeant Caviness both seen the Injuns," Jones said, correcting himself for using Sergeant Caviness's first name.

"Is that true, Caviness?" Scott asked.

"Yes, sir."

Scott nodded. "All right, Sergeant, if both of you saw them, I'll take your word for it. Let's get back down and get the men mounted. It's time to get started."

"Sir, I volunteer to ride as point man," Jones offered, as they started back down the slope.

"We won't be using a point man."

"Beggin' your pardon, sir, but we have to use a point man," Sergeant Caviness said. "If we've seen the Injuns, it's a damn sure thing that they've seen us."

"Did you get that from Lieutenant Pershing?" Scott asked.

"No, sir, it's somethin' I learned on my own," Caviness said. "Same as Lieutenant Pershing I reckon, I mean what with him being down in Arizona with Cook, like he was. That's why I'm sayin' that we need a point man. Without a point man, why, we could be riding right into an ambush! And I can't think of anyone in our detachment that I'd rather have riding point that Jones."

"We *are* riding into an ambush, Caviness. That's the whole point, don't you see?" Scott said. "An ambush for the Indians." He laughed.

"Sir, with all due respect, we have to have someone riding point," Jones said. "We'd be absolute fools not to have one."

"Trooper Jones, you are forgetting your place," Scott said. "You may have been given the Medal of Honor for fighting the Apache, but right now you aren't wearing that medal or sergeant's stripes. Here, you are just a private, and as such, you don't presume to tell an officer what to do. Do you understand that?"

"Yes, sir, I do," Jones said.

"Any more disagreements from you and I'll have you on charges when we return."

"Sir, I don't think Trooper Jones meant any disrespect," Caviness said. "It's just that he's been around a long time and—"

"I've heard quite enough," Scott interrupted. "Now, get back down there and be prepared to get mounted!"

"Yes, sir," Caviness said as he and Jones started back down toward the others.

"All right, to horse!" Caviness shouted as he was coming back down from the hill, and the soldiers moved quickly to their mounts.

With Yellow Hawk

"How many soldiers are there?" Yellow Wolf asked.

Standing Bear, the Indian who was reporting the sighting, flashed both hands twice. "They are following the water this way." Standing Bear pointed toward the north.

"We are only twelve, the soldiers have too many. We should go this way so that they will not see us," Spotted Eagle suggested, pointing toward the west.

"No," Yellow Hawk said. "We will go to the place on the water with the high sides. Ride swiftly, we must get there before they arrive."

Yellow Hawk slapped his legs against the side of his horse and the agile animal leaped forward at a full gallop. The others followed, and the small band of Indians closed the distance between them and the "place of the water with the high sides" very quickly.

The water they were talking about was Raw Hide Creek, and the "high sides" were the one-hundred-foot high bluffs that created a rather narrow passage for the creek. Just before they reached the bluffs, Yellow Hawk called for a stop.

"Spotted Eagle, you will take some and go on the other side of the water. I will stay on this side with the others. When the soldiers enter into the place between the two high sides, they will be below us, and there will be no place for them to hide."

"Ayiee!" Spotted Eagle said with a broad smile. "That is good! We will have the soldiers trapped and we can kill many!"

"Let us move quickly so that we can be ready when the soldiers ride into the place between the two high sides."

Spotted Eagle led five men across to the other side of the creek. Then the Indians on both sides moved quickly until they reached the top of the bluffs, Yellow Hawk on one side, Spotted Eagle on the other.

Moving their horses back so they couldn't be seen, the Indians took up positions and waited.

In the distance, they could see the army troops approaching in a long, orderly column of two abreast.

"Ha!" Yellow Hawk said. "The soldiers line up and make it easy for us." He jacked a round into the chamber of his Winchester.

* * *

"Lieutenant," Sergeant Caviness called. "I recommend we leave the creek."

"Do you, now?" Scott replied.

"Yes, sir."

Scott held his hand up to stop the column, and Sergeant Caviness breathed a bit easier because it appeared as if Scott was going to take his suggestion.

"Men," Scott said, standing in the stirrups to address the others. "We will continue to ride up the creek bed. We will start at a canter, continue the canter for ten minutes, then slow to a trot. Above all, keep it closed up, and keep moving!"

"Sir, you don't mean the creek bed, do you?" Caviness asked. "Surely, you mean we are going to be riding along the ridgeline, following the creek bed."

"I most definitely do mean the creek bed, Sergeant. We can move much faster by staying in the creek bed than we can by riding up on the ridgeline where we will constantly be traversing gullies."

"Lieutenant, that's not a very good idea," Trooper Jones said. "If we're on the creek bed, we'll—"

"Trooper Jones, if you question my orders one more time, I'll have you in the stockade as soon as we return to garrison," Scott said, angrily.

"Yes, sir, I'll say nothin' else, sir," Jones said in a quiet and acquiescing voice.

"Forward, ho!" Lieutenant Scott ordered, and the platoon started forward at the canter.

"Sam," Trooper Jones said to Caviness a short time later, "look up ahead. See how them walls close in on the creek bed like that? Once we get in there, it will be too narrow for maneuvering. That's what I was tryin' to tell the lieutenant, but you better believe I ain't goin' to say nothin' to him now."

"Yeah, you're right," Caviness said. "Maybe I'd better see what the lieutenant has planned."

Caviness rode ahead to catch up with Lieutenant Scott.

"Lieutenant Scott, may I recommend that we leave this creek bed and take the high ground, just until we are through that restricted canyon ahead?"

"Return to your position, Sergeant," Scott ordered.

"Sir, I'm pretty sure the first sergeant selected me because he wanted me to give you the benefit of my experience. And I strongly recommend that we not go through there, what with them walls so close and all."

"I am perfectly aware of your recommendation, Sergeant Caviness," Scott replied. "Now, kindly return to your position."

"Yes, sir," Sergeant Caviness replied.

Caviness dropped back to ride alongside Jones.

"What did he say?"

"What do you think the son of a bitch said?" Caviness replied quietly.

"He's goin' to get some folks killed," Jones said.

"Yeah, well, if we're lucky, he'll be the first one to go down," Caviness said with a low growl.

On top of the bluffs that looked down onto the stream, Yellow Hawk smiled as he saw the soldiers advancing. He looked across the creek to the bluff on the other side, and saw Spotted Eagle. He pointed to the approaching soldiers, and Spotted Eagle nodded. Then, the Indians all got into position behind rocks and shrubbery so that they couldn't be seen by the approaching soldiers.

They watched as the soldiers continued to come toward the narrow pass. Yellow Hawk saw a soldier with yellow stripes on his sleeve approach the soldier who had yellow boards on his shoulders, so Yellow Hawk knew that this was a chief.

The soldier with the stripes pointed toward the place between the two high sides, and for a moment, Yellow Hawk feared that the soldiers might not come into the ambush he had waiting for them. But the soldier who was the chief shook his head, and they continued to come. Yellow Hawk smiled. This would be a great victory, and not just against unarmed farmers and travelers. This would be a victory against the long knives.

As Yellow Hawk waited for the soldiers, he thought of what it would be like around the campfires as stories were shared about his victories. Some said that the day of the Indian warrior was over, but he would prove that it is not.

Scott and the others were halfway through the narrow canyon and it was beginning to look as if they might make it all the way without incident, when one of the soldiers suddenly shouted.

"Lieutenant! Injuns atop the hills!"

Immediately after the soldier's shout, the steep walls of the bluff reverberated with the sound of rifle fire. Looking up, Scott saw Indians firing down from the top of the bluffs, on either side of the narrow draw.

"Dismount! Dismount!" Scott ordered.

"Lieutenant, no! We can't dismount! If we do that, we'll be trapped in here! We've got to keep moving!" Sergeant Caviness shouted.

"Goddamnit, Caviness! Quit questioning my commands!" Scott screamed.

Caviness looked into Lieutenant Scott's eyes and he wasn't sure what he saw. Was it confusion? Panic? Whatever it was, it wasn't confidence.

"I said dismount!" Scott ordered again.

First Sergeant Cobb had selected the troopers of this scout from a cadre of seasoned cavalrymen who knew that the moment a body of cavalry dismounted, it would lose one-fourth of its effective fighting force by virtue of the fact that every fourth man was detailed to hold the horses of the other three.

"What the hell, Sergeant?" one of the more seasoned troopers said. "Does the lieutenant have any idea what the hell he's doin'? If we dismount here, we're goin' to be sittin' ducks!"

"You plannin' on disobeying the lieutenant, are you, Reeves?" Caviness asked.

"Lieutenant, we've got to get the hell out of . . . unh!" That was as far as Trooper Jones got before he was struck down by a bullet.

"J.C.!" Caviness shouted as he saw his friend go down.

Two other soldiers were struck down as well. The Indians had the superior position, and not only were they pouring down accurate fire on the cavalry troopers below, their own position was such that it was nearly impossible for the soldiers to return fire.

"Lieutenant! Lieutenant! We've got to get out of here now!" Caviness shouted.

"Uh . . ." Scott replied, but he was completely unable to speak.

"Lieutenant, give the command to withdraw!" Caviness said. "If you don't, you're goin' to lose ever' man!"

Scott nodded. "Y . . . Yes," he said. "Yes, we'll withdraw."

Caviness waited for a moment for Scott to give the command, but Scott seemed frozen in place, unable to make a sound.

"Troopers! Mount up!" Caviness ordered. "Withdraw with fire!" he shouted and, pointing his pistol toward the top of the overhang, he began firing as he urged his horse into a gallop. The others, including Lieutenant Scott, followed.

"Yip, yip, yip, yee, yee, yee!" Yellow Hawk shouted and he and the others stood and fired at the retreating soldiers. Then, when all the soldiers were gone, Yellow Hawk and his men climbed down the side of the bluff and hurried over to the fallen soldiers. The Indians began firing into the bodies of the soldiers, and then they stripped, scalped, and mutilated them.

Chapter Ten

Fort Laramie

By the time the detail returned to the fort, Scott had recovered enough from the paralysis induced by his fear that he was once more in charge of his column. Just as he approached the gate, he halted his men, then orchestrated their entry in the way he wanted them to proceed for what he knew would be a pass in review.

When the entire detail was inside the post, the massive gates were closed behind them. Practically the entire post had turned out to watch their return, and some had already noticed that there were fewer soldiers returning, than had departed.

Scott, mindful that he and his men were the center of attention, led them to the center of the parade ground, near the flagpole. There, he halted his command, brought them around in parade front formation, called them to attention. Then he galloped to the flagpole to render his report to

Colonel Gibbon, who, with the others of the post, had turned out to welcome the troops home.

"Sir, Lieutenant Scott reporting the return of the scouting party, authorized by you to search out, and engage the enemy. I am pleased to report that we did locate a large force of Shoshone Indians, under Yellow Hawk, and did engage them in battle, resulting in numerous Indian casualties. I now request the privilege of leading my command in a pass in review."

Colonel Gibbon returned Lieutenant Scott's salute, then invited him to pass in review.

Scott galloped back to the men who were in one long, company front formation.

"Form column of twos to the left! Pass in review!" Scott said.

Pershing and Holbrook were standing out on the porch of the supply room, watching the proceedings out on the parade ground.

"That's a little grandiose, isn't it?" Pershing asked. "Passing in review with only twenty men?"

"Seventeen men," Holbrook corrected. "Three are missing, and I don't see Trooper Jones. I wonder what happened."

"Apparently, they engaged hostiles," Pershing said.

After passing in review, Lieutenant Scott dismissed his men, and they left the parade grounds, leading their horses to the stable. One of the privates took Scott's horse, so Scott could render a more complete report to Colonel Gibbon.

Pershing and Holbrook remained out on the porch as the soldiers, leading their horses, came walking by. The expressions on their faces were difficult to read. They weren't joyful as one might expect of returning troops.

"Sergeant Caviness," Holbrook called down.

Caviness stopped, but he didn't come over to the supply room.

"Yes, sir?" Caviness asked.

"I count three men short. Will they be in later?"

"No, sir, they won't be comin' back."

"Where are they? What happened?"

"They was all three kilt, sir."

"Trooper Jones?"

"Yes, sir, he was kilt."

"What happened?"

"Lieutenant, I'm just a sergeant. It ain't my place to be a' givin' any report. You want to know that, you'll have to be gettin' it from Lieutenant Scott."

"Very well, Sergeant. Carry on."

"By your leave, sir," Caviness said, saluting.

Both Pershing and Holbrook returned the salute.

"I don't know what happened," Holbrook said. "But I've got a feeling that your classmate didn't do all that well."

"Yes," Pershing said. "From what little bit Sergeant Caviness told us, or more precisely, didn't tell us, I think you are right."

* * *

In the commandant's office at Old Bedlam, Scott was giving his report.

"We encountered the hostiles and exchanged gunfire. During the ensuing battle, I regret to say, we sustained three killed: Troopers Jones, Travis, and Calhoun."

"Trooper Jones was killed?"

"Yes, sir."

Colonel Gibbon stroked his chin. "Trooper Jones will be quite a loss. Of course, so will Troopers Travis and Calhoun. But Jones was an old soldier and, despite his occasional lapses into the bottle, he was very much a stabilizing influence on the younger soldiers. Where are they?"

"They are where they fell, sir."

"You mean to tell me that you abandoned three troopers?" Colonel Gibbon asked.

"We had no choice, Colonel," Lieutenant Scott replied. "We were under direct fire from Indians who held the high ground to either side of us. Also, we were outnumbered."

"How many Indians were there?"

"I'd say there were at least fifty, Colonel, and maybe more. And remember, I had only twenty men with me."

"Well, we can't just leave our men out there," Colonel Gibbon said.

"They're dead, sir," Scott said. "They were dead when we left, or I would never have left them."

Colonel Gibbon nodded, and stroked his chin. "Yes," he said. "Still, I don't know what's left of them now. Those devils do love to mutilate bodies."

"Give me an entire troop to command this time, Colonel, and I'll retrieve the bodies."

"I will send an entire troop, but I'm going to put Captain Kirby in charge. I want you to go as his second in command, since you have now had experience with the Indians."

"Colonel, I hope you aren't blaming me for this," Scott said. "When the Indians attacked, I harkened back to some of the tactical classes I took while at West Point, and realized that being badly outnumbered by a foe that held the high ground, situation and terrain were against me. I felt that it was my duty to look out for the safety of my men. I didn't want to wind up like Custer or Fetterman."

"No, I'm not blaming you," Colonel Gibbon said. "I'm sure that, under the circumstances, you had no choice. In fact, you are to be commended for not losing any more men than you did."

"When will we be going out again, sir? I'm anxious to recover the bodies of those brave troopers."

"Tomorrow morning," Colonel Gibbon said. "I want you to get with Captain Kirby tonight and give him as much information as you can about what you encountered today. Also, write out a report about the action, so I can send it up through channels. There has been some talk of closing Fort Laramie because, and I'm quoting the War Department here, 'All Indian hostilities have ceased and the need no longer exists for a military presence in the Territory of Wyoming.' Perhaps information from your experience will convince them that closing Fort Laramie now might be a bit premature."

"Yes, sir," Scott said.

When Scott stepped out of the company headquarters building, he heard the bang of the signal cannon. Then, as the bugler played retreat, the flag was lowered. Scott came to attention and saluted, holding his salute until the music stopped.

A few minutes later, Lieutenant Scott and Captain Kirby were in the sutler's store sharing a table at the officers' bar.

"Perhaps it was my fault to ride into a narrow draw like that," Scott admitted. "But the information I had was that we were after only a few Indians, no more than ten, or so. And, quite frankly, it was my intention to draw them out, to entice them to attack us. I was certain that my superior manpower, and firepower, would win out.

"What I didn't realize was that he had not ten, but at least fifty men with him, and every one of them was armed with a repeater rifle. The next thing I knew, we were facing a veritable hurricane of bullets."

"Damn! What did you do?" Kirby asked.

"I did the only thing I could do," Scott said. "I ordered us to engage the hostiles as we withdrew."

"I understand that Trooper Jones was one of the three men who was killed."

"Yes, Jones, Travis, and Calhoun. Jones, as I'm sure you know, was one of our most experienced men."

"Yes, with a Medal of Honor," Captain Kirby said. He raised his beer. "Here's to Troopers Jones, Travis, and Calhoun. May we meet them again at Fiddler's Green."

"Fiddler's Green," Lieutenant Scott replied, lifting his own beer.

Over in the barracks, Sergeant Caviness was going through the belongings of Troopers Jones, Travis, and Calhoun. First Sergeant Cobb was with him, and the two sergeants were alone in the barracks.

"Here's J.C.'s medal," Caviness said, laying the ribbon-suspended star on Jones's bunk.

"What are we goin' to do with it?" Cobb asked. "Does he have any relatives that you know of?"

"He's got a sister back in Ohio that he's spoke about some. She's married to a preacher man. I figure we can send the medal to her."

"What about Travis and Calhoun?"

Caviness shook his head. "I tell you the truth, Top, I ain't even sure that's their real names. We get folks like that in the army, you know. They're runnin' away from somethin': the law or, more times than not, a wife, and they give some phony name to join the army. I've done been through their things and there ain't neither one of 'em got anything worth sendin' anywhere, anyhow. Same as Jones, 'cept for the medal."

"I reckon you're right."

"They didn't have to die, you know," Caviness said after a moment.

"What do you mean?"

"I mean they didn't have to die. Lieutenant Scott damn near the same as kilt them. Jones and me both tried to tell him he didn't have no business ridin' in between them two bluffs like that, but the son of a bitch wouldn't listen to us. Then, next thing you know, they's Injuns on either side, shootin' down at us."

"Yes, well, as many Indians as there were, it probably would've happened whether you rode into the draw or not," Cobb said.

Caviness looked up in surprise. "What do you mean, as many Indians as there was?"

"Well, there were fifty Indians to your twenty."

"Where did you hear that?"

"I overheard Lieutenant Scott tell. Are you telling me that isn't true?"

"The lieutenant said they was fifty Injuns?"

"Yes. Are you saying there weren't that many?"

Caviness didn't answer. Instead, he merely continued folding Jones's spare uniforms and long handle underwear.

"Caviness, how many Indians were there?"

"If the lieutenant says they was fifty, I ain't goin'

to say they wasn't. I don't intend to get into no pissin' contest with 'im."

Cobb nodded. "Smart idea," he said.

Back in his quarters, Lieutenant Scott was sitting at the kitchen table, writing the report Colonel Gibbon had requested. Sue was kneading bread dough and setting it to rise.

"Sue," Scott said. "Listen to this after-action report I'm writing for Colonel Gibbon, and see what you think."

Sue quit kneading the bread, and looked over at her husband, whose eyes were gleaming with excitement, as he began to read.

"On August 15, 1887, Lieutenant Clayton M. Scott set off from Fort Laramie in command of a small cavalry detachment, to pursue a Shoshone raiding party that had murdered as many as eleven innocent white civilians during their brutal rampage.

"Lieutenant Scott pursued the Shoshones fifteen miles into a place where the river passes between two high bluffs. There, Lieutenant Scott encountered a much larger force then he had been told to expect. Though he attempted to surprise the Shoshone, his soldiers had been spotted and the hostiles, who had the advantage of high ground and cover, began firing down onto Lieutenant Scott's small detachment, killing three soldiers, they being: Troopers J. C. Jones, Edward Travis, and Marcus Calhoun.

"Lieutenant Scott ordered that fire be returned, directing the soldiers' efforts in such a way as to inflict very heavy casualties on the hostile force.

"But, as the cavalry detachment was greatly outnumbered and unable to mount a successful attack as long as the Shoshone had the advantage of position and numbers, Lieutenant Scott ordered a retreat. As his men galloped out of the confined area, Lieutenant Scott remained back, being the last one to leave, so that he might cover the withdrawal of his troops, and to prevent any further casualties."

Scott looked up after he finished reading the report. "What do you think?" he asked.

"I don't know," Sue said. "Why did you write the report, speaking of yourself in the second person?"

"I felt it would be more professional, that way."

"Or, perhaps you found it easier to praise yourself so highly."

The smile left Scott's face and, angrily, he moved toward her. Sue backed away from him, frightened by his appearance and action.

"You ignorant, worthless bitch!" he shouted. He picked up the bread dough and threw it against the wall. "I should know better than to ask you your opinion about anything!"

Scott stormed out of the kitchen and Sue, after waiting for a moment to be sure he wouldn't be coming back, went over to retrieve the bread dough.

Chapter Eleven

Wind River Reservation

Using grasshoppers for bait, Ska Luta had a good day of fishing, and as he left the banks of the swiftly moving Wind River, he was carrying three golden trout home for Elk Woman to cook, and he could already taste them.

"*Unci!*" he called as he returned to the small, one-room cabin where he was raised. "*Unci*, I have fish for our supper!" Even though he knew that Elk Woman was not his grandmother, she was the one who had raised him from infancy, and he had addressed her as such for his entire life.

When he stepped inside though, he saw Elk Woman lying on the floor.

"*Unci!*" he shouted. "*Unci!* What is wrong?"

Quickly, he knelt beside her and, putting his hand on her face, felt her move.

"Ska Luta," Elk Woman said, her voice so weak that Ska Luta could barely hear the words.

"What happened, *Unci?* Why are you on the floor?"

"I feel that my time has come, Ska Luta. Help me to my bed. I do not wish to die on the floor like a *tonkala*."

"You are not a mouse, *Unci*. But I will help you to your bed."

Ska Luta picked her up and laid her on the bed.

"*He-ay-hee-ee, hecheto aloe!*" Elk Woman said, singing the words, "Great Spirit, it is finished."

Elk Woman took Ska Luta's hand and squeezed it as hard as she could, but so diminished was her strength now that she could barely squeeze.

"I am thankful to the Great Spirit for bringing you to me," she said. "You have given my life purpose."

"*Unci*, you have done more than that for me. You have given me life, for surely, I would have died."

"Your white father's name is Glee Jon," Elk Woman said. "I do not know if he is alive." This was the first time in Ska Luta's entire life, that Elk Woman had ever spoken the name of his white father.

"I have no white father, *Unci*. I have only you."

Again, Elk woman squeezed his hand, then her hand grew loose, and Ska Luta saw the last breath leave her body.

Elk Woman was dressed in her finest clothes with a beaded necklace around her neck. Lying on the burial platform with her were her most treasured possessions: a copper kettle, a mirror, and a silver hairbrush.

The *pejula wacasa,* the medicine man, sang prayers to the Great Spirit as the drums maintained a steady beat in the background, the beating of the drums representing the connection between "the creature and the creator."

"Who speaks for the life of this woman?" the medicine man asked.

"I speak for this woman," Ska Luta said.

"How is it that you have the power to speak for this woman?"

"I speak for her because she is my grandmother," Ska Luta said.

"Can you speak well for her? Can you tell *nagi tanka,* the Great Spirit, why he should welcome Elk Woman?"

"I can."

"Then, speak for her, Ska Luta."

"The Great Spirit did not provide Elk Woman with a child. He did that, because the Great Spirit knew that Elk Woman would be needed to care for another child, one without mother or father, and she would treat that child as her own.

"I am that child, for it was as a small one, with no mother and no father that I came to Elk Woman."

Others spoke for Elk Woman as well, one of the men saying that, because she never had a husband, that every man was a husband to her. This was not said, nor was it understood to be, any kind of a sexual innuendo, but was said and understood to mean that she was a woman who was respected by every man. Several of the women said that because she had no sister, that every woman was a sister to her.

Finally, the funeral service was completed, and Ska Luta returned to the cabin where he had been raised and sat there, feeling very alone. He thought about the name of his father, the name Elk Woman had given him long ago.

Glee John.

With the cattle drive

Elmer Gleason was the first to awaken and, even before dawn, had laid a fire, started a pot of coffee, and started baking biscuits. Duff was the next one up, and he walked over to the fire and looked at the coffeepot that was sitting on the iron frame that was over the glowing coals.

"Coffee's ready, biscuits ain't," Elmer said.

"Coffee's enough," Duff said, using his gloved hand to pick up the pot. He poured himself a cup, then walked around to the other side of the chuck wagon and leaned back against it, drinking the coffee as he looked out over the plateau.

The first gray light of morning was just breaking upon the herd, and the sun, which was still low in the east, sent long bars of light slashing through the ponderosa pine trees, and the morning mist curled around the tops of the trees like wisps of smoke.

The two thousand head of cattle now milling

about on the plateau were acutely aware of smells, sensations, and pines, and though Black Angus were less apt to stampede than Longhorn, or even Hereford, Duff was well aware that they could be spooked by a wolf, a lightning flash, or just about any loud noise. Finishing his coffee, he tossed out the remaining grounds, then saddled his horse.

"Here," Elmer said, handing him a bacon biscuit. "You more'n likely won't be comin' back for breakfast."

"Thanks," Duff said, taking the proffered sandwich.

As Duff rode around the herd this morning, he listened with an analytical ear to the crying and bawling of cattle and, hearing nothing out of the ordinary, turned his thoughts to Meagan. He found himself thinking a lot about her lately, and he realized that if he let her, she could replace Skye in his heart.

But if he did let that happen, would that be dishonoring Skye's memory?

No, Skye wasn't here any longer, and if she were able to look down on him, to speak to him from beyond the grave, he had a feeling that she would approve of Meagan. And why shouldn't she? Meagan certainly felt no jealousy about Skye. She had let Duff know, in clear and unequivocal terms, that she respected the love that he had for Skye, as well as the fact that she still occupied a place in his heart.

Within half an hour, the others were up, had their breakfast, and were taking up their positions.

Looking toward Meagan, he knew that she was totally unaware that she was the subject of his ruminations. Instead, Meagan was concentrating on getting the herd ready for today's drive. Duff watched her dash forward to intercept three or four steers that had moved away from the herd. She stopped the stragglers and pushed them back with the others, and Duff watched with admiration. They had gone riding together before, so he was well aware of her equestrian skills, but never had it been morc apparent than it was right now. It was almost as if she and the horse were sharing the same musculature and nerve structure.

Though it was common practice for men to make fun of how much a woman had to have with her when traveling, Meagan had shown up for this drive with only what she could carry in her saddlebags. On the other hand, Duff, Elmer, and the other three men who had come with them had a wagon to haul their stuff. The vehicle was being drawn by a particularly fine-looking team of mules, and it was serving them well.

When first they left Sky Meadow, it had been the policy for Elmer to detach himself from the drive after breakfast and push on ahead at a faster rate. But since encountering Sergeant O'Riley and the soldiers from Fort Fetterman, where he learned of a warring party of Indians, Duff was keeping the wagon with the rest of the herd.

With whistles, shouts, and prodding, the herd got underway, moving forward as one great, black wave, slowly but steadily, making approximately four miles per hour. They were capable of traveling faster, but Duff was aware that if they traveled too fast, they would walk off some of their weight. And though his contract with the army was per head, and not per pound, he felt honor bound to get the cattle to them in as good a condition as possible.

He had come a long way since moving to America from Scotland. He had raised cattle in Scotland, but he had never made long trail drives there, as he had, so often, since coming here.

He looked back over at Meagan, and smiled. She was wearing the same clothes as all the other drovers, doing so because, she told him, she wanted to "fit in." But with the form-fitting denim trousers, and the clinging shirt, she was far from fitting in.

Meagan, totally unaware of Duff's scrutiny of her, couldn't recall when she had been so tired. It was a bone-aching, backbreaking tired, and yet there was an exhilaration that transcended the tiredness. The exhilaration came from the excitement of the drive and from the feeling of doing something that was beyond her normal scope of activity.

She wasn't the only one who was feeling the excitement of the drive. She could see it in the eyes and on the faces of the other drovers as well. The excitement was infectious and self-feeding, and it seemed to grow as the drive progressed. It was all around them, like the smell of the air before a spring shower, or the smell of wood smoke on a crisp fall day. But it wasn't fall or spring. It was summer, and as the day progressed, the sun would beat relentlessly down on the drovers and the animals below.

Meagan knew, though, that the yellow glare of the early summer sky would mellow into the steel blue of late afternoon by the time the herd reached the place where it would be halted for the night, and then she would be refreshed with a breath of cool air. But that would be twelve hours from now.

Fort Laramie

The bright, crisp notes of "Reveille" reached into every barracks, BOQ and married officers' quarters. Lieutenant Scott rose from bed and started putting on his field uniform.

"Do you want me to fix some breakfast for you?" Sue asked, sleepily. She was still in bed.

"No. Captain Kirby has asked that I join him in the officers' mess," he said. "I don't know why Colonel Gibbon didn't give me command of the troop. I'm the one who found the Indians."

"Why should he, Clay? Captain Kirby is commander of A Troop. Of course, if the entire troop goes, it should be his command."

"This is army business, Sue. What do you know about it, anyway?"

"Clay, you've only been in the army for two years,

six if you count West Point. Remember, I've been a part of the army for my entire life."

"Being an army brat doesn't make you part of the army," Scott said with a derisive sneer.

"Perhaps not. But it certainly gives me an awareness of protocol and procedure. And I know that it would be a severe violation of protocol to give you command of A Troop, as long as Captain Kirby is its commanding officer."

"Sometimes, Sue, I wonder whose side you are on? You're my wife. You make a big thing about being part of an army family. Well now you are part of my family, and you should want what is best for me."

"But of course, I do," Sue said.

"I'm not always so sure. If you really did want what is best for me, you would convince your father to bring me back to Washington."

"Oh, Clay, let's not go through all this again."

"Don't worry. It may not be necessary now. We've got a real Indian war to fight." He smiled. "There's not another officer in my graduating class who has the opportunity I have now. I intend to get the Medal of Honor out of this."

"The Medal of Honor? Clay, you have to do something very outstanding for that. And, you have to be put in for it."

"I will be," Scott said, confidently. "Just you wait. I will be."

* * *

Outside Lieutenant Scott's quarters, the fort was awakening to a new day. From the stable came the whinnies of horses, and the brays of mules. "Assembly" was played, then he heard the echoing voices of the commanders giving their morning reports, from distant and barely audible, to voices that sounded so close it was if he was on the parade ground with them.

"A Troop all present and accounted for, sir!"

"B Troop all present and accounted for, sir!"

"C Troop all present and accounted for, sir!"

The sequential reports continued until every troop and every battalion was heard from.

As he walked toward the officers' mess, he looked over toward the dismounted formation of the Fifth Cavalry Regiment, the formation being taken this morning by Major Allison. It was quite impressive, and he imagined himself standing in front of this very formation being awarded the Medal of Honor.

As Scott thought of the report he had written for Colonel Gibbon, he smiled. Who knows? Perhaps he would be put in for the medal as a result of the action he had described in that report.

Out on the parade ground, Major Allison took the reports from the battalion commanders, and then gave the order to present arms. When arms were presented, Allison did an about-face and, with his saber, rendered a salute. At that moment the signal cannon fired, and, as the bugler played "To the Colors," the flag was run up the pole.

Scott came to attention and rendered the hand salute.

"Order, arms!" Major Allison called, and Scott could hear the sounds of carbines being returned to the order arms position.

Major Allison then dismissed the regiment, and his dismissal was followed almost immediately by the bugler playing "Mess Call."

Captain Kirby was waiting inside the officers' mess and Scott joined him at his table. An orderly brought their breakfast.

"Eat quickly, Lieutenant," Captain Kirby said. "'Boots and Saddles' in half an hour."

"Yes, sir. Oh, Colonel Gibbon asked that I present a battle report of the detachment I commanded. Will I have time to do that?"

"Yes, no problem."

"Would you like to read it?"

"Yes, it might contain some information that would be helpful to this scout."

Kirby read the report. "You left out any specifics as to how Jones and the other two troopers were killed."

"Nothing specific to say about it," Scott said. "They were killed during the battle."

"And you say you believe you killed several of the Indians?"

"Yes, sir, I'm sure we did."

"Do you have any idea how many?"

Scott shook his head. "No, sir. As I point out in

* * *

Leaving Fort Laramie, they approached the spo
where Scott had been ambushed, reaching it b
mid-afternoon. There was no question as to whethe
the bodies would still be there, because long befor
they actually got there, they saw dozens of ugl
black buzzards making circles in the sky.

"Damn," Kirby said. "I hope the buzzards and th
animals have left us enough to recover. Where wer
you, exactly, when the Indians attacked?"

"We were following the creek bed," Scott replie
He pointed. "We were there, in the draw betwee
the two bluffs."

"My God, Scott, you took your command into
confined space like that?" Kirby asked, surprised b
Scott's response.

"Yes, sir, I deemed it necessary to fulfill th
mission."

"How was that necessary?"

Scott grew defensive under the questioning an
he looked back toward the troop of men who wer
following them. The bugler was right behind Scot
and Captain Kirby, First Sergeant Cobb, and th
guideon bearer were next, then Sergeant Caviness
as riding in the first rank of the troop. He didn't
ink anyone had heard the captain's question.

"Lieutenant Scott?"

"Sir?"

You were going to tell me how it was necessary

the report, the Indians had the advantage of high ground and cover, so we were never able to reconnoiter the area and, of course, we had to leave the three troopers who were killed."

"I just hope there's enough left of those poor devils to bring home," Kirby said as he took a drink of coffee.

"Captain Kirby, you aren't blaming me for leaving those three men there, are you?"

"No. From what I have read in this report, under the circumstances, I think you did exactly the right thing. You had no choice but to get out of there when you did. The enemy held the high ground, and you had no room for maneuver. The wonder is that you didn't lose more men."

"I thank you, Captain, for your understanding."

Chapter Twelve

Colonel Gibbon had turned out the entire regiment to see A Troop off this morning, and ordered the Fifth Cavalry Band to provide music. The band played a bouncy rendition of "The Girl I Left Behind Me." To the accompaniment of the music, A Troop, in mounted columns of two, rode around the parade ground of Fort Laramie as it performed its departure parade. Despite the fact that only one troop was deploying, there was a surprisingly large turnout of spectators to watch, as well as those who watched from the windows of the houses of the married officers and the soap-suds row quarters of the noncommissioned officers.

A short while later, as the troop rode through Millersburg, the small town that was just outside the gates, the citizens of the town were gathered on either side of the street to wish them well. They, like most of the civilians in the area, had been

frightened by the marauding Indians, and were anxious to see peace restored.

"Take care of them Injuns!" one man shouted.

"Hang 'em! Hang 'em high!" another yelled.

The concerned citizens weren't the only ones who had turned out. As they rode by Maxine's House of Delight, there were several young women in attire that could only be referred to as risqué standing on the upper balcony of the two-story edifice. They leaned over the banister to look down on the passing body of men, and in doing so, unashamedly displayed their cleavage for the enjoyment of the soldiers.

As they recognized some of the soldiers, they would call out to them, causing some of the younger troopers some embarrassment.

"Trooper Canfield, don't you go getting your thing shot off now! Me 'n' you have been having a lot of fun with that," one of the girls shouted, and the soldiers riding closest to Canfield began to tease him.

"Well now, Canfield, just what have you and th girl been doing with your thing?" someone ask and several of the soldiers laughed.

"At ease in the ranks!" First Sergeant called. "This ain't no church picnic we're goi

"First Sergeant, I don't think church pic anything to do with whatever Canfield doxie was talkin' about," Sergeant Cavine and the men, including even Captain Ki out loud.

for you to lead your command into a restricted area like that in order to fulfill your mission."

"Yes, sir. Well, my mission was to find the renegade Indians, and we did that, Captain. We had spotted the Indians and I saw that they were retreating. I believed that the best way to overtake them was to take the most direct route, and that led me up the creek bed."

"Didn't you say there were fifty Indians? What on earth would make you go into an area like that when both terrain and enemy forces were against you? Didn't you learn anything about tactics at the Point?"

"Yes, sir, and I also learned that sometimes a commander has to be flexible and take the initiative if the mission is to be accomplished. With all due respect, sir, you weren't there."

Captain Kirby took his hat off and ran his hand through his graying hair. "You're right, Lieutenant," he said with a sigh. "I wasn't there. And Sergeant Caviness and Trooper Jones were, and I know they would not have let you go in if they didn't think it was all right. I'll not sit in judgment over you."

"Thank you, sir. As I said, I was only trying to fulfill the mission in what I thought was the best way possible."

"Truth is, Scott, I guess you should be commended for not losing any more men than you did. You were smart, once you were engaged by superior forces under such conditions, to leave the battlefield."

They saw the three bodies as soon as they entered the draw. It was easy to see them, because all three of the cavalrymen had been stripped naked. Their naked bodies were very white against the dark sand.

"Oh!" Scott said, turning head aside as they approached.

All three of the slain soldiers had the top of their heads removed, not just the scalps, but the entire cranium. The brains of the three men were spilling out onto the ground. The chest cavities were open as well, and the hearts of the three men had been cut out. They had also been emasculated, though their penises were nowhere to be found, probably having been eaten by wild animals.

"Oh, my God!" Scott said. He dismounted quickly, then stood beside his horse with his head pressed hard against the saddle.

"Are you all right, Clay?" Captain Kirby asked, concern in his voice.

For a long moment, Scott didn't answer.

"Lieutenant Scott?" Kirby asked, even more concerned now.

"Yes, sir," Scott finally said, his voice weak. "Who in heaven's name would do something like that? And why?"

"Indians do it to keep their enemies from going to heaven," Kirby said.

"Savages," Scott said, spitting the word. "Bloody, ignorant savages."

"Cap'n," Sergeant Caviness said. "May I suggest

that we put men on top of both bluffs, keepin' an eye open?"

"Yes, good idea, Sergeant, thank you," Captain Kirby said.

Lieutenant Scott perceived that Caviness was looking at him, no doubt in judgment, as if pointing out that a good officer will recognize a good idea, when it is proposed by an experienced NCO.

"Get some tarpaulins out, and get these men wrapped up," Captain Kirby ordered.

"Wrapped up?" Scott said. "Do you mean you plan to take them with us?"

"Of course, I intend to take them back with us. Why do you think we came here, Lieutenant?"

"Well, to recover the bodies, yes, sir. But I didn't think we would be taking them back."

"What would you do with them, Lieutenant?"

"We came across a family of settlers that were massacred, and we buried them where we found them," Scott said.

"You buried the whole family?"

"Yes, sir."

"Well, there you go, Lieutenant, they were buried with family. We can do no less for these men. They are our family, and we are going to take them back to the post and give them a decent burial."

"Yes, sir," Scott said. He nodded. "Yes, you are right, of course. That is exactly what we should do."

"I'm glad I have your concurrence," Kirby said. His reply was sarcastic, but Scott just nodded, as if not recognizing the scorn.

"First Sergeant," Kirby called, and First Sergeant Cobb hurried over and saluted. "Yes, sir?"

"Select ten men to take these bodies back to the post."

"You want them to start back today, Cap'n?"

"No, we'll leave this confined area and make camp on high ground somewhere. The detail can start back tomorrow."

"Yes, sir. If it's all right with you, Cap'n, I'd like to send Sergeant Caviness back in charge of the detail. I mean, bein' as him and Jones was such good friends, and all."

"Of course, it's all right," Kirby said.

"Captain Kirby, if you send ten men back, it will decrease our strength while we are in pursuit," Scott said.

"How many Indians did you see, Lieutenant Scott?" Kirby asked.

"I . . ." Scott looked back toward Caviness, and saw that Caviness was waiting for him to answer. "I'm not sure, Captain. We were under fire at the time, and the Indians were holding the high ground, which made it difficult to ascertain their strength."

"We will have ninety men remaining, even after we send the burial team back to the post," Captain Caviness said. "If you are uncomfortable facing the Indians with ninety men, I can put you in charge of the burial detail and you can return to the post, while we continue our scout."

"No! No, sir, I didn't mean that at all!" Scott said,

quickly. "I'm quite certain that we have enough men to deal with any Indians we might find."

"I'm glad to see that you feel that way," Captain Kirby said.

As it was now nearly five o'clock, the troop made camp for the first night on the high bluff. Lieutenant Scott and Captain Kirby bivouacked in a Silbey tent. The Silbey tent was twelve feet tall and eighteen feet in diameter at the base. It was held up by a single pole in the center. The front door was eight feet, nine inches tall, with a rear ventilation doorway that was five feet high. The base of the tent was secured with reinforced brass spur washer grommet, which made the tent quite comfortable.

In contrast to the tent the two officers occupied, the rest of the soldiers stayed in small, two-man tents, each soldier carrying a "shelter half," or one side of the tent. For supper that evening, Captain Kirby and Lieutenant Scott sat at a field table that was laid with china and silver, as comfortable with this familiar setting as if they were in their own dining room.

"Would you like some jam?" Kirby asked.

"Yes, thank you, sir," Scott replied, taking the jar of jam from Kirby. He spread it on a piece of buttered bread.

"I hope the men are enjoying their supper this evening," Kirby said. "For the rest of the scout, we'll be dining on hard tack, bacon, beans, and coffee."

"Captain Kirby, have you been in battle before?"

"A few times," Kirby said. "I was with Colonel Gibbon during the Little Big Horn fight. If Custer had followed orders—if he had waited until we, and General Terry joined up with him, we would have had four thousand soldiers at the site of the battle, and the Indians would have been trapped between us."

"We studied Custer's blunder in tactics at West Point," Scott said. "I must confess that, when I encountered the Indians the other day, and realized that we were in an untenable position and facing superior numbers and firepower, the idea that I might wind up like Custer passed through my mind.

Kirby chuckled. "Well, I think that if we encounter any Indians during this scout, they will not constitute such a threat. From the information we have received from the chiefs at Wind River Reservation, Yellow Hawk's band has grown since he first left the reservation, but supposedly he doesn't have more than fifteen or twenty warriors with him."

"I think that number is very wrong," Scott said. "I am sure that I counted more than that. I counted at least forty."

"You may have thought so," Kirby said. "But the Indians are very good at deception. If you were in the draw, and they had the high ground on each side of you, it would be easy for them to appear in one place, and then quickly appear again, to make it seem as if there were more."

Scott shook his head. "No," he said. "I'm sure I counted more than forty."

"Well, no matter. As I said, even after we dispatch the burial team, we'll still have ninety men," Kirby said. "So even if Yellow Hawk does have forty men with him, I doubt that he will attempt to engage us. Indians don't like to fight unless they have an absolute confidence that they have the advantage. No doubt our biggest problem will be in locating them."

"I want to find them, and I want to do battle with them," Scott said.

Kirby chuckled. "I understand. You want to record some experience to enhance your chances of promotion."

"Yes," Scott said.

"Well, there's nothing wrong with that, I guess. After all, that's why we have an army."

"Captain, when we engage the enemy, you will give me an opportunity to prove myself, won't you?"

"Prove yourself?"

"I mean, uh, well, if there is an opportunity to be awarded the Medal of Honor, I want to take it. I know that if I were to receive the Medal of Honor, it would make a big impression on my father-in-law."

"You know, Clay, I've been in the army a long time," Kirby said. "I'm still a captain, though some of my classmates from the Academy are majors and lieutenant colonels now. And I have seen my share of battle. I'm not sure that being in battle is all that it takes."

Outside they heard the bugler blow "Taps," and Captain Kirby leaned over to extinguish the candle.

"We'd better get some rest. We've a long ride tomorrow."

Chapter Thirteen

With the cattle drive

Mercifully, the yellow glare of the summer sky mellowed into the steel blue of late afternoon by the time the herd reached the place where it would be halted for the night, and Meagan and the other drovers were refreshed with a breath of cool air.

To the west, the sun dropped all the way to the foothills, while to the east evening purple, like bunches of violets, gathered in the notches and timbered draws. Behind the setting sun, great bands of color spread out along the horizon. Those few clouds that dared to intrude on this perfect day were under-lit by the sun and they glowed orange in the darkening sky.

"All right, folks, supper's ready," Elmer called.

"Damn, that looks good, Mr. Gleason," Jimmy Sherman said, checking out the fare.

"Ha! Sherman, you are such a chow hound that

if he cooked up a pot of cow dung, you'd be the first one in line," Jory Bates said.

The others laughed, then Bates remembered that there was a lady in their midst.

"Beg your pardon, Miss Parker, for sayin' cow dung," he said.

"Mr. Bates, considering what you could have called it, I think no pardon is needed."

The others laughed.

That night, Muley Harris and Ira Adams could smell the herd before they could hear it, and they could hear it before they saw it. Because the cattle were black, the herd looked like a large shadow within a shadow.

"Let's move in real quiet, and take off about a hunnert cows from the end that's the farthest away from where they're a' campin'," Harris said.

"How we goin' to do that? We goin' to count 'em, or what?" Adams asked.

"No, we ain't goin' to have to actual count 'em," Harris said. "I figure we can purt' nigh guess at how many there is. Then, what we'll do is, ride in real slow and real quiet, and just kind of start 'em movin'."

"What about the nighthawk? What if he sees us?"

"Well, if he sees us, there ain't no need to be quiet no more, so we'll just shoot the son of a bitch, then take our cows and maybe stampede the herd.

They'll be so busy tryin' to save the rest of the cows that we'll get away with what we've took."

"All right," Adams said.

"Quiet, now. No more talkin'."

The two men rode down the ridgeline toward the herd of cattle that were bunched alongside the Chugwater. Harris pointed to the place in the herd where he thought they could go to carve out about a hundred head.

As they cut the cows from the herd, the cows passed over a layer of rocks that lay alongside the stream. When they did so, there was a clacking sound of hooves on rock.

Duff was riding nighthawk when he heard the faint sound. Since the herd was at rest, he looked around to find the source of the sound and saw a long dark line moving away from the main herd.

It took him a moment to realize exactly what was happening, but once he figured it out, he reacted quickly.

"Cattle thieves!" he shouted. "Everyone up! We're being robbed!"

Duff's shout awakened Elmer and the drovers, but it also alerted the thieves, and one of them fired a shot toward him. Duff saw the muzzle flash, then heard the bullet whiz by, amazingly close for a wild shot in the dark.

Duff shot back, aiming toward where he had seen the muzzle flame. The sound of two guns in the middle of the night didn't disturb the main herd, but it did set the pilfered cows to running.

Duff looked through the dust raised by the swirling cattle, trying to find one of the thieves. He saw a horse, but its saddle was empty, and he believed he may have scored with the shot he had directed toward the muzzle flash. Then another horse appeared, this time with a rider. The rider fired at Duff, and Duff returned fire. The rider fell from the saddle, and the horse galloped off, to join the other riderless horse.

It appeared as if there had only been two thieves, because he saw no one else, but the cattle the thieves were trying to steal were now running. The main herd, though made restless by the flashes and explosions in the night, milled around, but resisted running.

Elmer and Jory appeared then.

"Where are the rustlers?" Elmer asked.

"Only two, I'm thinkin'," Duff said. "And I got them both. Elmer, stay here with the main herd, keep them from stampeding. Jory, would ye be comin' with me, lad? We'll run these down."

"Yes, sir!" Jory answered, spurring his horse into a gallop toward the fleeing cows.

Duff urged his own horse into a gallop, and within a minute he and Jory were riding alongside the running, lumbering animals.

"We've got to get to the front!" Duff shouted.

The cows were running as fast as they could run, which was about three-quarters of the speed of the horses, and that meant it was fairly easy to overtake them. Within a few minutes, Duff and Jory rode to the front, where they were able to turn them. Once the cows were turned, they lost their forward momentum, slowed their running to a trot, and finally to a walk. When that happened, it was fairly easy to turn them around and start them back.

By the time Duff and Jory got the cows that had been cut out back, Elmer, Ford, and Sherman were riding around the standing herd, keeping them calm. The cows that had been cut out seemed happy to be back in the comfortable company of the herd, and within another half hour, all was quiet and things returned to normal.

"Have you seen the rustlers?" Duff asked.

"Yeah," Elmer answered. "That is, we seen what's left of 'em. Both of 'em was run over by the herd. They're cut up pretty good."

"I don't suppose you recognized either of them?" Jory asked.

"Jory, their own mama wouldn't recognize 'em," Elmer said.

"What'll we do with 'em, Mr. MacCallister?" Jeff Ford asked.

"We'll bury them," Duff said.

"Somehow, it don't seem right to be burying folks that we don't know. I mean without no marker or anything," Ford said.

"Son, I've seen hundreds of unmarked graves out here—men, women, and children," Elmer said. "These here will just be two more."

"I reckon so," Ford said.

"I may as well get the biscuits and coffee goin'," Elmer said. "It'll be light soon."

"Go ahead, Elmer, we'll take care of this business," Duff said.

When Elmer returned to the encampment, he saw Meagan standing by the tongue of the wagon.

"I take it everything is under control now?" she asked.

"Yes, ma'am, there ain't nothin' for you to be a'worryin' about now," Elmer said. "It's all over with."

"Elmer, I'm not some dainty schoolgirl. I heard Duff call out that there were rustlers. I just want to know what happened, is all."

Elmer chuckled. "No, ma'am, I reckon you ain't exactly no schoolgirl at that," he said. "Truth is, a couple of fellas tried to run off some of our cows. Then, when they saw that Duff seen 'em, they took a couple of shots at him. That's where they made their mistake."

"Duff is all right, isn't he?" Meagan asked, anxiously.

"Oh, yes, ma'am, Duff is just fine. Like I said, when them two shot at Duff, they made a big mistake."

"Duff shot them?"

"He shot both of 'em. Two shots, in the dark, and he got 'em both. I tell you the truth, I've known some pretty good shots in my day, but I ain't never seen anyone as good as Duff. He can shoot a gun, pistol, or rifle, like nobody's business."

Elmer started pulling out some pans.

"Are you starting breakfast?"

"May as well, it's too late to try and go back to bed now. Sun will be up in another hour."

"I'll help."

"You don't need to do that."

"I know," Meagan said with a broad smile. "I want to."

Fort Laramie

Lieutenant Pershing was on temporary duty to Fort Laramie where, along with Lieutenant Holbrook, according to the written orders that assigned him here, he was charged with the following task:

> *Write a TO&E for a cavalry regiment, and a cavalry troop. Upon completion of the assignment, the finished paperwork, including all information used to make the allocations, will be sent to the Department of Army for final approval and general distribution to every cavalry regiment and troop within the United States Army. Time authorized for this task is two months.*

The TO&E, which stood for "Table of Organization and Equipment," would lay out in the most minute detail the job of every assigned soldier from private, farrier, hospital steward, bugler, corporal, sergeant, first sergeant, sergeant-major, surgeon, lieutenant, captain, major, and lieutenant colonel to be assigned to a cavalry troop. In addition to the personnel requirements, Pershing and Holbrook would also be responsible for deciding upon the equipment to be issued: sabers, rifles, pistols, ammunition, lanterns, field stoves, packs, shelter-halves, ropes, tent stakes, ponchos, web belts, entrenching tools, canteens, mess kits, number of horses, saddles, and wheeled vehicles. The work was detailed and painstaking, and because what they did here would apply to every cavalry unit in the entire United States Army, they had to be very particular.

Lieutenant Holbrook had been "keeping company" with Mary Meacham, daughter of the post surgeon. Then, when Holbrook's sister, Clara, came to Fort Laramie for a visit, Holbrook invited Pershing to join him, Mary, and Clara for a picnic down by the Laramie River. Pershing accepted.

With a picnic lunch loaded in an army buckboard, the four drove down to the river. The trail passed through a stand of aspens, across a level bench of land peppered with fluttering yellow, red, and blue wildflowers, and then up a small rise. When they reached the top of the rise, Holbrook stopped and set the brake. The four got out, and as the ladies began to spread out the blanket and take out the basket of food, Pershing and Holbrook looked out over the junction of the Laramie and Platte Rivers, both of which were shining silver in the noonday sun. Behind them lay Fort Laramie, where the flag caught a breeze, then lifted out in full spread, a bright patch of color against the pale blue sky. Involuntarily, Pershing stood a little straighter, almost as if he were coming to attention. Clara noticed Pershing's reaction, and she chuckled.

"You love it, don't you?" Clara said.

"The West? Yes," Pershing answered. "I'm from Missouri, and there are parts of Missouri that are as beautiful as any other place in the Union. But there is something about the West, something about the gray light of early morning when it's quiet. And I like it in the middle of the day, when wildflowers carpet the plains in every color of the rainbow. But I also like it in the evening, when the clouds are lit from below by the setting sun so that they glow pink and gold against the purple sky. And the stars at night? Why, they sparkle like diamonds on velvet."

Clara laughed, softly. "Why, John Pershing, you've a bit of the poet in you. It's obvious by the way you put it into words that you love this West of yours. But when I said you love it, I was talking about the army."

"Yes," Pershing said. "I like the army."

"That's not what I said either. I said you *love* it."

Pershing chuckled, then nodded. "All right. It's not something that is easy to put into words. But I guess I don't have to put it in words, not if you can see it."

"I don't see how anyone could not see what the army means to you."

"All right, people, our lunch is ready," Mary said.

"Good, I'm hungry," Pershing said, glad to be pulled away from a conversation he felt was getting much too personal.

The lunch was a bountiful one, consisting of sliced ham, potato salad, deviled eggs, fresh bread, and, for desert, chocolate cake.

As they were eating, the sound of a distant call floated to them.

"Oh, listen to the bugle," Clara said.

"It's not a bugle, it's a trumpet. Bugles are for dismounted troops," Pershing said. "Trumpets for mounted troops, each regiment is authorized six trumpets and six buglers."

"And you want to know why they are authorized six trumpets and six buglers?" Holbrook said. He pointed toward his chest with this thumb. "Because John and I *say* they are. That's part of the TO&E."

"Wait a minute, I don't understand," Mary said. "Six trumpets and six buglers? Wouldn't they be trumpeters?"

"No, they are buglers who play trumpets," John said.

"Now I'm really confused."

Holbrook laughed. "That's the purpose of the army. It is our intention to confuse people, thus such things as trumpets for mounted troops, buglers for dismounted troops, but the man behind the instrument, be he mounted or dismounted, is a bugler. You have to learn how to confuse people when you are doing something like writing a TO&E."

"That's the second time you've used those initials," Clara said.

"It's the table of organization and equipment. It's like a guidebook for every troop in the cavalry."

"Oh, my, that's quite important, isn't it?" Clara said.

"You better believe it is," Holbrook said. "When you go back home, you can tell Dad that his son is about to be published."

"Really?"

Now it was Pershing's time to laugh. "In a manner of speaking. But you won't see our names anywhere."

After dinner, another bugle call floated up to them from the fort.

"What is that call?" Clara asked.

"It's 'Fatigue Call,'" Holbrook said.

"'Fatigue Call'? What an unusual name for a song. What is it for?"

"It tells the men that it's time for them to begin their afternoon details, stable duty, working on the grounds, that sort of thing," Holbrook explained. He laced his hands behind his head, then lay back on the cloth.

"Don't you feel guilty, loafing around up here when you think you should be doing, what is it . . . stable duty? Oh, that sounds very unpleasant."

"Mucking stalls?"

Clara made a face. "Mucking stalls? I don't know what that is, but it sounds extremely unpleasant."

"Believe me, you don't want to know what it is. And it is extremely unpleasant," Pershing said.

"I can't believe you would miss doing something like that. I mean, don't you have to be there?" Clara asked.

Holbrook laughed. "Fortunately, my dear sister, officers don't actually perform fatigue call. We tell the sergeants what we want done, the sergeants tell the corporals, the corporals tell the privates, and the privates do it."

"So, what you are saying is, the privates do all the work?" Mary asked.

"Heavens, you don't expect me to do it, do you?" Holbrook asked, with a laugh.

"I wonder when A Troop will get back," Pershing said.

"I think they're supposed to be out for three or four days. That is, if they don't run into any trouble," Holbrook said. "I don't like to talk out of turn, but I feel a lot better about the troop with Captain Kirby in command. Nobody has said anything directly, but I have a sneaky feeling that Scott didn't exactly shine on his last scout."

"Yes, I sort of got that feeling as well," Pershing said. "Although I did read the report he rendered. It was . . . well for want of a better word, I'll say it might have been a bit embellished."

Holbrook chuckled. "Don't tell me that a member of our mess, and your classmate, exaggerated his report."

"Let's just say that his prose would have been appropriate if he had been writing a report on the battle of Gettysburg," Pershing said.

This time Holbrook laughed out loud. "I'll have to read that," he said.

"I do pray that all return safely," Mary said.

"Amen," Holbrook said, growing more serious.

The picnic party returned to the post just as Sergeant Caviness and his body-retrieval party was returning. The last three horses of the column were pulling hastily constructed travois, and on each travois was a body, wrapped in canvas.

Everyone on the post knew, not only what the objects on the travois were, they knew who they were, and the friends and acquaintances of the dead soldiers—Troopers Jones, Travis, and Calhoun—stood out on the porches of the barracks, the sutler, and the dependent housing to watch as the solemn formation returned.

Sergeant Caviness led them to the parade ground right in front of the flag. Then he halted them, and ordered them to dismount.

"Stand by your horse," Caviness ordered.

The men dismounted and stood by, as Lieutenant Bond, who was acting as Officer of the Day, took the report.

"Sir, Sergeant Caviness, with a detail of ten detached from Captain Kirby's command, reporting with recovered bodies."

"Thank you, Sergeant," Lieutenant Bond responded, returning the salute. "Assign three men to deliver the bodies to the post mortician. Dismiss the others."

"Yes, sir," Caviness said. He did an about-face. "Schuler, Waters, MacMurtry, stay in place." These were the three men to whose horses the travois were attached. "The rest of you, dismissed."

"Me for a beer!" someone shouted, and others joined in the shouts of appreciation for the stand-down.

"Schuler, you, Waters, and Mac, deliver the bodies to the post mortuary. As soon as the mortician receives them, you're free to join the others."

The three men who were assigned the gruesome duty nodded, and then led their horses toward the mortuary.

Chapter Fourteen

Pershing was sitting at a table in a cleared-out room of the post supply building. The room was cleared of the normal elements of a supply room, the extra blankets, sheets, pillows, shelter-halves, canteens, tent pegs and poles, and the other items that normally filled a supply room. But that didn't mean the room was empty, because there were books, reports, paper, pens, and pencils scattered on tables all through the room. At the moment, Pershing was computing the number of rounds of "ammunition, ball, caliber .45" needed for the M1873 carbine that was the standard issue of the enlisted men except for the bugler and guideon bearer. With a basic load of 40 rounds per man, and 95 men, each troop would need 3800 rounds.

Pershing had just made the entry when he looked up to see Holbrook coming in.

"We're going to have a memorial service and a burying first thing in the morning," Holbrook said.

"They're going to bury all three men here, on the post?"

"Yeah. Not one of them have a next of kin listed, so we don't know how to get hold of anyone."

"That's probably just as well," Pershing said. "If they're buried here, they'll at least have some friends at the service. Even if we knew where to send them, like as not they would get a lonely burial when they got there."

"Yeah, that's pretty much the way I see it as well," Holbrook said.

Along the Platte River

The Shoshone called Black Crow was on his knees with his arms spread out wide to each side. He was staring up, looking right into the sun. It was necessary that he do this, because he had to prove himself before he could rejoin Yellow Hawk and the warriors who were with him.

When Yellow Hawk had attacked the farmhouse, Black Crow took the scalp of the boy, but Black Crow hadn't killed the boy. Yellow Hawk banished him because what he did was without honor.

But now Black Crow knew how he could come back to Yellow Hawk with honor. He had seen what he first thought was a herd of buffalo, even though there were no buffalo left. As he came closer, though, he saw that the animals were not buffalo, they were cattle. Though they were a kind of cattle that Black Crow had never seen before. They didn't have horns, and they were black. Perhaps this was a new kind of buffalo.

As soon as Black Crow located the herd of cows that looked like buffalo, he began preparing himself for what he must do. He would steal one of the small buffalo and take it back to Yellow Hawk. They would kill the animal and eat it, and Black Crow could tell the story of how he stole it from a herd of many, right from under the eyes of the white man.

Finally, he looked away from the sun, but he couldn't see. He was not worried. He had chosen this way of purifying himself a long time ago, and he knew that there would be a time when he couldn't see, and then his vision would return. Unafraid, he lay there with his eyes closed for a long moment until finally, he opened them again, and when he did, he could see.

Black Crow mounted his horse and rode to where he had seen the strange-looking cattle. He would stay out of sight until the sun was gone from the sky.

Meagan waited until she was certain everyone was asleep, then she climbed down from the wagon. They had left the Chugwater and were now on the Platte River and Meagan felt almost as if the river were calling to her. She had gotten hot and sweaty, and she could feel the dirt just caking up on her. She wanted a bath more than just about anything she could think of. But she knew that the only way she could take a bath would be to do so in the middle of the night.

She thought now that it was late enough that she would be able to sneak into the river and bathe, and be back in the wagon before anyone noticed. Of course, there would be a nighthawk working the herd, but since the cattle thieves had attempted to run off some cows the other night, the nighthawk would be so attentive to the herd that she was sure that he wouldn't even notice her.

Meagan dug through her saddlebag until she found a bar of Pears Soap. She actually sold this soap in her shop and the ladies particularly liked it because it had the scent of lavender.

It was the middle of the night, and she was in the middle of nowhere, so she was certain there was no one around to see her. Stripping out of her clothes, she walked, naked, out into the water, carrying the perfumed bar of soap with her. She began splashing the water on her skin, luxuriating in the wonderful feeling of cleanliness. She was cognizant only of the delightful feeling of the water and the soap, and she paid absolutely no attention to the picture she might be presenting, since she was alone.

Black Crow was startled when he saw a woman take off her clothes and walk out into the water. Getting down from his horse, he tied it to a tree and then walked, quietly, down to the river's edge.

If he killed the woman, then waited until her body was discovered, the men who were tending the herd would be drawn to the site of the dead woman, leaving the herd unwatched. Then it would be easy for him to get away with one of the cows.

Black Crow carried, not his rifle, but a bow and quiver of arrows with him, because whatever he did, would have to be done quietly. He moved down to the water's edge and saw her standing in the water, lathering herself with soap. He would wait for a few more minutes before shooting her.

Duff was riding nighthawk, and as he came around the front of the herd he thought he saw someone slipping through the line of trees near the edge of the herd. Whoever it was, he saw only briefly in the moonlight. It concerned him, because he realized that it might be another attempt to rustle the cattle.

Dismounting, Duff ground tied his horse, Sky. Then, pulling his pistol, he climbed to the top of the knoll, then slipped down on the other side. He advanced along the edge of the water, ready for whatever was ahead. Suddenly, he stopped and stared in disbelief. There, clearly visible in the bright splash of moonlight, was Meagan Parker.

What in the world was she doing here? Then, he answered his own question. Obviously, she was taking a bath, for she was standing in the water, lathered with soap and, at the moment, stark naked!

His first thought was, what was she doing taking such a chance? What if someone happened onto her? And his second thought was, wait a minute, someone had happened onto her. He had.

Even as he was considering this, he found himself mesmerized by the scene of a beautiful young woman with long, lean limbs, high-lifted breasts, and small, budding nipples. He stood there for a long moment, enjoying the beautiful scene before him, thinking of a painting he had once seen, "Aphrodite Bathing." Then, realizing that his undetected observation was a vulgar invasion of her privacy, he turned his back to the water, and called out to her.

"Meagan?"

"What?" Meagan shouted, shocked at being discovered. She spun around toward the sound of the voice, crossing her arms across her breasts in a vain attempt to cover herself as she did so. She saw a man standing on the bank of the stream and, though she couldn't make out his features because he was standing in shadows, she had recognized his voice.

"Duff, you—you should have made your presence known."

"I did," Duff replied. "I called out to you."

Meagan chuckled. "Yes, I guess you did at that, didn't you?"

Duff could hear the ripple of water from behind him as Meagan walked out of the stream. "Would you mind keeping your back to me until I am dressed?" she asked. "Although, I suppose it's too late now."

"Too late for modesty perhaps, but 'tis nae too late for me to be a gentleman and keep my back turned."

"Just how much of a gentleman are you?" Meagan asked, a touch of seductiveness in her voice.

"And what is it ye would asking me, lass?"

"You can turn around now," Meagan said.

Duff turned back around just as Meagan was packing her shirttail into her pants. Not fully buttoned, the shirt gapped open, and he could see droplets of water glistening on the globes of her breasts. He stared, unabashedly.

"I thought you said you were a gentleman," Meagan said, with a lilting laugh in her voice. "But here you are, staring." She continued to button up her shirt, gradually denying the view that had been afforded him when first he saw her.

"I'm a gentleman, aye, but 'tis also a fact that I'm a man."

"That's good to hear," Meagan said as, fully clothed now, she came walking up the side of the berm. She held her hand out for him to help her to the top.

"Now what do we do?" Meagan asked.

Duff smiled. "Well, we could . . ."

At that moment, Duff saw on the opposite bank of the river an Indian. The Indian was holding a bow and he had it pulled back, aiming toward Meagan. Acting quickly, Duff jerked Meagan toward him, then pulled her down to the ground, just as the arrow was released.

"What are you . . . ?" Meagan started, and then she saw the launched arrow vibrating in the tree into which it had just been shot. She realized then that if Duff had not brought her down, the arrow would be sticking out of her, rather than the tree.

The Indian was fitting a new arrow into his bow for a second shot, but Duff, who had put his pistol back in his holster, pulled it again and fired. The Indian fell and rolled down into the river. Duff ran across the river, then climbed up to the bank on the other side and looked in both directions, but he saw no more Indians.

Returning to the river, he pulled the Indian's body out of the water, and dragged it up onto the bank. By now Elmer, Jory Bates, Jimmy Sherman, and Jeff Ford were running up, all with pistols in hand.

"What is it?" Elmer asked. "What was the shot for? More rustlers?"

Duff pointed to the body of the dead Indian, lying on the near bank.

"This rather unpleasant fellow had it in his mind to stick an arrow in me," Duff said. He pointed to the arrow, sticking out of the tree.

"Or else me," Meagan added.

Elmer walked over to the Indian's body. Then, with his foot, he rolled him over.

"He's a Shoshone," Elmer said.

"You can tell by looking at him?"

"Look at the paint on his face," Elmer said. "Bright red, with white and yellow. That's the way it is with Shoshone."

"Well, Sergeant O'Riley told us there were some Indians on the prowl," Duff said.

"Yeah, but this is a little strange," Bates said. "I recollect that it's always been said that Injuns don't like to fight at night. It's got me a'wonderin' what this buck was doin' out here, all alone."

"Are we sure he's all alone?" Ford asked.

"Aye, I've looked, and see nae more of the devils."

"Like as not, he wasn't out makin' war," Elmer said. "I figure he was prob'ly plannin' on runnin' a couple head of cows off for food. If this group really has gone out on their own, I don't think they're likely to be gettin' much help from the people back at the reservation. I'm thinkin' the reservation Injuns don't want nothin' to do with them."

"Do you think we're likely to be bothered with them again?" Meagan asked.

"It could be," Elmer said. "I reckon that all depends on how hungry they are, and how much they're hankerin' for a little beef."

"We'll be at the fort in about three more days," Duff said. "For the rest of the drive we'll sleep in our clothes, with weapons handy. And 'tis thinkin' I am, that we'd best keep two on at night."

"We don't have four of us for that duty, boss," Ford pointed out. "And that's countin' you. That means we'll all be pullin' duty half the night, ever' night."

"But only for two more nights," Duff said. "I'm thinkin' we'll reach Fort Laramie by mid-afternoon, three days from now."

"When we get there, I plan to sleep for about three days," Ford said.

"I plan to have about three beers," Bates said.

"Yeah . . . me, too. Then sleep," Ford said.

Chapter Fifteen

Fort Laramie

By order of the post commander, when the colors were raised the next morning, they went to the top of flagpole, then were lowered to half-mast. The funeral was held in the post chapel as the three coffins, which were made of polished and shining pine, were on sawhorses at the front of the church, separated from the chancel by the communion rail. Because the bodies had been mutilated, the coffins were closed, but the hats and tunics of each of the three soldiers were placed on top of the coffins.

In the case of Jones, Colonel Gibbon had given him a posthumous promotion, and the three stripes of a sergeant had been sewn back onto the sleeves of his tunic. Pinned to Sergeant Jones's tunic was the Medal of Honor.

The burial rite was read only once, so that, when it came time to insert the name of the deceased, all three names; Jones, Travis, and Calhoun were spoken. There was no eulogy, but Colonel Gibbon did get up to speak to those assembled in the chapel.

"During the late war, there was a poem that appeared in the February 7, 1863, edition of *The Poughkeepsie Telegraph.* The poem spoke to me and I think, being as we are all soldiers, that it will speak to you as well. With your permission, and with a nod of recognition to the unknown author, I would like to quote it now.

"Breathe not a whisper here,
The place where thou dost stand is hallowed ground;
In silence gather near this upheaved mound
Around the soldier's bier

"Here, liberty may weep,
And freedom pause in uncheck career,
To pay the sacred tribute of a tear
Over the pale warrior's sleep."

After the service in the chapel, Pershing went with the others to the soldiers' cemetery and stood by as the three coffins were lowered into graves that were dug side by side. Seven soldiers, carrying carbines, stepped up to the graves, with Sergeant Caviness in command.

"Ready!" Caviness called, and the seven soldiers brought the weapons to their shoulders as one and, aiming them up at a forty-five-degree angle, held them.

"Fire!"

The seven carbines cracked as one.

"Reload."

The seven soldiers opened the trapdoor breech which ejected the empty cartridge and reloaded, doing it very quickly.

"Ready!"

Again, the soldiers raised the carbines to their shoulders and at the command fired a second time. Then the whole procedure was repeated a third time.

After the three volleys, which represented a salute of twenty-one rounds, the post bugler stepped up to play "Taps." There was, it seemed to Pershing, a difference in tone and tint to the character of "Taps" when it was played over a deceased soldier, as compared to what put the soldiers to sleep at night, even though the notes played were exactly the same.

The soldiers were dismissed then, and given one hour to change into their work uniforms. Pershing and Holbrook returned to the supply room to resume their work on the TO&E.

"John, do you think you'll stay in the army?" Holbrook asked.

"I don't know," Pershing said. "To be honest, I went to West Point because I thought it offered a better education than the college I was attending in Missouri. And, I do think the education was better. I didn't intend to get so involved with the army in the beginning, but there are things about it that I very much like. And you can sum it all up in the motto of the Academy."

"'Duty, honor, country,'" Holbrook said.

"Yes. Somewhere along the line, they became more than just words for me. They became the core of my being. Like today, burying these three soldiers. They weren't just soldiers to me. They were my family, my brothers, and I was very moved by the service."

"You know what I think, John? I think I had better call you by your first name while I still can. One of these days, I'll have to call you General Pershing."

Pershing laughed. "Right now, I'd settle for first lieutenant."

Holbrook joined him in laughter. "You and me both, John. You and me both."

The two officers heard the distant sound of rolling thunder, and Holbrook walked over to the window to look outside.

"We're going to have some rain," he said.

With the troopers in the field

On this, the third morning they were out, A Troop was up and on the go by six a.m. It began raining just before noon, and the rain turned into a thunderstorm, including hail, by early afternoon. The ice pellets stung and bruised man and beast alike, but there was little the men could do about it except hunker down in their ponchos and ride it out. The inclement weather was hard on the soldiers, for despite the ponchos they wore, the rain managed to get through to soak their wool uniforms. As a result, even when the rain stopped in the late afternoon, the men were still miserable in their water-soaked, heavy, chafing wool uniforms.

"All right, we'll make camp here for the rest of the day," Captain Kirby said.

"Cap'n, would it be all right if we stripped out of these uniforms and spread 'em out to dry?" First Sergeant Cobb asked.

"Sure," Captain Kirby said. "Go ahead."

They made camp then, and for the rest of the afternoon the men were half naked as they had their wet uniforms spread out on the grass to dry.

"Hey, Sarge! What if the Injuns attack us while we're near 'bout nekkid?" one of the solders asked. "They won't know who's the officers and NCOs and who's the soldiers."

"Maybe the sergeants should sew their stripes on their long handles," one of the other soldiers suggested.

The others laughed.

"Trooper," First Sergeant Cobb said, pointing to the sleeve of his long handles. "What do you see here?"

"I don't see nothin' there, Top."

"Yeah, you do," Cobb insisted. "What you see are stripes and rockers."

"No, I don't. I don't see nothin' there."

"Let me put it this way. You either see stripes and rockers, or I see you doing three days of mucking the stalls."

"Oh. You mean *those* stripes and rockers," the trooper said. "Well, sure, I see them now. I just wasn't lookin' close enough."

Again, the other soldiers laughed.

The next day was an easy march. The trail was wide, flat, and free of any obstacles. The weather was hot and dry, but there was plenty of forage for the animals, and they were near water. They made twelve easy miles, then stopped for camp at two o'clock that afternoon. By now the novelty of going out on a scout against Indian warriors was beginning to wear off, especially as they had not encountered any Indians.

With Yellow Hawk

The fact that the cavalry troop had not encountered any Indians didn't mean they weren't there. Yellow Hawk and his men had seen the soldiers and were keeping track of them as they were on the move. Yellow Hawk had but eighteen men with him, and he had counted nearly one hundred soldiers.

There were far too many soldiers to attack as a body, but he was hoping they might split up into smaller groups, and if they did that, he would merely pick the smallest group to engage.

That is exactly what did happen the second day when ten soldiers broke away from the main group to take the bodies back to the fort. Yellow Hawk considered attacking them, but the soldiers were well armed and, Yellow Hawk perceived, better led than had been the first group he had attacked. Also, the soldiers stayed on flat open ground and never presented an opening for an attack, so Yellow Hawk followed a tried and true tactic. He would not engage the soldiers unless he had such superior numbers that victory was assured.

He let the smaller body pass, and kept the larger body under constant observation. Yellow Hawk and the others laughed at how easy it was for them to keep track of the soldiers. Many of the Indians with Yellow Hawk had attended the agency school that was on the reservation, as had Yellow Hawk himself. There they learned not only to speak English, but to read as well, and one of the stories they could remember was about some mice who had managed to put a bell on a cat. That way, the cat could never sneak up on them.

They made jokes, saying that it was not necessary to put bells on the soldiers, they were already wearing bells. The Indians were referring to the metal bridle bits and harness accouterments, the canteens, mess kits, and sabers. In fact, it was the cacophony of sound that warned them of the approach of the soldiers, and that allowed them to keep track of them.

Then, midway through the third day, the soldiers

turned around and started back. Yellow Hawk was disappointed that not once, during the entire time, had there been an opportunity to attack. The best they could do now was follow along behind and hope that one or two soldiers might, for some reason, drop out of the march.

But that didn't happen, and when they got too close to the fort, Yellow Hawk broke off the contact.

With the herd

As Duff had predicted, he and his herd reached Fort Laramie by mid-afternoon of the third day after their encounter with the single Indian.

"Where do we go from here?" Elmer asked.

"To tell you the truth, Elmer, I'm not all that sure. I agreed to bring the cows to the fort, and here we are. I think I'll ride in and speak to the commander of the establishment and see what he has in mind. I'd like you and the men to stay here and keep an eye on the herd."

"We'll keep 'em here," Elmer said.

"Meagan, would you be for wanting to ride into the fort with me?"

Meagan smiled. "I thought you would never ask," she said. "But if I had known I was going to meet the commanding officer, I would have brought something so I could dress as a lady, and not a cowboy."

"Sure'n it makes no difference what ye be

wearing, lass, for 'tis pretty enough ye are that t'would be for making a blind man look twice."

Meagan chuckled. "You do have a way with words about you, Duff Tavish MacCallister."

An hour later, Duff and Meagan were challenged at the gate of the fort by the guard on duty.

"Halt, and state your business," the soldier said, bringing his carbine up to the port arms position.

"Aye, 'tis a foine soldier ye be, lad, challenging us like that. I'll be for putting in a good word for ye. The name is MacCallister, and if ye would be so kind, would ye get word to Colonel Gibbon that MacCallister has arrived with the cattle the army has ordered."

The solder nodded. Then he turned his head to the left, and bellowed out, "Corporal of the guard! Front gate!"

Meagan was a little surprised to hear him call out in such a fashion, and even more surprised when she heard the call being repeated across the open area of the post.

"Corporal of the guard! Front gate!"

After a moment, a soldier with two gold chevrons on his sleeve came trotting up to the gate.

"Why the call, Pounders?"

"This gentleman and the lady wish to call upon Colonel Gibbon," the gate guard said.

"Is the colonel expecting you, sir?" the corporal asked.

"Aye. 'Tis a herd of cows I've brought."

"Very well, sir, follow me, I'll take you to Old Bedlam."

"Old Bedlam?"

"It's what everyone calls the post headquarters building," the corporal replied. "It's also the colonel's quarters."

Because the corporal was walking, Duff and Meagan dismounted, and they, too, walked across a broad, green field toward "Old Bedlam," a two-story white building, with a porch that spread all across the front.

"If you two would wait here, I'll see Sergeant Major Martell," the corporal said.

A moment later, the colonel himself stepped out onto the front porch, and the man who was standing guard came to attention and raised his rifle to present arms. Colonel Gibbon returned the salute.

"Mr. MacCallister," the colonel said. "Come in, come in. This would be Mrs. MacCallister?"

"No, sir, this is Miss Parker," Duff said. "Half the cows I'm delivering to the army belong to her."

"Well then, she certainly has every right to be here then, doesn't she?"

Colonel Gibbon led Duff and Meagan back to his office. "As soon as we take delivery of the cattle, I'll wire Cheyenne to make arrangements for you to be paid. Where are the cattle now?"

"They are about two miles south of here in a field that has enough grass and water to keep them from wanting to wander."

"We have already built feeder pens. I'll send some men to pick them up tomorrow. You and your men are welcome to come onto the post with them. I don't look for the disbursement officer to arrive from Cheyenne for at least another week, maybe ten days. In the meantime, we will be happy to accommodate you and your men."

"Ye've m' thanks, Colonel," Duff said. "But the men will be starting back in a couple of days. 'Twill just be Miss Parker, Elmer Gleason, 'n' myself remaining."

Colonel Gibbon walked back out into the orderly room with Duff and Meagan. As he did so, Sergeant Major Martell and the company clerk stood.

"Sergeant Major, if you would please, go with this lady and this gentleman, and make arrangements to send some men out tomorrow, to help bring in the herd."

"Yes, sir," the sergeant major replied. "Ma'am, sir, if you would come with me?"

After making arrangements for some soldiers to come get the cows the next day, Duff and Meagan returned to the herd. As Duff had explained to the colonel, the cows were in an area with ample food and water, and seemed quite content to stay as long as Duff wanted to leave them there. Here, a belt of bright green ran alongside the Platte River which flowed by in a soft, almost majestic whisper. To the west, a ridge of purple mountains thrust into the sky.

They were all in a good mood, the drive having been completed, and tomorrow being a payday, not only for Duff and Meagan, but for the cowboys as well. Elmer surprised them all with a pie that night, and Jeff Ford had an even bigger surprise, when he produced a guitar and sang a few songs for them. He proved to have quite a good voice.

When Meagan turned in to her bed in the wagon that night, she was unable to go to sleep. She didn't know why she couldn't go to sleep; she certainly was tired enough. But no matter how many times she turned and repositioned herself, sleep continued to elude her. She sat up and looked out the back of the wagon at the sleeping men. She could hear snores from some of them, so she knew they were sleeping well.

She withdrew back into the wagon. She recalled the words of Colonel Gibbon when he had met them, this afternoon.

"Mr. MacCallister," the colonel said. "Come in, come in. This would be Mrs. MacCallister?"

Would she ever be Mrs. MacCallister? Did she want to be? She wasn't sure what she wanted from this relationship. She wanted more than she had now, of that she was certain. But she also didn't want to lose her independence. She liked owning The Ladies' Emporium. She genuinely enjoyed designing and making dresses, looking at it as an expression of art.

Finally, with those thoughts tumbling about in her head, she fell asleep.

Chapter Sixteen

Meagan got up early the next morning, and along with Duff and Elmer she watched as the first pink fingers of dawn spread over their camp. The last morning star made a bright pinpoint of light in the southern sky, and the coals from the campfire of the night before were still glowing. Elmer threw chunks of dried wood onto the fire, and soon tongues of flame were licking against the bottom of the coffeepot. A rustle of feathers caused her to look up just in time to see a golden hawk diving on its prey. The hawk soared back into the air carrying a tiny scrub mouse, which was kicking fearfully in the hawk's claws. A prairie dog scurried quickly from one hole to another, alert against the fate that had befallen the mouse.

Elmer poured each of them a cup of steaming black coffee and they had to blow on it before they could drink it. They watched the sun turn from gold to white, then stream brightly down onto the plains.

"What time do you think them soldier boys will be out here to get the herd?" Elmer asked.

"I expect they'll be here by mid-morning," Duff said. "The colonel said they had built feeder pens on the post, so after breakfast, I propose that we take the herd all the way up to the walls of the fort."

"Sounds like a good idee to me," Elmer said.

After breakfast, Elmer hitched the team to the wagon, and started on toward the post. Duff and the others got the herd moving, though this morning they were moving at a much more leisurely pace than they had at any time during the drive.

As the herd drew close to Fort Laramie, Elmer saw an officer and half a dozen soldiers coming from the fort to meet them.

"Who is in charge here?" the young lieutenant asked when he and the soldiers reached the wagon.

"It's that feller back there, sonny," Elmer said, enjoying the fact that the lieutenant winced at being called "sonny."

Duff saw the small group of soldiers stop and talk to Elmer. Then he saw the lieutenant leave the wagon and come toward him. Duff rode out toward the lieutenant to halve the distance between them.

The young lieutenant saluted. "Your pardon, sir, but would you be Mr. MacCallister?"

"Aye, Duff MacCallister," Duff replied. "And you be from the fort to take the cows, would ye, Leftenant?"

"Yes, sir. Lieutenant Bond is the name. Colonel Gibbon sent me with a contingent to show you where to take the cattle."

"When I met with the colonel yesterday, I was told that ye had feeder pens constructed."

"Yes, sir, we do have feeder lots, and our own abattoir," the lieutenant said. "We'll be processing the beef ourselves."

An hour later, all the cattle were in feeder pens and the drive was officially over.

"Mr. MacCallister," Lieutenant Bond said. "As I believe the colonel explained, it'll be a few days before the disbursement officer comes up from Cheyenne. In the meantime, I've been instructed to offer you and your men the comforts of the post. You and your foreman can stay in the BOQ, and your men are welcome in the barracks."

"And the young lady who is with us?"

"Yes, sir, the colonel has made arrangements for her as well. He asks that she stay in Old Bedlam as the guest of the Colonel and Mrs. Gibbon."

"That's very nice of the colonel."

"Tell me, Lieutenant, is there any place on this here army post where a fella can get a beer?" Bates asked.

Lieutenant Bond chuckled. "There is, indeed,"

he said. "I'm sure the sutler will be glad to take your money."

The first thing Duff did, after being assigned a room in the BOQ, was to take a bath, and get into clean clothes. He had just finished getting dressed, and was looking into the mirror, combing his hair, when there was a knock at the door. When he opened it, he saw a young, familiar-looking lieutenant, and he smiled, and stuck his hand out.

"Lieutenant Pershing," he said. "It's good to see you again."

"It's good to see you, too, Mr. MacCallister," Pershing replied. "That is, as long as I don't have to shoot against you."

"Oh? I thought perhaps a sportsman and competitor like you might want another go."

Pershing smiled, and nodded. "I might," he said. "On the other hand, I'm not all that anxious to be shown up again."

"'Twas a lucky shot, Lieutenant. A lucky shot is all."

"Ha," Pershing said. "One thing I do know is shooting. And believe me, Mr. MacCallister, when I say that was no lucky shot. I've no doubt but that you could have made that shot three out of three times, if you had to."

"What are you doing here? I thought your post was Fort Assiniboine."

"I'm on temporary duty here," Pershing said,

without going into specifics. "But the reason I'm here, standing outside your door, is to extend an invitation from Colonel Gibbon. He is hosting the officers of the Fifth and their ladies for dinner tonight and he has asked me to invite you. Your lady, I understand, is already the colonel's guest."

Duff smiled. "Aye," he said. "She is at that, isn't she? Please tell the colonel for me that I would be glad to be his guest this evening."

"Oh, but I can't attend a formal dinner like this," Meagan said. "I don't know what I was thinking, but I brought only working clothes with me, and when I say working clothes, I mean pants and shirts, like men."

"My dear, not to worry," Kathleen Gibbon said. "You are about the same size as Mary Meacham, and she has a beautiful wardrobe. Mary is our surgeon's daughter and I know she would be happy to lend you something that would be appropriate."

"Oh, do you think so? I would be ever so grateful," Meagan said.

"Come with me, and I'll introduce you."

The table in the commandant's quarters was perfectly balanced as far as men and women were concerned. On one side of the table, Pershing was sitting with Jason Holbrook's sister, Clara, and Holbrook was sitting with Mary Meacham. On the other side of the table Duff was sitting with Meagan, and Major Phil Allison, who was second in command of the post, was sitting with his wife Julianne. Colonel Gibbon was at one end of the table and his wife, Kathleen, was at the opposite end.

The meal had been cooked and served by orderlies, enlisted men for whom this was their job.

"I've left instructions for one of the cows to be butchered, and carved into halves," Colonel Gibbon said. "Tomorrow, Sergeant Beck, who informs me that he was the best pit master in the state of Texas, has agreed to undertake the task."

"Ah, so we'll have barbecued beef tomorrow night," Pershing said.

"Not tomorrow night," Colonel Gibbon said. "Sergeant Beck says that it will take him twenty-four hours to do the job properly, so it must be for the following day. I must say, I am looking forward to tasting Angus beef. I've not had it before."

"If you haven't tasted it before, Colonel, then you are in for a treat," Meagan said.

Colonel Gibbon chuckled. "You don't have to sell me, Miss Parker. The army has already committed to buy the beef." Then, to the others, he explained, "Miss Parker owns half of the cows that were delivered."

"Maybe we won't have a barbeque tomorrow night, but we will have a dance," Kathleen Gibbon said. She smiled at Clara and Meagan. "And believe me, as there are so few women on the post, you two young ladies will be a most welcome addition."

"She isn't just saying that," Mary said. "There are so few women on the post that we have to dance every dance with someone different."

"Oh, my dear, I wouldn't say we *have* to. I would say that it is our privilege to do so," Kathleen said.

"Yes, ma'am, of course that is the way I meant it."

"Tell me, Mr. MacCallister, did you encounter any Indians on the way here?" Colonel Gibbon asked.

"Aye, but t'was only a minor encounter."

"Minor? He tried to kill me," Meagan said.

"Heavens, he tried to kill you, personally?" Kathleen asked with a gasp.

Meagan smiled and put her hand on Duff's arm. "If ever you have read a novel where the hero comes in the nick of time to save the lady, that's what happened. Duff saved me."

"How did he save you?" Clara asked.

"Why, he shot the Indian," Meagan said easily.

"Oh, my. How awful," Clara said.

Holbrook laughed. "Sis, if you think Mr. MacCallister shooting the Indian was awful, how much more awful would it have been had the Indian shot Miss Parker?"

"Oh," Clara said. "Oh, yes, I see what you mean."

"So, you did encounter hostiles," Colonel Gibbon said.

"Aye, but t'was only one, and I think his purpose may have been to steal a cow."

"But he took a shot at you?" Major Allison asked.

"I think he saw Miss Parker and me, and may have felt that he had been discovered. And instead of running away, he took a shot at us."

"I swear the Indians are getting so bold again," Julianne Allison said. "I thought the Indian question was all settled."

"It is all settled," Colonel Gibbon replied. "These are isolated incidents, and the Indians who are causing the trouble now are as much outlaws among their own people as they are among us. And remember, we have our own outlaws to deal with."

"Yes," Meagan said. "We encountered some of those as well."

"My goodness," Clara said. "Your trip up here sounds as if it were quite"—she paused in her sentence, as if looking for a word—"exciting."

"I wonder if Captain Kirby and Lieutenant Scott have encountered any Indians," Holbrook said.

"I doubt it," Pershing said.

"Why do you doubt it, Lieutenant?" Major Allison asked.

"Because the detachment is too large. Indians never initiate the engagement unless they are absolutely sure they will prevail. And since what we are dealing with here is but a small band of renegades, I am sure that they will not initiate any action against Captain Kirby."

"Yes, but suppose Captain Kirby initiates the engagement?" Major Allison asked.

"He won't be able to. An army unit under march is only slightly less noisy than a parading band."

Duff laughed out loud.

"Hrrumph!" Major Allison grunted in dissatisfaction.

"Lieutenant Pershing is correct, Phil. If the Indians don't want to be engaged, they won't be," Colonel Gibbon said.

"Then I don't understand. What was the purpose of sending out the expedition?"

"It had two purposes," Colonel Gibbon replied. "One was to recover the bodies of our fallen comrades, and the other was to present a show of strength, to let the renegade Indians know that they continue their adventure at their own peril."

Although Elmer had been invited to dinner as well, he begged off saying that the dinner would be a "bit too hoity-toity" for him. He preferred the sutler's store, which was the social hub of Fort Laramie. Here, the officers and men could buy anything from a razor to a can of peaches, to a beer or whiskey. The latest books and newspapers from the East were also on sale, though as they came up by coach from Cheyenne after having arrived in that city by train, they were normally two weeks old. Tonight, while Duff and Meagan were having dinner with the post commandant, Elmer was at the sutler's, eating pickled pigs' feet, and enjoying a beer.

Sherman, Bates, and Ford had come to the sutler's store with him, and the four men found a table and were enjoying drinks and conversation.

"You the fellas that brought in the cattle?" a sergeant asked, coming over to their table.

"That we are, Sergeant, that we are," Elmer said.

The sergeant smiled, then stuck out his hand. "The name is Beck," he said. "Roy Beck."

"I'm Elmer Gleason, these here boys is Sherman, Bates, and Ford. It's good to meet you."

"Well, Mr. Gleason, tomorrow I intend to barbeque one of those steers. I hope you boys can stick around long enough to be able to taste it. I guarantee you, it's goin' to be the best thing you've ever put in your mouth."

"Tell me, Sergeant Beck, have you ever cooked Angus beef?" Elmer asked.

"No, not so's I can remember."

"Believe me," Elmer said. "If you had cooked it, you would remember. Now me, I've et just about ever' thing from rats to buffalo hump . . . and the best thing I've ever et is Angus beef. So I hope you know what you're a' doin'."

"I could barbeque a boot and make it good. So if Angus is as good as you say it is, then we are goin' to have some prime eatin'."

"Good enough," Elmer said. "Why don't you join me 'n' my friends?"

"I'd be glad to," Beck said, reaching over to get an empty chair from an adjacent table.

"Rats?" Sergeant Beck asked.

"Down in Louisiana, it was. Some folks call 'em nutrias, but what they is is big rats. They taste a lot like possum."

"Well now, I have barbecued possum," Sergeant Beck said.

Sherman started talking about how his mom used to cook possum and as the discussion continued, Elmer spotted a face at the far end of the bar and he was sure he had seen that man before. It took him awhile, then he remembered when, and where, he had last seen him.

Chapter Seventeen

As Elmer continued to study the sergeant who was standing at the far end of the bar, he recalled when, where, and how he had seen him. It had been over twenty years ago.

1866

Just north of New Madrid, Missouri, on the road called El Camino Real, Elmer Gleason and four other men were waiting under a cluster of trees. It was raining, and the road was covered with water and flushed with the black mud that was so indicative of the Southeast Missouri swampland.

Like Elmer, the four men with him were veterans of the recent war. They had served under him during the conflict, and so were used to working together, easily and efficiently. They were like soldiers embarked upon a specific mission, just like the many missions Elmer had led them on during the war. The big difference now was there was no war and this wasn't a mission. This would be a robbery, plain and simple.

Elmer stood in his stirrups, scratched his crotch, and then settled back again. He looked over at the men who, as he was, were wearing oil slickers and wide brimmed hats, pulled low to keep out the rain.

"Lieutenant, you know what I'm a' thinkin'? I'm a' thinkin' that maybe them Yankee soldiers ain't goin' to be comin' out in this kind of weather," one of his men said. Elmer was no longer a lieutenant, and the man who had spoken was no longer a Confederate soldier, but old habits died hard.

Elmer took off his hat and poured water from the brim, then put it back on. He reached down and patted his horse soothingly.

"Oh, they'll be here all right," he said. "They got near six months of tax money they've stole off all the farmers and businesses, an' they'll be wantin' to put it on a train up at Sikeston, so's they can send it back to Washington."

A few minutes earlier, Elmer had sent one of his men down to the curve in the road to keep a lookout. He came riding back now, at a gallop, the hooves of his horse throwing up clods of mud and dirty water from the covered roadbed.

"I seen 'em, Lieutenant. They're a'comin' just like you said they would."

"How many are there?"

"Yeah, well, that's the thing. They's a coach with a driver and a shotgun guard, and they's also four outriders with 'em, two ridin' in front of the coach, two ridin' behind it."

"Hold on, here," one of the others said, the expression in his voice showing his obvious anxiety. "I didn't know nothin' 'bout no soldiers. I thought it was just goin' to be somethin' simple, like stoppin' a coach."

"Maybe you figured that all we would have to do is pass the hat," Elmer said.

"No, I mean, I know'd it wasn't goin' to be easy. It's just that I wasn't countin' on us a' runnin' up ag'in a bunch of soldiers is all."

"Hell, they's as many of us as there is of them," one of the other men said. "The fact that they got soldiers don't bother me none a' tall. Hell, when you think about it, we fought ag'in the damn Yankees for purt' nigh four years and we didn't get nothin' more'n food for it, and lots of times not even food. At least this time we'll be gettin' something out of it."

The man who had lodged the protest looked at the others, then realized that he was alone in his fears. He nodded. "Hell, don't you boys go getting' no idea that I ain't a' goin' to be with you. All I was doin' was just makin' talk about it."

"Anyone else got anything to say?" Elmer asked.

When no one replied, Elmer nodded. "Good, I'm glad you are all still with me. Now, we've talked it over, and ever'one knows what to do. Finely, you got that tree ready?"

"Oh, yeah," Finely replied. "All I got to do is give

it a couple of whacks and a shove and it'll lay down just like we want."

"That'll keep 'em from goin' on ahead, but what about behind 'em?" one of the men asked.

"That ain't no problem," Elmer said. "With all the mud and such, they can't pull off the road to get the coach turned around. Besides, we'll be behind 'em."

"Why don't we just shoot the sons of bitches and get it over with?" someone asked. "Hell, they ain't nothin' but a bunch of damn Yankees anyhow."

"We'll take the money, but we ain't goin' to shoot 'em. Hell, even durin' the war we didn't shoot men that was just doin' their jobs, unless they was shootin' at us, and I don't see no need to change it none," Elmer said.

By now they could hear the sound of the approaching coach, though because it was around a bend that was shielded by trees, they couldn't yet see it. That also meant that they couldn't be seen.

"All right, ever'body get in position," Elmer ordered.

Elmer and the others slipped back into the woods and waited for the coach. From the shouts and whistles, Elmer knew that the driver had to work the team exceptionally hard to pull the heavy coach through the thick mud.

A moment later the coach appeared.

Because Elmer had ridden with both Bloody Bill Anderson, and Quantrill, he was well experienced at setting up an ambush, and now, from his position in the trees, he studied the coach and its escort detail. As his lookout had stated, two of the soldiers were riding in front of the stagecoach and two more were riding behind the coach. In addition to the military detail, the coach driver and the guard were also armed.

By now the rain was falling so hard that visibility was limited to a few hundred feet, which meant that Elmer's men, hidden in the trees and masked by the rain, were completely out of sight.

Elmer was just about to give the signal to drop the tree across the road when one of the soldiers in front, a sergeant, held his hand up stopping the coach.

"What's he doin'?" one of the men asked quietly.

"I don't know," Elmer replied. "Looks to me like he's maybe got him an idee that he'd better be careful."

The sergeant came riding up the road ahead of the coach and the others of the escort detail. He looked around carefully. Elmer twisted in his saddle to make certain that his men were well concealed. He motioned for Finely, who was standing by his notched tree, to get out of sight. Finely did so, and Elmer was reassured by the fact that he couldn't see him, even though he knew where to look.

He knew that the Yankee sergeant was experiencing a gut feeling.

"I know what you're feeling, Yankee," Elmer said quietly. "I've felt it a few times myself."

Finally, the Yankee sergeant gave the order to

proceed, and Elmer watched the coach and its escort approach, waiting for just the right moment.

At the appropriate time, Elmer brought his hand down. There were two loud thumps, loud enough to get the attention of the sergeant in charge of the escort detail. Then, with groans, creaks, and loud snapping noises, the huge cypress tree started down, falling across the muddy road with the crashing thunder of an artillery barrage. At the same time the tree hit the road in front of the coach, Elmer and his men moved out onto the road behind the coach and fired several shots into the air.

"Hold it up right there!" Elmer shouted. "I've got ten more men in the trees!" Elmer pointed his pistol at the soldiers. "Throw down your guns and put up your hands."

"We're bein' held up!" one of the soldiers said and he threw down his rifle. The other soldiers, perhaps taking their cue from him, threw their weapons down as well. Only the sergeant refused Elmer's order. Elmer turned his pistol toward the sergeant. "Drop your gun, Sergeant! Do it now!"

Reluctantly, the sergeant lowered his pistol, then let it drop into the mud.

Both the driver and the shotgun guard had their hands up, but neither had yet dropped their weapons.

"Throw down them guns!" Elmer said, now pointing his pistol toward the two men up on the box. They complied.

"Now, I want you four Yankee boys to get down off your horses," Elmer ordered.

Grumbling, the men got down. As soon as they did, two of Elmer's men moved up to take the horses.

"You're stealing our horses?" the Yankee sergeant asked.

"We're not stealing them, we're just denying you the use of them," Elmer explained. "We're going to take 'em with us for a mile or so, and then we'll let 'em go. Like as not, they'll wind up back in your own stable. You four boys can finish your ride in the coach. Driver, throw down the money box."

"What money box? I ain't got no money box," the driver said.

"You've got an armed escort, but you don't have a money box?"

"That's the truth."

"Here's the thing, driver. I don't believe you," Elmer said. "So what I'm goin' to do is make you two boys climb down, and I'm goin' to climb up there and have a look myself. If I find the box, that'll mean you was lyin' to me, and I don't like liars. I'll just have to shoot you both."

"Throw down the damn box, Abe," the shotgun guard said anxiously.

The driver threw down the box, and Elmer smiled. "I thought you might see things my way," he said.

One of Elmer's men shot off the lock, then opened the lid. Inside the box were several stacks of bound greenback dollars.

"You realize, don't you, mister, that you ain't

just stealin' money from a stagecoach," the sergeant said. "You'll be stealin' money from the United States Government."

"Who stole the money from the people," Elmer said.

While Elmer held the soldiers at bay, two of his men started scooping the money out of the box and putting the bills into a cloth bag. When all the money was taken from the box, they gave the bag to Elmer, who tied it to his saddle horn.

"That's all of it, Lieutenant," one of Elmer's men said.

"Lieutenant?" the sergeant asked. "Wait a minute, are you men in the army?"

"We was in the army," Elmer said. "But not your army."

"Rebels," the sergeant grunted. "You do know that the war is over, don't you? Lee surrendered."

"Yeah," Elmer said. "Lee surrendered. We didn't."

1888

"Lee surrendered, we didn't," Elmer said aloud.

"What's that, Mr. Gleason?" Sergeant Beck asked.

"What? Oh, nothing. I was just sort of thinkin' out loud is all." Elmer pointed to the soldier who had held his attention for the last few minutes. "Tell me, Sergeant Beck, what's that fella's name down there? The sergeant that's standin' off by hisself."

"His name is Havercost," Sergeant Beck said. "He's got more'n thirty years in now, and is 'bout ready to retire."

"Sergeant Havercost, you say?"

"Yes. Do you know George?"

"I can't exactly say that I know him," Elmer said. "But we have met." Elmer got up from the table and walked across the room to talk to the sergeant.

"Hey, Jimmy, what you think that's all about?" Ford asked.

"Beats the hell out of me."

"Maybe they know'd each other durin' the war," Bates suggested.

"Not unless that sergeant was a Confederate," Sherman replied.

Sergeant Beck laughed. "Believe me, George Havercost wasn't a Rebel."

When Elmer stepped up to the bar, Sergeant Havercost turned toward him and smiled. "You're one of the men that brought the cows in, aren't you?"

"Yes," Elmer replied.

"It will be good to get some beef again. Mr. Clark, give this gentleman a beer on me," he said. He stuck out his hand. "The name is Havercost," the sergeant said.

"Yes, I know. Sergeant Beck told me. The name is Gleason. Elmer Gleason." Elmer took Havercost's hand.

"You know, Mr. Gleason, I have the strangest sensation that we have met before," Havercost said.

Elmer looked sideways at him. He knew that the sergeant was trying to piece together where they had met, and if he studied it long enough and hard enough, he was likely to come up with it. Elmer decided to give him some confusing hints. "It could be that we have met before," he suggested. "I just come up from Texas a year or so ago. Were you down there?" In fact, Elmer had not been in Texas in several years, but he was purposely giving the sergeant misinformation.

The sergeant shook his head. "No, I'm afraid not. I've never been to Texas. But it could be that maybe we met durin' the war. You look to be about my age, so I reckon you served."

Elmer chuckled. "I did at that, Sergeant," he said. "But if this is the same color uniform you was wearin' then, we was on opposite sides. I was a soldier of the Confederacy, a private in Cobb's Legion."

Elmer had never been in Cobb's Legion, another bit of misinformation.

The sergeant shook his head. "No, I never run into Cobb's Legion, near 'bout all my experience was west of the Mississippi."

"Was it? Well, sir, don't see how we could have met durin' the war, then. I never come west of the Mississippi until 'bout ten years ago."

"Well, I'm old and forgetful," Sergeant Havercost said. "I reckon I've just run across too many men in my day to remember 'em all. But it's good meetin' you, Mr. Gleason, especially with you bringin' the beef like you done."

Elmer smiled. "You wait till you taste it, Sergeant. Why, you'll think you've died, and gone to heaven."

"After our fare for the last few months, near 'bout anything is goin' to be an improvement," Sergeant Havercost said.

Elmer picked up his beer. "Thanks for the beer, Sergeant Havercost. But I reckon I'd better get back to my men, now."

Havercost nodded, and held up his beer in salute at Elmer turned away.

Elmer smiled as he returned to his table. Havercost had not recognized him.

Chapter Eighteen

By late afternoon of the following day, there were two beef halves on spits that were suspended over glowing coals. Sergeant Beck was in charge of the cooking, which was just getting started. Morale on the post was high, not only because of the barbeque all would enjoy the next day, but also because there would be a dance tonight.

The dance was for everyone on the post, enlisted and officers alike, and it would be held at the sutler's store, the meeting room in the back being turned over for that purpose.

Duff, Meagan, Elmer, Ford, Travis, and Calhoun had been invited to attend. The dances were somewhat restricted, due to the lack of women. The wives of the post did their part by allowing their dance cards to be filled by the bachelor officers and men, and it wasn't all that unusual to see Colonel Gibbon's wife, Kathleen, dancing with a young private.

There were few single women at the post, mostly laundresses who lived on Soapsuds Row washing and ironing the post laundry. As a rule, the laundresses did not stay single very long. They were prime candidates for marriage to the noncommissioned officers of the post, and the salary of a laundress, combined with the pay and allowances of a sergeant, could give some of the senior NCO households incomes to be envied by all but the highest ranking officers.

The four unmarried laundresses and Mary Meacham were the only permanent single women on the post. At present Clara Holbrook, Lieutenant Holbrook's sister, and Meagan Parker, both but temporary guests, brought the total number of single women to six. Six single women, and eight officers' wives, fourteen NCO wives, and Mrs. Ethel May Clark, wife of the sutler, brought the total number of women to twenty-nine. There were on the post four hundred and fifty men.

Again, Meagan bemoaned the fact that she—who as a seamstress and owner of a dress shop was always prepared for any social event—had nothing to wear to the dance.

"I have part of a dress," Mary said. "I started to make it from a pattern I got from Godey's Lady's Book, but I'm not very good at it. I just wasted my money buying the material, I fear."

"Really? Suppose I buy it from you, and finish it myself?"

"You can do that?" Mary asked.

"Yes." Meagan laughed. "I know, you see me in denims and a man's shirt, and you know that I helped bring up a herd of cows. But herding cattle is not what I do. I'm a seamstress, and I own a dress store."

"My!" Mary said. "Oh, how wonderful! Yes, you can buy the material. It will be worth it, just to see the dress completed. The picture of it in Godey's was very beautiful."

"Do you have a sewing machine?"

"I don't, but Mrs. Allison does, and she said I could borrow it, anytime."

"Good. I'd better get busy if I want the dress to be ready in time for the dance tonight."

When Meagan, Mary, and Clara arrived at the dance that night, the three beautiful ladies turned many a man's head. One who had his head turned was Duff MacCallister, and he didn't think he had ever seen Meagan more beautiful than she was tonight. He hurried over to meet her.

"You must have done an awfully good job of packing your saddlebags," Duff teased. "This is the second dress I've seen you in since we arrived."

"I borrowed the dress I wore last night. I bought this one," Meagan said.

"Did ye' now? And a lovely dress it is, too."

The music for the dance was provided by the regimental band and they sat with their instruments on a raised platform to one side of the big room.

The band leader, a sergeant, was wearing a uniform that had more gold on it than any of the officers who were present. At a signal from Colonel Gibbon, he lifted his baton, and the music began.

Because there were so few women and so many men, many of the younger soldiers would tie a handkerchief around their left sleeve, indicating that they would be willing to be dance partners with the other soldiers. No one thought the less of any soldier who did this. It was not considered effeminate, it was considered practical.

The two visiting women, Meagan Parker and Clara Holbrook, because they were young, single, and very pretty, quickly became the hit of the dance as the single officers, and even some of the bolder enlisted men, lined up to put their names on their dance cards.

"I can see right now that I'll nae be able to claim ye for many dances," Duff said.

"Well, you aren't in uniform, Duff. And you know how much women are attracted to uniforms," Meagan teased.

"Aye, I dinnae think to bring my kilts. Sure 'n' they would have made a big hit here," Duff said with a laugh.

"Well, I think you look adorable in your kilts," Meagan said.

"Adorable, is it now? Och, adorable is nae a term that I find agreeable."

Smiling, Meagan put her hand on Duff's arm. "Sure now, and dinnae ye be such a child about a bit of a compliment." Again, she perfectly imitated Duff's Scottish brogue.

"Miss Parker, I do hope there is yet room for my name on your dance card," Lieutenant Pershing said as he approached her.

"Of course there is, Lieutenant," Meagan replied.

Captain Kirby's wife, Nancy, and Lieutenant Scott's wife, Sue, were also present at the dance, even though their husbands were in the field. Once the dance started, they were on the dance floor doing their part to alleviate the shortage of women.

At one point during the evening, Pershing took his leave of the sutler's store. He had danced with Holbrook's sister more than he had danced with any other woman present. Clara had a way about her, a smile, a lingering touch, a provocative scent that managed to penetrate his carefully constructed reserve. He was afraid that if he was around her too much, he would wind up doing something that would rupture the camaraderie he had established with Jason Holbrook, and that he definitely didn't want to do. For one thing, the two men had become good friends, and for another, a ruptured relationship would interfere with the work that the two men were doing.

Pershing walked out onto the quadrangle, then sat down by the signal cannon and leaned back against the wheel. The music of the regimental band floated across the quadrangle, and he sat there in the dark, listening.

The band played "Lorena." He knew that "Lorena" had been one of the favorite ballads of the soldiers on both sides of the Civil War and, as he heard it, he couldn't help but think about the many young men who had listened to the song during the war that were no longer alive, not only those who were killed in the war, but those who had died since. He knew that he would never be able to hear this tune again without thinking of them. He was only five years old when the war ended, but he had known a lot of Civil War veterans, and because he was born and raised in Missouri, he knew veterans from both sides of the conflict.

He looked around the post and saw the hospital, Old Bedlam, and the BOQ all gleaming white in the moonlight. All of the officers' quarters were well lit by kerosene lamps, and the windows were shining brightly, projecting squares of glimmering gold onto the ground outside. On the far side of the quadrangle the light was considerably dimmer from the enlisted men's barracks and from the married NCO's quarters as most of them burned the cheaper candles for light, rather than the lanterns that required fuel.

Finally, Pershing got up and returned to the dance.

"Where have you been?" Meagan asked, when he returned. "Your name is on my dance card, and I was about to think you might stand me up."

"Ha!" Pershing said. "Disabuse yourself of that thought, Miss Parker. As you can see, I am here, bright eyed, and ready to claim my turn." He glanced toward Duff. "Of course, with your permission, Mr. MacCallister."

Duff laughed. "Leftenant, ye dinnae know the young lady all that well, do ye? 'Tis nae my place to grant or deny permission about anything she does. She is a woman with a strong will. To that, I can attest."

The music started and, with a broad smile, Meagan offered her arm. Pershing took it and led her out onto the dance floor.

At the gate, the gate guard was moving around, dancing to the music, when he heard horses approaching.

"Corporal of the guard! Riders approaching the gate!" he called.

The call was repeated across the quadrangle so that the corporal of the guard reached the gate just as Captain Kirby and A Troop came riding up.

"Welcome back, Captain!" the corporal of the guard said, as he and the gate guard saluted.

Both Captain Kirby and Lieutenant Scott returned the salute.

"Thank you, Corporal McMurtry," Captain Kirby said. He pulled to one side as the troops came riding in, and as he sat there, he could hear music from the sutler's store.

"Is there a dance tonight, Corporal?" he asked.

"Yes, sir," McMurtry said. "And I'd be there if I didn't have duty tonight."

When the last of his soldiers came through the gate, Kirby wished Corporal McMurtry a goodnight, then urged his horse to catch up. He called the troop to a halt in the middle of the parade ground.

"I know some of you might want to go to the dance, but you make certain your mounts are rubbed down before you go," he ordered. "First Sergeant, post."

First Sergeant Cobb rode to the middle of the formation and Lieutenant Scott, who had been behind, rode away quickly to leave the formation as command was about to be turned over to a sergeant, and a sergeant could not command a formation that included an officer.

"First Sergeant, dismiss the troop."

Cobb saluted, and then turned toward the mounted troop.

"Troop, dismount!"

The soldiers dismounted as one.

"Fall out!" he called.

"Horse, you're goin' to qet a quick rubdown, 'cause I'm goin' to that dance!" one of the soldiers shouted.

"Hell, Gilbert, why don't you take your horse to the dance? You ain't goin' to get no woman to dance with you," one of the other soldiers said, and there was a general laughter as the soldiers led their horses to the stable.

The dance had been going for about an hour when several new men came in. These were the soldiers who had gone out with Captain Kirby and Lieutenant Scott. Kirby came over to report to Colonel Gibbon.

"Captain, it is good to see you back," Colonel Gibbon said. "Did you encounter any Indians?"

"No, sir, Colonel, not a one," Kirby said. "If you want to know what I think, I think it might have just been a bunch of young bucks that got themselves drunk on contraband whiskey, then left the reservation to go wild for a while. Like as not, they're back on the reservation, and except for Yellow Hawk, we won't be seein' 'em again."

"You may be right, Captain. But still, we can't just let them go unpunished."

"No, sir, I don't reckon we can," Captain Kirby said. He smiled. "By the way, did I see some spitted beef when we came back?"

"You did indeed," Colonel Gibbon said. "Sergeant Beck is in charge, and I'm told it will be ready to serve by noon tomorrow."

"All right, after a week of field rations, that is something I look forward to with great pleasure. And, as soon as I wash off some of this dirt, I intend to come back and have at least one dance with my wife, if I can pull her away."

"It's good to have you back, Bill," Colonel Gibbon said.

Out on the dance floor, Sue was dancing with a young private when Lieutenant Scott stepped in.

"You won't mind, will you, Private, if I claim my wife?" Scott asked in a tone of voice that was both sarcastic and callous.

"No, sir! No, sir! I'm sorry, sir!" the private said, jumping back quickly, and in fear.

Scott took Sue by the arm and led her off the floor.

"Clay, what are you doing? You are embarrassing me," Sue complained, though she said the words quietly.

"I come back from a weeklong campaign against the Indians, and I find you, not at home welcoming the soldier home from the wars, but on a dance floor, cavorting with the enlisted men. And you say that I am embarrassing you?"

"I'm sorry. You know how few women there are on the post. Mrs. Gibbon herself asked us to be generous with our dances. Why even she dances with everyone, officer and enlisted alike."

"When I make colonel, you can do the same thing. For now I'm tired. I want to take a bath, and I want to go to bed. I have had a very hard week."

Chapter Nineteen

"What happened to Mrs. Scott?" Pershing asked Holbrook. "I believe my name is on her dance card."

"You didn't see?" Holbrook asked.

"See what?"

"Clay stormed out on the floor like the cretin he is, grabbed Sue by the shoulder, and pulled her away."

"Oh, no, I didn't see it."

"John, I know that Scott was your classmate, and believe me, I know the camaraderie that exists between members of the same class at the Point. Hell, I remember him as well, and I had no particular grievance with him then."

Pershing chuckled. "You were two classes ahead of us, Jason. Nobody in my class would have dared give you cause for grievance."

Holbrook chuckled as well. "Yes, but be that as it may, he has certainly done nothing since his arrival out here to earn anyone's respect, or admiration. The best I can say about him is that he is tolerated."

"Why is that, do you suppose?"

"Oh, I don't have to suppose, I'm sure I know why it is. Clay Scott thought that by marrying General Winfield's daughter, he would receive only the most desirable assignments, and be promoted quickly, but it hasn't happened. What in the world a beautiful, refined young woman like Sue Winfield saw in Scott, I'll never know." Holbrook laughed, but it was a derisive laugh. "I've no doubt but that he is surprised that he isn't a captain yet."

"I must say that in the time I've been here, he has exhibited a degree of entitlement," Pershing said. "But I thought that was just me."

"I overheard Captain Kirby say that they encountered no Indians during this patrol, so Scott wasn't tested. I would give anything to know how he behaved on the scout where Jones, Travis, and Calhoun were killed. Sergeant Caviness was with him, but he won't say anything."

"Caviness is loyal to Scott, is he? That speaks well for Scott, don't you think?"

"No, it doesn't speak well for Scott. It speaks well for Sergeant Caviness," Holbrook said.

At that moment the band played a fanfare. Then Sergeant Major Martell stepped out in front of the raised platform.

"Ladies, officers, and men," the sergeant major said. "Our troops have returned from their scout without one casualty. Let us give them a cheer. Hip, hip!"

"Hooray!"

"Hip, hip!"

"Hooray!"

"Hip, hip!"

"Hooray!"

"And now, as is our custom here, we will conclude this dance with the grand march, led by Colonel Gibbon and Mrs. Martell, and brought up by me, and Mrs. Gibbon."

The soldiers hurried to claim their place in the grand march, and then, with the downbeat of the band leader's baton, the march began. At the end of the grand march, the band concluded the evening by playing "The Girl I Left Behind Me." After that song, officers and their ladies, NCO's and their wives, single officers and single ladies, left the sutler's store to return to their quarters.

Meagan was a guest of Colonel and Mrs. Gibbon, and her room was on the top floor, left-hand side of Old Bedlam, with a door that led from her room out onto the balcony. After Meagan dressed in her white nightgown, she opened a window to catch the night breeze, and because it felt so good she decided to walk out onto the porch for a few moments. From this elevated position, she had a very good view of the entire post and she saw the glow of the burning coals, over which the beef was being cooked. Beyond that she saw the dependent housing, the quarters for the married soldiers, both noncommissioned and commissioned officers. Looking in the other direction, she saw the BOQ, then the barracks, and beyond the barracks, the stables.

Directly in front of her she saw a wide-open expanse of grass, in the middle of which was a flagpole which was devoid of its banner, and a single cannon. The barrel of the cannon gleamed softly in the moonlight.

Over in his room in the BOQ, Duff extinguished the lantern, then looked out the window. He saw something white and gleaming on the upper terrace of Old Bedlam, and realized at once that it was Meagan. In the moonlight, there was almost an angelic aura around her. Meagan had proved herself during this drive, holding up her end of the work like any of the other drovers, not complaining when the hours were long, and the days hot. And when exposed to danger, she didn't flinch.

Duff watched as she just stood there on the porch, looking out over the post, and enjoying the night air. He wished there was some way he could be standing there, right beside her now, without causing talk. Duff had given no real consideration to marriage since Skye had been killed, and he didn't really think it was the time to think about it now. But if he did think about it, Meagan would be the first person he would consider.

As he was watching her, Meagan turned to look toward the BOQ, and Duff got the distinct feeling that she was looking right at him, that she knew he was here, looking at her.

He held her gaze for a long moment, even though he knew that she couldn't actually see him. Then she turned and went back inside.

Over in the married officers' quarters, in the house occupied by Lieutenant Scott and his wife, Sue, the evening wasn't as peaceful. As soon as they stepped inside the door, Scott slapped her.

"No! Please, no!" Sue shouted, holding her arm up and cringing in fear.

"Shut up!" Scott said. He slapped her again. "You make one more sound and I'll really give you something to scream about! You want everyone on the post to know about our private affairs?"

Sue began crying quietly. "Why are you doing this, Clay?"

"Why am I doing it? Well, let me ask you. How do you think it makes me feel to return home, and find you with another man?" Scott asked bitterly.

"With another man? Clay, what are you talking about?" Sue replied, shocked by the accusation.

"You know damn well what I'm talking about. I'm talking about you on the dance floor with an enlisted man. An *enlisted* man, mind you. Do you have any idea what an insult that is to our marriage?"

"Clay, I must have danced with a dozen or more people tonight! I don't even know that young private's name, for heaven's sake!"

"And because you are a slut with a dozen or more men, instead of one private, that's supposed to make me feel better?"

"It's not like that, Clay. I told you, even Mrs. Gibbon was dancing with the soldiers."

"Yes, but Colonel Gibbon was there!" Scott said. "I wasn't!"

"I don't see what difference that should make."

"If you don't see the difference, then you are even more of a slut than I thought," Scott said. "Fix me something for supper."

"Supper? Now? It's after eleven o'clock."

"I don't care if it's three o'clock in the morning," Scott said with a growl. "You are my wife. When I ask you to fix my supper, you damn well better do it."

"Are bacon and eggs all right?" Sue asked in a trembling voice.

"I guess they will have to be," Scott said. He sat down and pulled off his boots, then stretched his feet out. Then he watched as Sue, still sniveling, started a couple of pieces of bacon to frying.

"Oh, quit your crying, I'm not going to hit you anymore," Scott said.

"You had no right to hit me in the first place."

"Sure I did. I'm your husband. I have every right to hit you, whether you give me a reason or not."

For the next few minutes neither of them spoke. Then Scott got up and walked into the kitchen behind Sue, who was cooking. She flinched.

"I told you, I'm not going to hit you again." He reached out to put his arms around her. "I'm sorry I hit you. I'm just frustrated. It's your father's fault, Sue. He needs to get me away from this post. He needs to bring me back to Washington to be on his staff. Wouldn't you like to be back with your friends and family again?"

"Yes."

"Well, all you have to do is ask him to bring me back. I know he will listen to you, Sue. I tell you what, don't even mention me. Just tell him that you want to come back. That's probably all it will take. Will you write the letter?"

"I'll write the letter."

"That's a good girl," Scott said. He kissed her on the forehead, totally oblivious that she was still shaking in fear.

By the time "Reveille" was sounded the next morning, the entire post was permeated by the aroma of meat that had been cooking all night long. When the men were dismissed after reveille formation, many of them went over to examine the cause of the wonderful smell. There, they saw two soldiers slowly turning the spits, each of which held half a steer, the beef halves dripping juice onto glowing coals, while Sergeant Beck was busy brushing some sort of sauce onto the brown, glistening meat.

"Hey, Sarge, how about a bite?" one of soldiers said, reaching out to pull off a piece of the meat.

"You pull off any of that meat and I'll cut off your hand," Sergeant Beck said, and though the soldier knew he was joking, there was enough seriousness in the remark to cause him to jerk his hand back.

"I just wanted a taste."

"You'll get a taste," Sergeant Beck said. "You'll get all you want at dinnertime."

Because this was to be a post celebration, the meal wasn't going to be served in the mess hall, but out on the parade ground where, for the enlisted men, long tables had been set up and set with plates, spoons, knives, and forks from the mess hall.

There were three tables set up for the officers, and they were covered with tablecloths, and set with china, crystal, and real silver, supplied not only from the household treasures of the married officers, but from the officers' open mess as well. Elmer was invited to eat with the officers of the post, but Sergeant Havercost had given him a special invitation to eat with him, Caviness, First Sergeant Cobb, and the rest of the unmarried NCOs. And because Elmer felt a sense of guilt over having once robbed Havercost, he agreed to join them.

The soldiers were on their best behavior, standing in line to present their plates to Sergeant Beck, who carved generous portions of the meat for them.

"Whooee, Beck, what'd you do to this here beef?" Sergeant Caviness asked, putting into words what everyone was thinking. "This here's the best tastin' meat I ever ate."

"It's the sauce," Sergeant Havercost suggested. "What kind of sauce are you usin'?"

"The sauce is nothing but vinegar, lemon juice, brown sugar, and some ground cayenne," Sergeant Beck said. "That's the same sauce I always use."

"Well, you've done somethin' different."

"Ask him," Sergeant Beck said, pointing to Elmer.

"Did you do something to this meat, Mr. Gleason?"

Elmer shook his head. "It's not how it's cooked," he said. "It's what is cooked. The beef you are eatin' came from a Black Angus."

"The hell, you say," Caviness said. He looked at the meat on his plate. "And this here is what you and MacCallister brought to us?"

"Yes."

"Well, I'll be damn. Whoever thought the army would be eating this good?"

After the meal, there was a baseball game with players from A and B troops playing against C and D troops. Meagan was sitting beside Duff, and she realized that as he was watching the game, he had absolutely no understanding of it.

"Why is it that sometimes they hit the ball and

run, and other times they hit the ball and don't run?" Duff asked.

"Because if the batted ball is caught, it is an out," Megan explained.

"An 'out'?"

Meagan laughed. "Most of the time it is the men who must explain a sport to the women. I'm having a great time reversing the roles."

Sherman, Ford, and Bates, the cowboys who had brought the herd down, remained for the barbeque, then stayed around to watch the baseball game. Elmer was staying at the fort with Duff, so the three men would be taking the chuck wagon back to Sky Meadow. After the game, the three came over to see Duff and Meagan.

"Mr. MacCallister," Sherman said, speaking for all of them. "We're goin' to get on back to the ranch now. We'll keep an eye on things till you get back."

"Don't spend all the money afore you get back home now," Ford teased. "Keep enough of it back that you can make the payroll."

"Don't you worry any about that, Mr. Ford," Meagan said with a little laugh. "Half the money is mine. If Duff spends all his money, I'll have enough to make the payroll."

"That's right, ain't it?" Ford said with a broad grin. "Well then, Mr. MacCallister, you just don't mind what I said. If you want to spend all your money on a glorious drunk, why, you just go right ahead and do it."

"Well, 'tis thanks I'm giving ye for the permission to spend m' own money," Duff said.

Ford got a distressed look on his face.

"Oh, law, Mr. MacCallister, I din't mean it like that. Why, I ain't got no right to say what you do with your own money."

Meagan laughed. "Mr. Ford, I know it's hard to tell because he's a Scotsman, and Scotsmen are hard to understand sometimes, believe me I know. But he is teasing you."

Not until Duff smiled did Ford realize he was being teased, then he laughed easily as well.

"You had me goin' there for a moment," Ford said.

"Jory, Jimmy, Jeff, ye boys be careful going back home. Dinnae get into any trouble anywhere. 'Tis good lads ye are, and I'm honored to have ye working with me."

The three cowboys nodded their good-byes. Then with Jimmy Sherman driving the wagon, Jory Bates, and Jeff Ford on horseback alongside, the three started toward the gate. Sherman had left his horse behind for Elmer to ride when it was time for Duff, Meagan, and Elmer to leave.

Duff watched them until they passed through the gate, then he turned to Meagan.

"Meagan, would ye be for taking a bit of a stroll down to the river?"

"Why, I would love to," Meagan replied, taking his arm.

A moment later, as they stood there looking out over the water, Meagan began to sing.

"The water is wide, I cannot cross o'er
But neither have I the wings to fly
Give me a boat, that will carry two,
And both shall row, my love and I."

Her voice was a pure, sweet soprano and Duff looked at her in surprise as she continued.

"There is a ship, and she sails the sea
She's loaded deep, as deep can be,
But not as deep as the love I'm in.
I know not if I sink or swim."

"Why, Meagan, and were ye for knowin', lass, that it is a Scottish tune ye be singing?"

"'O Waly, Waly,'" Meagan said. "But I don't know what that means."

"You sang it, Meagan. The water is wide," Duff said.

As Duff looked at her, Meagan saw a smoldering flame in his eyes, and she felt a tingling in the pit of her stomach. He moved toward her, paused for a moment and, encountering no resistance, entangled his hand in her hair and pulled her lips to his.

The kiss began innocently enough, no more than the brush of lips they had shared on that night at her apartment, when he first told her that he had sold some cattle to the army. It was soft and tentative, as if he were exploring the bounds. But when she offered no resistance, the kiss deepened.

Meagan lost all control of herself then, becoming a creature who was totally subservient to Duff's will and demand. She could no more break off this kiss than she could fly, and though a weak cry far back in her mind warned her against going too far, every emotion and sensation in her body silenced that voice.

It was Duff who established the boundaries. "I think perhaps we should return to the fort," he said.

With all that was in her, Meagan wanted to ask, why? But as he put his hand gently on her arm and turned toward the fort, she acquiesced without comment.

It began to rain.

Chapter Twenty

Argonne Forest, October 3, 1918

The Germans had a piece of artillery they called "Big Bertha," a huge gun that fired 1,800 pound shells for a distance of seven miles. Occasionally, they would launch one in the direction of the Château de Chaumont, where General Pershing had established his headquarters. Fortunately, none of those shells actually struck the castle. But often they would land close enough, within less than a quarter of a mile, that the concussion of the explosion would rattle the windows.

Sergeant Duff Tavish MacCallister, Jr. had been invited by General Pershing to spend the night at Château de Chaumont castle, and at the moment, he was the general's guest at the dinner table. Tavish felt very awkward, being served by the same orderlies who were serving the general. And though Tavish was but a sergeant, these orderlies were serving him with as much care and respect as they were showing the general.

Pershing chuckled. "You seem a little self-conscious, Sergeant," he said.

"I'm not used to dining with generals," Tavish replied.

"Maybe not. But you have dined with Governor Brooks, Governor Carrey, and President Roosevelt. I believe, in fact, that you were President Roosevelt's guide on a hunting trip he took."

"Well, yes, sir, but they were my dad's friends."

"I consider myself a friend of your father."

"It's not the same. I was a civilian then. Now I'm a sergeant in the army, and you are a general."

"Let's put that aside for a moment, shall we?" General Pershing asked.

"General, that's easy for you to say. But I haven't been in the army all that long and respect for officers has been drilled in me . . . respect for a general officer? Well, to be honest with you, that's not anything I ever even thought I would have to deal with. And now, here I am, having dinner with one."

"I haven't always been a general, Sergeant."

"No, sir, but you've always been an officer."

Pershing chuckled. "Evidently, you have no idea what it is like to be a plebe at West Point."

"No, sir, I don't know what it's like."

"Trust me, Sergeant, as plebes we had to put up with such things as: 'What is the definition of leather?'"

"Leather? You mean like my boots? From a cow?"

General Pershing chuckled. "It's been a long time since I was a plebe, but I still remember all the inane questions we were asked, and would have to remember, or walk punishment tours. You think of leather as your boots, but this is what leather is." Pershing cleared his throat, and began to speak. "'If the fresh skin of an animal, cleaned and divested of all hair, fat, and other extraneous matter, be immersed in a dilute solution of tannic acid, a chemical combination ensues; the gelatinous tissue of the skin is converted into a nonputrescible substance, impervious to and insoluble in water; this is leather.'"

Tavish laughed out loud. "General, if you don't mind my asking, what does that have to do with making a man a good officer?"

"Sergeant, you are asking the very same question I asked thirty-six years ago. And the answer I gave myself then is the same answer I'll give you now. It doesn't have a damn thing to do with making a man a good officer."

Tavish laughed again.

"Tell me, Sergeant, are you enjoying the beef?" General Pershing asked.

"Yes, sir, it's quite good."

"Do you recognize it?"

Tavish got a surprised look on his face. "Do I recognize it?"

Pershing laughed. "I thought perhaps that you might, being that it's your father's beef," he said. "I approved the purchase by the army of ten thousand pounds of beef from Sky Meadow Cattle Company. And, as you know from the story I've been telling you, this isn't the first time your father has supplied beef to the army."

"I know that while I was growing up, my dad supplied beef not only to the army, but to the Indian Agencies," Tavish said.

"It's too bad he didn't supply fresh beef to us during the war in Cuba," Pershing said. "A parsimonious Congress provided the army with the cheapest meat possible, and what we received in Cuba was so poorly preserved, chemically adulterated, and spoiled, that it not only tasted awful, it was actually quite toxic and dangerous to eat. The meat caused an ungodly number of illnesses and death from dysentery. In fact, food poisoning wound up killing twice as many men as were killed in battle with the Spanish."

"Yes, sir, I was but a boy at the time, but I remember my dad talking about it. He thought it was disgraceful."

"It was disgraceful, but at least as a result of that, the army gets better treatment when it comes to the food supply. Like this," he said, holding up a piece of just carved steak.

"When I get back to A Company, I'll have to tell the rest of the boys where their meat comes from. Heck, General, who knows, when I was still helping at the ranch, I may have prodded this very steer in the ass."

General Pershing laughed out loud, laughing so

hard that he had to grab a napkin to catch the meat he was chewing.

"You may have indeed," he said. He wiped his mouth, and carved off another piece of steak. But before he lifted it to his mouth, he looked over at Tavish. "You don't have another gem like that, do you?"

"No, sir. I'm sorry, sir," Tavish said.

"Sergeant, may I ask why it is you aren't an officer? With your contacts, you could certainly be an officer."

"It's just not anything I ever considered, General. I have been perfectly content to help my dad run the ranch."

"As well you should be. I know that it is one of the most productive ranches in the nation. And I know that you are a very wealthy man, which is why I asked the question how you wound up here, and as an enlisted man."

"General, I volunteered to come into the army because I thought it was the patriotic thing to do. I don't intend to make a career of it, though I certainly have learned to honor and respect those who have made it a career."

Again General Pershing laughed. "That is a very nice recovery, Sergeant, seeing as I have made it a career."

"Yes, sir, thank you sir," Tavish replied with a chuckle.

"You say you came into the army because you thought it was a patriotic thing to do?"

"Yes, sir."

"Then if I give you a very difficult job to do tomorrow, one that will require a great deal of skill on your part"—Pershing stopped for a moment and stared directly into Tavish's eyes before he continued—"and, I might add, one that will put you in a great deal of personal danger, would you be willing to accept the challenge?"

"We are all in danger, General."

"No, Duff," General Pershing said, and it didn't escape Tavish's attention that the general had called him by his first name. "I mean you, personally, will be put into an extremely dangerous situation in order to carry out the mission. And, I'm asking if you will accept the mission, because it isn't something I feel I can I order you to do."

"There is no need for you to order me to do it, General. If it is something that you believe is necessary for us to accomplish what we are here to accomplish, and if it is something you feel I can do, I volunteer to do it."

"It will require a marksman of exceptional skill. That's why I had you perform for us this afternoon."

"Yes, sir, I thought it might have something to do with that."

"Tomorrow, I'm going to ask you to make a very difficult shot. In a way, it won't be all that different from a shot that your father once had to make. Come out onto the terrace with me."

General Pershing and Tavish sat out in the

darkness, looking to the east. More than 2,700 guns of the American and French armies continued to exchange artillery barrages with the Germans. The flashes from the muzzle flames of the big guns were so frequent that there appeared to be one continuous, but flickering, light across the western horizon, while the guns made a constant, rumbling roar, like distant rolling thunder.

"Where was I in the story?" General Pershing asked.

"You had just had your first taste of Black Angus beef," Tavish said.

"Oh, yes. I've had it many times since then, such as tonight, of course, but I don't think I've ever tasted anything any better than the beef that Sergeant Beck cooked for us that night, so long ago, in that distant, and now abandoned post."

"Are you talking about Fort Laramie, General?"

"Yes. Your father has told you about it?"

"Actually, Mr. Gleason is the one who told me about it."

"Gleason?"

"Elmer Gleason. He and my father have been friends for a long time, ever since my father came to America."

"Oh, yes, I remember Elmer Gleason. He was sort of a, well, how can I put it? A curmudgeon then."

Tavish laughed. "If you think he was then, you should see him now."

"You mean he's still alive?"

"Yes, sir. He's eighty-seven years old, and he has his own house on the ranch."

"As I recall, he was quite a colorful character," General Pershing said.

"Yes, sir. I believe Elmer Gleason may be just about the most colorful character I've ever met. He was an officer, you know."

"Mr. Gleason was?"

"Yes, sir, he was a lieutenant."

"I didn't know that. I don't believe he mentioned it while he was at Fort Laramie."

"No, sir, he probably wouldn't have, being as he was in the Confederate army. Sort of."

"Sort of?"

"He rode with Quantrill."

"Oh, my," General Pershing said. "Quantrill was quite a bad one."

"I made the mistake once of saying that to Mr. Gleason. But I only made the mistake once. I must say, he gave me a different perspective on the man.

"Before the war, Quantrill was a schoolteacher who was highly respected by everyone who knew him. When the war started, he organized and led up to four hundred men in what has become the best-known band of guerrilla fighters in our history, often winning battles against Union forces with far superior troops. The people supported him, entrusted their sons to him, and some served him as spies. Wives and mothers willingly tended his wounded. Mr. Gleason said that the victors have written the history, and that's why Quantrill has come down to us as such a monster. But he asked me a question that I couldn't answer. How was Quantrill able to get decent and righteous people to follow him, if he were, as he has been pictured, a depraved, degenerate, psychotic killer, devoid of the slightest tissue of humanity?"

General Pershing took a swallow of his wine before he responded.

"Son, you should teach military history at the Point. Or at least, give a guest lecture there on the subject of guerilla warfare. I've never heard a more succinct defense of Quantrill."

"There wasn't a very high bar for me to pass, was there, General? I mean, how many defenses of Quantrill have you heard?"

Again, General Pershing laughed out loud. "You've got me there, Sergeant. I don't think I've ever heard Quantrill defended."

"In all fairness, I must confess that I was but repeating the words of Elmer Gleason."

"I should have gotten to know Mr. Gleason better," General Pershing said. "Obviously, there was much more to the man than I was aware. But, back to my story. Barbecuing the beef that day did more for morale than just about anything I had ever seen, and I must confess that I stole the idea, and have used it many times since then. I mean, the soldiers didn't even appear to mind when it started to rain. They just—"

"General Pershing?" a voice interrupted and,

looking around, Tavish saw that a colonel had just stepped out onto the veranda.

"Yes, Colonel Patton?"

"I've got the information on the German colonel you wanted."

"Let's hear it."

"Our information is correct, General, in that Johannes Georg von der Marwitz is commanding the lines. And his chief of staff is Colonel Fritz von Krueger."

"Von Krueger, yes, I thought so."

"I'm sure you know, General, that von Krueger has spent a lot of time in the U.S., including two years as a liaison officer at Fort Monroe. General, he has the book on every senior officer in your command, all the way down to colonel."

"Including you, George?" Pershing asked.

"Yes, General, including me. He is, without doubt, Marwitz's most valuable asset. Marwitz won't make a move without von Kruger's input. And, because he made a study of every staff and command officer under you, he is our greatest danger."

"Yes, I thought as much. That's why I had you put together a file on him. Won't you join the sergeant and me for a glass of wine?"

"Thank you, General, but I need to get back. I've more work to do."

"Very well," Pershing said.

Pershing watched as Colonel Patton went back into the castle. "Mark my words, Sergeant, we are going to hear from that colonel someday. He is the most undisciplined and reckless officer I've ever known but there is something about him . . . an innate willingness . . . no . . . a necessity to fight."

"Yes, sir, even I have heard of him and his tank corps," Tavish said.

"Well, let's get back to my story of how I met you father, shall we? Where did I leave off?"

"It had started to rain," Tavish said.

"Oh, yes. And quite a rain it was, too."

Chapter Twenty-one

Fort Laramie

The rain came up suddenly and unexpectedly, not starting with a gentle sprinkle, but opening with a deluge. Even though the meal was over and most of the people were watching the baseball game by then, the tables were still set with cloth and the dinnerware. Men and women hurried back to the place where the picnic had been held and began to pick up the tablecloths and dinnerware, doing so as quickly as they could. Those who weren't involved in the recovery of the dinner items hurried into some shelter.

Elmer took shelter in the sutler's store, and buying a beer, found a table in the corner. Sergeant Havercost came over to join him.

"I see you knew where to go when the rain started," Havercost said.

"Like they say, Sergeant, any port in a storm."

Elmer took a swallow of his beer. "It's just that some ports are better in a storm than other ports."

"To be sure," Havercost said with a little chuckle. "Tell me, Mr. Gleason, how long have you been with Mr. MacCallister?"

"Ever since he come to America, I reckon," Elmer answered. "I helped him get Sky Meadow started."

"Sky Meadow?"

"That's his ranch."

"That's funny," Havercost said. "I would never have figured you for a rancher."

"Oh? Well, I ain't always ranched. I've trapped some. I was a sailor on a clipper ship for a while. I done some prospectin' and some minin'. I even deputy sheriffed some, down in Texas."

Havercost took a swallow of his own beer, then wiped his mouth with the back of his hand.

"And, as I recall, you was also a road agent for a bit, back in Missouri, oh, around '66 or '67, I think it was," Havercost said.

"Beg your pardon?" Elmer said.

"I remember now when it was that I last seen you. And I know where it was, too," Sergeant Havercost said. "It was on a road in southeast Missouri, about halfway between New Madrid and Sikeston. What was it, '66 or '67?"

"You think you recall somethin', do you?"

"Yeah, you know what made me remember?"

"What?"

"The rain," Havercost said. "A while ago when I

seen that rain drippin' off the end of your nose, I remembered. I'd seen rain drippin' off that same nose once before. It was rainin' that day, too, if you recall."

For a long, quiet moment, the two men just stared at each other. Then Elmer smiled.

"Oh, yes, I do recall. And now that you got me to thinkin' about it, seems to me like it was rainin' like a son of a bitch," he said.

Havercost laughed. "Well, I'm glad to see that you ain't tryin' to deny it."

"No sense in denyin' it," Elmer said. "You got me dead to rights. So what happens now? Do you turn me in, or what?"

"Turn you in to who? Turn you in for what? That was then, and this is now, and besides, it wasn't my money in the first place." Havercost laughed again. "Anyway, it was damn near worth it, just to see the expression on Sollinger's face when I told him that all the tax money had been took."

"Sollinger?"

"Yeah, Robert Sollinger. He was the revenue man the money was s'posed to go to."

Elmer chuckled. "Well, I'm glad I was able to give you that pleasure."

"Don't tell me, Gleason, that you give all that money back to the people that the tax collectors took it from."

Elmer laughed. "Well now, you know Sergeant Havercost, damn me if I didn't give that some thought. But there was a problem, you see. There weren't no way I was able to know who the money come from. So I done the next best thing."

"What was the next best thing?"

"Me 'n' the boys that was with me spent it," Elmer said.

Havercost laughed again, louder this time than before, and he slapped the table. "You know what, Gleason? I hope you had a fine old time with that money."

"Oh, I did, Sergeant, I truly did," Elmer said. "Now how about lettin' me buy the next drink to make up for robbin' you?"

"Don't mind if I do," Havercost said. "And I'm curious. What did you spend it on? I hope it was wine, women, and song."

Elmer shook his head. "Nope."

"No?"

Elmer smiled. "Now you tell me, Sergeant Havercost. Why the hell would I want to waste any of that money on song?"

Havercost laughed again. "Well, as long as you didn't waste any of the money," he said.

Sergeant Caviness came over to the table then.

"Do you folks mind if I join you?" he asked.

"I don't mind," Havercost said. "It's up to Mr. Gleason."

"Hell, I'm surrounded by Yankee solders," he said. "Why should I worry if another'n come along?"

"Mr. Gleason, one of the cowboys that come up

with you, tells me that you used to live with the Shoshone."

Elmer didn't answer right away. Instead, he took a drink of his beer and studied Caviness through narrowed eyes.

"You got a bone to pick with me over that?" he asked.

"No, no, don't get me wrong. I ain't got no bone to pick. I just got a question, and I'm hopin' you can answer it."

"All right, ask. If I know the answer, I'll answer it."

"Here's what I'm wantin' to ask you, and you'll need to think like an Injun to be able to answer it, which is why I'm askin' you, since I figure that since you lived with 'em once, maybe you can think like one.

"Suppose there was someone leading a group of soldiers, say he was an officer. And suppose that officer led them soldiers into a real narrow space, between two high places. And suppose there was Injuns up on top of them high places, just a' shootin' down onto the soldiers."

"The first thing I would ask is why some officer is dumb enough to lead his men into a place like that? He would just be waiting for an ambush."

"Yes, well, it could be that they was some people that told him he ought not to do that, but he didn't listen to 'em. Anyhow, here is my question. When the Injuns started shootin', how come they wasn't shootin' at the officer?"

"They weren't shooting at him because there was

no honor in it. See, here's the thing about Injuns. They don't hate their enemies. The enemies that put up a good fight, the Injuns honor and respect. They have no respect for cowards, and there is no honor in killin' a coward."

"Yeah," Caviness said. "Yeah, that's pretty much what I was a' thinkin' myself."

"Sam, you're talkin' about Lieutenant Scott, ain't you?" Havercost asked.

"I ain't a' talkin' 'bout no one in particular," Caviness said. "And I ain't plannin' on doin' it, neither."

Wind River Reservation

Ska Luta Glee John listened to the elders as they discussed Yellow Hawk and the others who had left the reservation.

"They have killed many," Howling Wolf said. "Many more of our young men have joined Yellow Hawk, and they have killed many. I fear they will cause the soldiers to attack us."

"I don't think the soldiers will attack us. We have done nothing. It is Yellow Hawk who has done the bad things," Standing Bear said.

"I was with Black Kettle at Sand Creek," Howling Wolf said. "We had done nothing, but that did not stop the white soldiers from attacking our village and killing many women and children. I fear that will happen again."

"I think we should join Yellow Hawk," Brave Elk said.

"Why should we do such a thing?" Standing Bear asked.

"If, as Howling Wolf says, the soldiers will attack us, I do not want to be here in the village with the women and children."

"I think the soldiers will not attack us," Ska Luta said.

These were the first words spoken by Ska Luta, and the others at the council looked at him in surprise and annoyance.

"Who are you to speak at the council of the wise?" Brave Elk asked. "Are we to listen to the words of the young, now?"

"I am young, this is true," Ska Luta said. "But I have studied at the agency school, and I have read the newspapers of the whites. I believe they know that Yellow Hawk is not one of us."

"Is it the white blood in you that speaks, or is it the red?" Brave Elk asked.

Glaring at Brave Elk, Ska Luta pulled his knife from his belt.

"Ayiee!" There were gasps of alarm among the others as they thought Ska Luta was issuing a challenge, and they were about to witness a fight. But the gasps of alarm turned to gasps of shock and surprise when they saw what Ska Luta did next.

Ska Luta held the knife out in front of him for a moment. Then he put the blade to his face, and pulled it across his cheek, opening up a rather deep wound, and drawing blood.

As the blood ran down his cheek, Ska Luta

glared at Brave Elk. "Tell me, Brave Elk. What color is the blood that runs from my wound?"

Brave Elk was too shocked to respond, but Standing Bear who was the chief, spoke for them all.

"The blood is red," he said. "And Ska Luta has proved by his wisdom and his boldness that he is one who can speak at our council."

Sasha Quiet Stream, a young, unmarried woman came quickly to Ska Luta's side and held a cloth to his wound to stop the bleeding.

Brave Elk glared at Ska Luta and the others.

"You would listen to a green willow but you will not listen to me," Brave Elk said. "I look at all of you and I ask, where are the men of courage? Where are the men of honor? And the answer is, the men of courage and honor are with Yellow Hawk. Only women and children remain here."

With that, Brave Elk spun on his heel and walked away from the council as those who had gathered opened up a path for him to pass through.

"Ska Luta," Standing Bear said.

Ska Luta felt a degree of apprehension at being directly addressed, and he looked toward the old chief.

"You are a young man wise beyond your years," he said. "It is good that you counsel against our young men joining with Yellow Hawk. I ask you now to join our council."

Again there were utterances of surprise, for never had one so young been asked to join the council of the elders.

"I am greatly honored that you have asked," Ska Luta said. "And I will join the council of elders."

The young woman who was tending to the wound on Ska Luta's cheek smiled in pride at being the one who was tending to Ska Luta.

"Come to the house of my grandfather," Sasha Quiet Stream said. "There I will tend to your wound."

"Thank you," Ska Luta said.

Sasha Quite Stream led him away from the council and, as they had for Brave Elk, those who had gathered to hear the discussion of the council now parted again, making a path through which the young woman and the young man could pass.

Like Ska Luta, Sasha Quiet Stream had neither mother nor father, and she lived in the house with Keytano, her grandfather. Keytano had fought with the Lakota in their great battle in the Time of Making Fat at the place of Greasy Grass, a place the whites called Little Big Horn. It was well known by all, that he had counseled against going to war with the whites, but it was equally well known that he had fought well, so there were none among the people at Wind River who felt no honor toward Keytano.

"I have said that no more should there be war between the Indian and the white man, because more whites will come, and then more will come until, like the blades of grass that cover the prairie, they will be everywhere."

"Yellow Hawk has said that he will kill many soldiers. He has already done so," Ska Luta said. "And now, many of our young follow him, and I fear that he will become a great leader, to be followed by many."

Keytano shook his head. "No. The time of the warrior leader is past. It is now time for the peacemaker. You are that peacemaker."

"Who, among the young, will listen to a peacemaker? They are drawn to the warrior."

"This is true," Keytano agreed with a nod of his head. "But it is also true that more courage will be required of the leader who would preserve peace than is required from he who would make war. And there is great honor in following such a path. Already, the council has seen this, and you have been asked to join them. But, even before the council saw this, I saw before, in a vision."

"What did the vision tell you?"

"The vision told me that your red blood will make you a great leader among our people, and that your white blood will make you a great leader among the white people. And you and Sasha Quiet Stream will be married."

"Grandfather!" Sasha Quiet Stream gasped. "How can you speak so? Ska Luta has made no request to take me as his wife."

"I have seen it in a vision," Keytano said. "And everyone knows that what comes to you in a dream is a vision that speaks only the truth."

Sasha Quiet Stream had bathed Ska Luta's face

with cool water, and now she was laying healing herbs on the wound. Ska Luta reached up and took her hand in his. She stopped what she was doing and looked down at him.

"If it is in a vision that your grandfather has seen, we cannot deny it," Ska Luta said.

"Ska Luta, are you asking that I become your wife?"

"Yes," Ska Luta said.

"Then I must make preparations for it."

"And I must bring gifts to your grandfather," Ska Luta said.

Chapter Twenty-two

When it was announced to the others that Ska Luta and Sasha Quiet Stream were to be married, there was a general happiness. And, because neither Ska Luta nor Sasha Quiet Stream had parents to make the arrangements for the marriage, and because Sasha Quiet Stream's grandfather was too old to do so, many in the village took upon themselves the task of preparing everything for the marriage.

With all preparations made, on the day of the wedding, Ska Luta arrived in his finest clothes—buckskin trousers and a fringed buckskin shirt, decorated with porcupine quills.

Sasha Quiet Stream was wearing a dress made of deerskin, softened and bleached white.

Both Sasha Quiet Stream and Ska Luta got on their knees to have their hair washed with a sudsy solution. Normally, the bride's mother would wash the groom's hair and the groom's mother would wash the bride's hair, but as neither of them had a mother, a couple of the village ladies assumed that responsibility. Then, with their hair washed, and rinsed, Standing Bear conducted the ceremony.

"Ska Luta, and Sasha Quiet Stream, you must now share the first step of this joining," Standing Bear said.

Ska Luta looked at Sasha Quiet Stream. "You will walk with me. Together we will share the responsibilities of the lodge, food, and children. May the Creator bless noble children for us to share. May they live long."

Sasha Quiet Stream replied. "Together we will share the responsibility of the home, food, and children. I promise that I shall discharge all my share of the responsibilities for the welfare of the family and the children."

"And now, the second step," Standing Bear said.

"Since you have walked with me, our wealth and prosperity will grow. May we be blessed by the Great Spirit. May we educate our children and may they live long," Ska Luta said.

"I will love only you, and treat all other men as my brothers. My devotion to you is pure and you are my joy. This is my commitment and pledge to you," Sasha Quiet Stream replied.

"And now, for the final step," Standing Bear said.

"As you have walked these three steps with me, our love and friendship have become inseparable and firm. We have experienced spiritual union in the eyes of the Great Spirit. Now you have become completely mine. I offer my total self to you. May our togetherness last forever," Ska Luta said.

"By the law of the Great Spirit, and the spirits of our honorable ancestors, I have become your wife. Whatever promises I have given you I have spoken them with a pure heart. All the spirits are witnesses to this fact. I shall never deceive you, nor will I let you down. I shall love you forever," Sasha Quiet Stream said.

Using his knife, Standing Bear cut a lock of hair from both Ska Luta and Sasha Quiet Stream. In front of everyone assembled, he tied the two locks of hair into a very tight knot, and then he gave the bundle to Jumping Rabbit, who was Sasha Quiet Stream's fifteen-year-old cousin.

"Go," he said to Jumping Rabbit. "Hide these locks of hair and let no one see where you hide them. Tell no one where you hide them." Jumping Rabbit took the locks of hair and ran off.

"Now," Standing Bear said to Ska Luta and Sasha Quiet Stream. "As long as the hair stays as one, you will both be as one. If you wish to break the marriage, you must find the locks of hair and, in front of witnesses, untie the hair. Go, as one. Start your lodge together."

Immediately, the drums began to beat in celebration and the entire village prepared for the marriage feast that was to follow.

Fort Laramie

By now every woman on the post knew that Meagan had sewn the dress she wore to the dance, finishing what Mary Meacham had only started. And, because of that, every woman on the post of Fort Laramie now knew that Meagan was not only an accomplished seamstress, but that she owned a dress shop. Mary, Clara, and Colonel Gibbon's wife, Kathleen, asked her if she would give them some tips on sewing and she agreed. But, she told them that would require a trip into the nearby town of Millersburg in order buy the material they would need.

The three ladies who had expressed an interest in learning to sew were always ready to go into town, and took every opportunity to do so. This opportunity was not different.

One of the problems with allowing the women of the post to go into town was that most visits into town required an army escort, and there was simply never enough men available to make up the escort. But Meagan believed she had a solution to that problem.

"I'll get Duff to go to town with us," she offered.

Not only Duff, but Pershing and Holbrook also went as well, the two lieutenants being off the normal duty rosters due to their dedicated assignment of writing a TO&E. They made the trip into town by a buckboard that had been fitted with three seats. Once in town, the women went off on their own while Duff, Holbrook, and Pershing decided to visit the Three Bell Saloon. There was a drunk passed out on the steps in front of the place and the three men had to step over him in order to go inside. The place smelled of whiskey, stale beer, and sour tobacco. There was a long bar on the left, with dirty towels hanging on hooks about every five feet along its front. A large mirror was behind the bar, but imperfections in the glass distorted the reflected images.

Behind the bar there was a sign which read: THIS IS AN HONEST GAMBLING ESTABLISHMENT. PLEASE REPORT ANY CHEATING TO THE MANAGEMENT.

In addition to the self-righteous claim of gambling integrity, the walls were also decorated with heads of game and pictures. One of the pictures was of a train rushing through the night, sparks spewing from the smokestack and every window of every car glowing with light. Another was of a sternwheeler steamboat, and yet another was of a three-masted sailing ship which could have been the *Hiawatha* that had brought Duff to America.

But the picture that was the *pièce de résistance* was one called *Custer's Last Fight*, a large lithograph that doubled as an advertisement for beer. Duff stopped to study it.

"I'm sure you've heard of Custer," Holbrook said. He pointed to the picture. "Here it is, a moment of history."

"Yes, of course I've heard of him," Duff said. "My cousin, Falcon, was there."

"Your cousin was killed with Custer?" Holbrook asked.

"No, I believe he was with the men who were not a part of Custer's final patrol."

"That would be Benteen or Reno," Pershing said. He pointed to the picture. "I will admit that this is a dramatic portrayal, though, quite fanciful. I took a special interest in this particular battle while I was at West Point. The Indians are not dressed properly, and Custer's hair wasn't long as it is here in the picture. He had it closely shorn before leaving Fort Abraham Lincoln; also, though he is wearing a red scarf in the picture, he was not wearing one on the day of the battle. But, the most egregious error is the location of the battle."

"What do you mean the location is wrong? It's at Little Big Horn. This is Little Big Horn, isn't it?" Holbrook asked.

"Yes," Pershing said. "But they are on the wrong side of the river."

Holbrook laughed. "John, did anyone ever tell you that you are a wiseass?"

"As long as the emphasis is on the 'wise' I will accept that as a compliment," Pershing said.

There were several large jars of pickled eggs and sausages on the bar.

Over against the back wall, near the foot of the stairs, a cigar-scarred, beer-stained upright piano was being played by a bald-headed musician, and a young soldier and one of the bar girls were standing alongside the piano, swaying to the music. There were at least six soldiers in the bar, but as neither Pershing nor Holbrook was in uniform, none of the soldiers in the bar noticed them.

Out on the floor of the saloon, nearly all the tables were filled. A half dozen or so bar gals were flitting about, pushing drinks and promising more than they really intended to deliver. A few card games were in progress, but most of the patrons were just drinking and talking.

The three men stepped up to the bar.

"What'll it be?" the barkeep asked as he moved down to greet them.

"Gentlemen, it would be my pleasure to buy the drinks," Duff offered.

"I never turn down a free drink," Holbrook said.

"Barkeep, would ye be for having any Scotch, now?"

"A Scotsman, are you?" the bartender replied.

"Aye."

"Well, you are in luck, sir, for one our neighboring ranchers is a Scotsman by the name of Brian McDonald, and Mr. McDonald insists that we keep a supply of good Scotch."

"Then if ye would, we'll have three drinks, and keep the bottle where you can get to it handily so that we can have a bit more if we are of a mind to."

"Yes, sir," the bartender said, and putting three glasses on the bar, he filled them with the pale gold liquid.

Duff picked up his glass and held it out toward the other two men. "Drink up, m' lads, and then

I've no doubt but that ye'll be tellin' me,'tis the finest thing ever ye've tasted."

The three men had just tossed down their drinks when Clara came into the saloon.

"Clara! What are you doing in here?" Holbrook asked. "Little sister, this is not a place for you."

"It's Mary," Clara said, her voice high pitched and full of fear.

"Mary? What about her?"

"There's a man holding her. Meagan is with them, and she sent me to you, Mr. MacCallister. She said you would know what to do."

"Where are they?"

"They are in the mercantile store. We were just in there, looking at patterns and material, when a man came in with a gun and grabbed Mary. He's holding her there now."

The three men didn't wait for any further explanation, but moved quickly out of the saloon, then ran down the street toward the mercantile. When they got there, they saw several people gathered around in front of the store, one of whom was wearing a city marshal's badge.

"Marshal, what's going on in there?" Duff asked.

"It's Harley Mack Jenner," the marshal said. "He's a mean drunk and I was about to put him in jail until he sobered up. I didn't think he'd give me any trouble, so I wasn't paying that much attention, but he grabbed my gun and hit me over the head with it. Next thing I know'd, he run across the street from the jail, and went into the store. He's got a couple of women that he's holdin' an' he won't let anyone else come in."

"Is there another way in?"

"Yes, there's a back door, but it's locked," someone said.

"Who are you?"

"The name is Waters. Charles Waters. This is my store, but he run me, my wife, and my clerk out."

"Do you have a key to the back door?"

"Yes, sir, but it's in the store."

"What about windows?"

"There's a window on the side."

"Is it open?"

"Yes, sir, it is, bein' as it's so warm I got it open to catch the breeze. But he's standin' so close to it that if you try 'n' crawl in through it, he'll see you for sure. And he's holdin' a pistol to that woman's head. I'm afraid if he sees someone tryin' to come in, he might shoot the woman."

"How close to the window is he?"

"He's real close. Not more 'n ten feet, I'd say."

"Ten feet?"

"Yes, sir, maybe closer. For sure he's no farther."

"What do you have in mind?" the marshal asked.

"I dinnae know for sure, but I plan to have a look and see if I can come up with an idea. What's your name, Marshal?"

"Emerson."

"Well, Marshal Emerson, ye just be ready."

"Ready for what?"

"Just be ready," Duff said.

There was a narrow passage between the mercantile store and the apothecary, which was next door to it. Duff went up the passageway to the window and then, very carefully, looked inside. As he did, Meagan saw him, and he held his finger across his lips.

"Why don't you let her go?" Meagan said to Jenner.

"Why should I let her go?" Jenner replied. "Long as I got her, there ain't nothin' nobody can do to me."

"Let her go and I'll stay here with you," Meagan offered.

Good girl, Duff thought. As long as you keep him talking, he'll nae be paying any attention to me.

"Nah, that won't do no good," Jenner said. "There don't nobody in town know who you are, so there won't nobody care what happens to you. I know this here girl is the daughter of the army doc, and ever'one in town knows her."

"What do you plan to do with her?"

"I don't rightly know. I ain't made up my mind."

"You haven't thought this through very well, have you?"

"I'll come up with somethin'."

Duff pulled his pistol, then aimed, very carefully, at the pistol Jenner was holding.

"You can't stay here forever," Meagan said. "You'll get tired, you'll get hungry, and you know you can't stay here forever."

"I can stay here long enough. Besides I—"

Whatever Jenner was going to say, he didn't

finish, because Duff pulled the trigger. His Colt .45 boomed, and the pistol Jenner was holding flew out of his hand.

"Ahh! Son of a bitch!" Jenner called out loud and grabbed his bloody right hand with his left. Quickly, Meagan picked up the pistol he had dropped.

"Marshal!" she called. "You can come in now!"

Emerson rushed in through the front door then, his pistol drawn. Half a dozen others came in behind him, propelled more out of a sense of curiosity than anything else.

"I need a doctor!" Jenner said. "My hand's been shot off!"

"No, it warn't," Marshal Emerson said. He chuckled. "But you sure lost the tip end of your finger."

"That ain't funny!"

"Come on across the street to the jail," Emerson said. "You was just goin' to spend the night till you sobered up. But I reckon you just bought yourself a little more time by what you done tonight."

"I wasn't really goin' to do anything to her," Waters said. "I just . . . I just got over here and the next thing you know I grabbed her without thinkin'."

By now Duff had come around the building and he was inside, along with Pershing and Holbrook.

"Damn!" Holbrook said. "That was quite a shot you made."

"Not for him," Pershing said. "I've seen him shoot before."

Chapter Twenty-three

Three days later, the colonel's orderly came up to Lieutenant Scott, who was overseeing a riding drill. The orderly came to attention and saluted, but Scott, who was examining a stirrup, took an inordinately long time to acknowledge the young soldier. Finally, he turned toward him and gave him a very casual salute.

"What do you want, Private?" he asked, as if irritated that a mere private had approached him.

"Beggin' the lieutenant's pardon, sir, but Colonel Gibbon wants to see you in his office."

"What does he want?"

The private's eyes opened wide in surprise at the question. "Sir, I don't know, the colonel didn't tell me nothin' but to come fetch you."

"No, Private, he did not tell you to 'fetch' me," Scott said. "I scarcely think that a private would do anything other than deliver a message."

"Yes, sir," the private said. "And that's what I done, sir. I just give you the colonel's message."

"Sergeant Caviness. Take over the drill," Scott ordered.

"Yes, sir," Caviness replied.

Scott started toward Old Bedlam, but the private overtook him. "By your leave, sir," the private said, saluting, and hold his salute until he was well beyond.

What did Colonel Gibbon want, anyway?

Sergeant Major Martell stood as Scott stepped into the orderly room. "Just a minute, sir, I'll tell the colonel you're in," he said. He came back a moment later. "Go right in, sir."

Scott stepped up to the desk and saluted.

"Scott, it looks as if you are going to get your wish," Colonel Gibbon said.

"What wish is that, sir?"

"You're being transferred away from Fort Laramie."

A big smile spread across Scott's face. "I'm going to Washington?"

"Washington?" Colonel Gibbon replied. "No, what in the world makes you think you're going to Washington?"

The expression on Scott's face turned from happiness to confusion. "But, I thought you said I was being transferred away from Fort Laramie."

"You are. You are going to Fort Huachuca, Arizona."

"Oh."

"The commander of D Troop there is Captain

Lindell. He will be leaving in three months, and you are being assigned as his executive officer. You will, more than likely, take command of his troop once he leaves."

Now Scott smiled again. "Yes, sir!" he said.

"How soon can you be ready to leave?" Colonel Gibbon asked.

"I can be ready by tomorrow morning."

"Very good. I'll make a spring wagon available for you and your wife, and I'll send a four-man detail to accompany you to Douglas. You can catch the train there."

"Yes, sir! Thank you, sir."

"My own command, Sue! Do you realize what this means? With my own command, I'm sure to get promoted. And once I command a troop, why other command positions will come available."

"I'm very happy for you," Sue said.

"Happy for me? Why, you should be happy for both of us. And you should also be happy that I won't be asking you to contact your father anymore. I got this on my own, Sue. General Winfield didn't have a damn thing to do with it."

"I'll be watching every move Captain Lindell makes while I'm his executive officer," Scott was saying to Duff, Pershing, and Holbrook that night in the officers' bar at the sutler's store.

"That's a good idea," Pershing said. "That way it'll be a smooth transition when you take over."

"Ha! There won't be anything smooth about it," Scott said, topping off his comment by tossing down his shot of whiskey.

"What do you mean, it won't be smooth?" Holbrook asked. "I thought you said you were going to be watching Captain Lindell."

"Oh, I am going to be watching him," Scott said, pushing his glass across for a refill. "But that's just so I can see all the mistakes he's making. Then, as soon as I take command, I'll adjust those mistakes."

"I know Captain Lindell," Pershing said. "I think he is a fine officer. The army must as well. He is being promoted to major and is going to the Cavalry School at Fort Riley. If I were you, I wouldn't be so quick to jump in and change everything."

"Well, that's the difference between you and me, John," Scott said. "I'm the kind of officer who is willing to take the initiative. You, obviously, are not. That's why I will make general officer one day, while officers like you will be lucky if you retire as a captain."

"That's a little harsh, isn't it, Clay?" Holbrook asked.

"Sometimes the truth is harsh," Scott said.

"Leftenant, I've had young officers like you in my command," Duff said. "And speaking as one who has held command, let me say that, while I admire your enthusiasm and self-confidence, I would look askance at one who would make such a jarring transition."

"What army would that be, Mr. MacCallister?"

"I was in a Scottish regiment in the British army."

Scott tossed down another whiskey before he answered.

"Ah, yes. And that would be the same British army that we defeated in two wars, would it?"

"Och, lad, but 'tis two mistakes ye've made there. 'Twas before our time, which means I was nae in the army that was defeated, and ye were nae in the army that won."

"Ha!" Holbrook said, laughing out loud. "Looks like Mr. MacCallister got you on that one, Clay."

Scott drank still one more whiskey. "Laugh if you want," he said. "But I'll have command of a troop while you two"—he took in Pershing and Holbrook with a wave of his hand—"will still be counting blankets, saddles, and such."

"It seems to me, Clay, that you might want to be nice to Jason and me," Pershing said with an easy smile. "We're writing the TO&E for all cavalry units. Why, with a stroke of the pen, we could take twenty men from your troop roster."

"Damn good idea, John. Let's do it!" Holbrook said.

"Yes, well, you gentlemen enjoy your . . . paperwork," Scott said. "I'd better go home now. Tomorrow will be a big day for me."

Scott started toward the door, weaving around a bit as he left.

"Damn," Holbrook said. "He sat right here and got drunk in front of us. I hope he makes it back to his quarters all right."

"I guess we can make allowances for it," Pershing said. "He's excited about getting a command."

"It seems to me that the lad has a bit of growing up to do," Duff suggested.

When Scott returned to his quarters he saw that Sue had already gotten everything packed for them, leaving out what she and Scott would wear for the trip.

"What is this?" Scott asked, seeing his uniform laid out on the bed.

"It's your uniform for tomorrow."

"You dumb bitch!" Scott shouted, picking up the uniform and throwing it at her. "We are going to be on the train tomorrow and, because I am in uniform, I will be representing the U.S. Army. I want to look my best! I may as well pull stable duty in this uniform."

"I thought you would want to keep your best uniform for when you report in for your new assignment," Sue said.

"Don't think!" Scott said. "You don't have the capacity for thinking. Now get this packed, and get out my best uniform."

"Do you want your mess dress uniform?"

"No, I don't want my mess dress uniform, you ignorant bitch! Are you insane? I want my best service uniform. How could you have been raised in a military family, and be so dumb?"

The next morning, Sergeant Caviness was in the stable saddling his horse when First Sergeant Cobb came out to talk to him.

"I understand that Sergeant Major Martell assigned you the job of leading the detail that will be riding guard for Lieutenant and Mrs. Scott this morning," Cobb said.

"That's right."

"Sam, I know that you and Lieutenant Scott don't get on all that well. If you'd like, I'll talk to the Sergeant Major and get him to assign someone else."

"Who else?" Caviness said as he continued to saddle his horse.

"I don't know. Maybe Sergeant Havercost."

Caviness shook his head. "Hell, George is comin' up on bein' fifty years old now," Caviness said. "We don't need to send an old man like him out on a detail like this. Besides," Caviness stopped in midsentence and took a look around the stable before he continued. "I'm so happy to be getting rid of that son of a bitch that I'll take this detail gladly."

First Sergeant Cobb chuckled. "I should report you for that, but I can't report you for saying the same thing I believe." He reached out to shake Caviness's hand. "Take care out there, Sam, and when you come back tonight, I'll buy you a beer over at the sutler's."

Caviness smiled. "You've got a deal, Top," he said.

Colonel Gibbon, Major Allison, Captain Kirby, and Lieutenants Pershing and Holbrook were standing out under the flagpole as Lieutenant Scott and his wife were preparing to leave. Scott's escort consisted of Sergeant Caviness and three other mounted soldiers, plus an additional soldier to drive the buckboard which would take Lieutenant Scott and Sue to the train depot in Douglas.

The other officers' wives were out there as well to tell Sue good-bye.

"Sue, I have a dear friend there," Julianne Allison said. "Her name is Tamara, and she is married to Captain Boyce. Do look her up, and give her my best. If you need any help getting settled in, she'll take care of it for you."

"Yes, ma'am, I will, and thank you," Sue said.

"Colonel Gibbon, with your permission, I am ready to depart this post," Lieutenant Scott said with a salute.

"Permission granted," Colonel Gibbon replied, returning the salute.

"Sergeant Caviness, give the order to your men," Lieutenant Scott said.

"Detail, forward ho," Sergeant Caviness said, and

the four riders and buckboard started forward. As it passed through the gate, the gate guard came to attention, and brought his carbine up in salute.

"Watch that son of a bitch," Holbrook said quietly to Pershing. "He'll make the guard hold the salute as long as possible."

As Holbrook stated, Scott waited until he had just about passed the guard before he returned the salute.

Duff and Elmer had watched the departure from the porch of the sutler's store.

"Elmer, I get the idea that Leftenant Scott was nae too popular among the officers," Duff said.

"I don't know about the officers, but I know the enlisted men hated him," Elmer replied. "I expect there will be a few beers hoisted tonight in celebration of his departure."

Chapter Twenty-four

With the Scott detail

As the steel-rimmed wheels of the buckboard rolled across the hard-packed earth, they picked up dirt, causing a rooster tail of dust to stream out behind them. The wood of the buckboard was bleached white, and under the sun it gave off a familiar smell.

Suddenly, the buckboard lurched so badly that the occupants were very nearly tossed out. "Oh!" Sue gasped in a startled tone of voice. She grabbed on to the seat.

"Whoa, horses," the driver called, pulling back on the reins. The team stopped and the buckboard sat there, listing sharply to the right.

"What is it, Private?" Scott asked.

"We dropped off into a hole, sir," the driver said. "I think we have broken an axle."

"Why, you idiot! Why did you drive through a hole?"

"Sir, I didn't see it!"

"Are you blind?"

"It ain't Private Castleberry's fault, sir," Sergeant Caviness said. Caviness had dismounted and was looking at the damage.

"What do you mean, it isn't his fault? He's driving the buckboard, isn't he?"

"Yes, sir, but this here hole was put here of a pure purpose, then covered up."

"Don't be ridiculous. Who would do such a thing?"

"Well, sir, Yellow Hawk would be my bet," Caviness said.

Yellow Hawk gave the reins of his pony to another, and then climbed to the top of the hill. Lying down behind the crest of the hill so that he couldn't be seen against the skyline, he scooted forward on his stomach, and then peered over. There, on the road below him, he saw the buckboard and the detail of army guards. There were six soldiers and one woman, and Yellow Hawk smiled. Some had criticized him because most of his attacks had been against civilians, and the one time he had attacked the army, most of them had gotten away from him. This time, nobody would escape. He returned to his horse, then remounted.

"Come," he told the others. "This is a good day."

* * *

"Listen," Sergeant Caviness said.

"Listen to what?" Scott asked, irritably. "I don't hear anything."

"Listen," Sergeant Caviness said again.

All three were quiet for a moment, with only the sound of the ever-present prairie wind moaning its mournful wail. Then they all heard what Caviness had heard, the distant thunder of pounding hooves.

"Get off the road and take cover, men!" Caviness said. "We've got company comin', and I don't think it's anyone we want."

"I'll be giving the orders here, Sergeant!" Lieutenant Scott said.

"Yes, sir. What do we do, sir?" Caviness asked.

"We, uh, had better get off the road and take cover."

Scott ran to the edge of the road, leaving Sue still sitting in the buckboard.

"Ma'am," Caviness said, reaching up for her. She came to him, and Caviness helped her down.

"Thank you, Sergeant," Sue said.

By now the Indians were on them, and Caviness and the four men with him started shooting. Lieutenant Scott was unarmed because he was in transit from one army post to another. Private Castleberry was unarmed because he was the driver.

"Lieutenant, here, take my pistol!" Caviness said, handing the weapon over to Lieutenant Scott.

Scott took the pistol, then ran to nearest horse and jumped on. "I'll go for help!" he shouted as he rode away.

"Scott! You cowardly son of a bitch! Come back here you . . . unngh!" Caviness's shout was cut short when he was hit in the head by a bullet.

"Sergeant Cav—" Castleberry shouted, then he, too, was cut down by an Indian bullet.

Now, Yellow Hawk had twenty men with him, against the three remaining soldiers. Yellow Hawk leaped over the rocks, and in and out of gullies, shouting with joy as he pursued the fight. The three soldiers fired at him, but it was as if he were impervious to their bullets. The buckboard was set afire. Yellow Hawk climbed onto it, even as it was burning, and looked at his handiwork, chortling in glee as the last soldier was put to the lance. Now that all the men were dead, he would go to each of them and touch them with his coup stick. That was because as the leader of this war party, he could count coup not only on those he had killed, personally, but on all who were killed. He began singing a victory song.

Sue had not been harmed, and she looked up to see about a dozen Indians around her.

"What are you going to do now?" Sue asked, her voice surprisingly calm.

Perhaps it was shock, the shock of the attack, of seeing all of the soldiers killed, and seeing her husband run away in cowardice that numbed her. Whatever it was, it took away all her own fear so that she asked the question, not as a person in hysterics, but almost as a person who was disinterested in the answer. If they told her they intended to kill her now, at this very moment, it would have meant nothing to her.

Yellow Hawk and the other Indians looked at each other in surprise. Never had they heard such a calm-sounding voice from one who was about to die. The fact that it was a woman's voice made it all the more shocking to them. They began speaking to each other and they spoke in their native language so Sue could not understand what they were saying.

"Yellow Hawk, this is a woman with powerful medicine. See how she does not fear to die?"

"I think she does not know she is going to die," Yellow Hawk said. "If she knows she is going to die, she will show fear."

"I think she knows, but does not care," Spotted Eagle said.

"She will show fear of me," Yellow Hawk said. "When I raise my coup stick to strike her, you will see fear in her eyes."

"No, I think not. I have looked closely, and I see no fear in her eyes."

Yellow Hawk did not like the way the conversation was going. He had led the battle and he had won a great victory, but because the woman was showing no fear, the glory of his victory was being challenged.

"She does not know I am going to kill her. When she realizes that, she will show fear," Yellow Hawk said. "This, I will prove to you."

"How will you prove it?"

"I will kill her. Just before she is to die, you will see."

"Yellow Hawk, if she shows no fear, I think you should let her live," Spotted Eagle said.

"Why?"

"Because she will be a woman of much medicine. Perhaps we can use some of her medicine."

"I will kill her, and there will be no medicine."

"If she shows no fear, do not kill her." This came, not from Spotted Eagle, but from Running Horse.

"I stand with Running Horse and Spotted Eagle," Strong Bull said. "If she does not show fear of dying, do not kill her."

"All right," Yellow Hawk agreed. "I will prove to you that she has not overcome the fear of dying. I will raise my war club over her head. If she shows fear, I will kill her. If she shows no fear, I will let her live."

"I believe that she will show no fear," Running Horse said.

Yellow Hawk raised his war club, and he let out a menacing, blood-curdling yell.

Sue had seen her husband run away in fear, and she had seen the soldiers die, one by one. She was resigned to dying now, and the strange, almost numbing calmness which had come over her before, was still present. If she was to die, let this be the moment. She stared into the abyss and didn't flinch.

"Show fear, woman," Yellow Hawk said in English. "Show fear, for I am about to kill you!"

The brief instant Yellow Hawk held the war club over her head might have been the only moment remaining between Sue and eternity. It was a fleeting moment in the lives of those who were standing there, watching, but it was a lifetime to Sue, and she was composed to live the rest of her life in dignity.

"Show fear!" Yellow Hawk shouted, and with that shout, Sue realized that, ironically, the final victory was to be hers!

"I have beaten you, haven't I?" she asked. She smiled at the thought.

"Look at the woman!" Running Horse said, speaking in his own language. "Look how she smiles in the teeth of death! Surely she has the greatest medicine."

Yellow Hawk, frustrated by the turn of events, turned and, with a shout of frustration, threw his war club away. He turned back to Sue, and with a look on his red-and-yellow painted face, a look that was far more frightening than anything Sue had ever beheld, he pointed at her.

"I will let you live," he said. "I will make you my woman."

"I would rather you kill me than to be your woman," Sue said.

"Would you rather be the woman of the coward who ran, and left you to die?"

"What?" Sue asked with a little gasp.

Yellow Hawk smiled. He had found a spot of vulnerability in this woman.

"That was your man, wasn't it? The coward who ran?"

"He was afraid," Sue said.

"Ayieee!" Yellow Hawk said, his mood considerably changed with the knowledge that he had found the woman's weakness.

"Come," he said to the others. "We will take this woman with us. Perhaps we can learn something of her strong medicine."

A couple of the Indians took Sue gently, and led her to a horse, then helped her to mount. She realized then that, for some reason, she was going to be allowed to live. What she did not realize was that her actions had caused Yellow Hawk to lose face. And she did not realize what the implications of that could be.

Chapter Twenty-five

When Lieutenant Scott came through the gate of the fort, he was still at a gallop and his horse was covered with a white, briny lather.

"We were attacked! We were attacked! Yellow Hawk!" he shouted. He continued to gallop the horse all the way across the parade ground, and didn't stop until he reached Old Bedlam. He slid down from the horse and turned it loose. The horse walked a few steps away, whickered, dropped to its knees, then rolled over onto its side.

Sergeant Havercost, who, along with several other soldiers of the fort, had been drawn away from their duties by the commotion, went out to the horse. He knelt beside the animal and put his hand over the horse's heart.

"He's dead," Havercost said.

"That's Sergeant Caviness's horse," First Sergeant Cobb said.

By now Colonel Gibbon had been drawn outside,

along with Lieutenants Pershing and Holbrook. Duff and Elmer came out to join the others.

"What happened, Lieutenant?" Colonel Gibbon asked. "Where are the others?"

"They're dead, Colonel. All are dead," Scott said. He put hands over his face. "My wife is dead. I watched the savages kill her."

"Oh, my," Julianne Allison said. "Not sweet Sue. Oh, you poor man."

"It was awful," Scott said. "I fought them off as best I could."

"How is it that you weren't killed, too?" Captain Kirby asked.

"I don't know," Scott said. "I know that I killed four or five myself. The last one I killed was after I ran out of ammunition, and we were fighting hand to hand. He had his war club. I was armed only with a knife that I'd taken from the body of one of the savages I had killed earlier.

"Then, when I looked up, the Indians were all withdrawing."

"Are you sure that Sergeant Caviness and your escort detail, all of them are dead?" Colonel Gibbon asked.

"Yes, sir, they are all dead," Scott said. "Sergeant Caviness fought bravely. He was the last to die, and he gave me his horse and wished me luck on coming back to tell the story."

"And your wife?" Captain Kirby asked.

"Yes, Sue," Lieutenant Scott said. Again, he covered his face with his hands. "She cried out to them, begged them not to kill her, but those savage bastards . . . they aren't human," he said. "I can't describe what they did to her, to my beautiful wife."

"Oh, you poor thing," Julianne said, walking over to put her arms around him.

"Lieutenant, take some time to get yourself cleaned up, then get some rest. When you feel up to it, I want you to submit a full report on what happened."

"Yes, sir," Scott said.

Sue had no idea why she hadn't been killed. Perhaps they would kill her later. She mounted the horse they brought for her, and went with the Indians, riding hard to keep up with them. She wondered that she hadn't lost her mind out of fear, and the only way she could maintain any composure was just to block her mind to everything she had seen and experienced—all sight, sound, memory, even all thought. She made the conscious decision to just take things moment by moment, not anticipating the next moment, but just letting it happen.

When they reached an encampment, Sue was surprised to see that there were women and children here. She knew that some Indians had left the reservation. She had read about it in the newspaper, and of course, Clay had encountered them before. But she had no idea that the renegade Indians would actually have women and children with them.

They were gathered along the banks of the stream, staring at her with eyes open wide in curiosity and wonder. She vowed to herself that she would show them no more fear than she had shown the one who had raised his war club to her. She may be killed, but she would not beg for her life. She would not let them see her fear.

The Indian who had threatened her with the war club, whom she assumed was Yellow Hawk, came up to her and, gruffly, pulled her down from the horse.

"Are you Yellow Hawk?"

To her surprise, the Indian smiled. "You have heard of me?"

"Yes."

Yellow Hawk made a fist of his right hand, and with his thumb, pointed to his own chest. "I am not surprised. Soon, all will have heard of me, and my name will be spoken with the names of Crazy Horse, Rain in the Face, Gall, and Sitting Bull."

"I doubt it," Sue said. "They were all great leaders of their nations. You are nothing but an egotistical fraud."

Yellow Hawk looked confused, and Sue realized that he had no idea what she meant. Then, even though he didn't know what the words meant, he perceived that it was an insult of some sort, so the confusion on his face was replaced by an angry frown.

"Come with me," he ordered.

Yellow Hawk led her past those who had gathered in curiosity and into a tepee, where he pushed her roughly to the ground. He spread out her arms and legs and tied them with rawhide thongs to stakes which had been driven into the ground and, for a moment, Sue feared that she was about to be raped.

"What is going to happen to me?" she asked.

"You are going to die," Yellow Hawk answered.

"Why must I die?" Sue asked. "I mean you no harm."

"Do you fear death?" Yellow Hawk asked.

The shock which had allowed Sue to take her fate so calmly before was now wearing off. Had she been killed immediately, she would have borne up to it. But she had been kept alive and now she was embracing life with an appetite she didn't know she possessed.

She wondered how best to preserve her life now. Should she plead for it? Or should she seem to show disdain?

Another Indian stepped into the tepee before Sue could answer. Though she couldn't be sure, because all the previous conversation had been in a language she couldn't understand, she believed that this was the Indian who had kept Yellow Hawk from killing her.

"What is your name?" this Indian asked in English.

"My name is Sue," Sue replied. "I am glad that you can speak English."

"Except for the very old, we all speak English," the Indian said. "We learned it in the Agency school."

"If you have gone to school, why are you and the

others doing this? Isn't there peace between our people now?"

"There can be no peace as long as the whites can tell the Indians what they can and what they cannot do."

"But aren't the laws that have been made for your own good?" Sue asked.

Yellow Hawk made a snorting sound, said something in disgust, then left the tepee.

"Yellow Hawk does not like you," the Indian who remained said.

"Yes, well I'm not that overly fond of him, either."

The Indian laughed.

"Well, at least you have a sense of humor," Sue said. "What is your name?"

"My name is Running Horse."

"Yellow Hawk wants to kill me, doesn't he?"

"Yes."

"But you argued against it. You kept him from killing me."

"Yes."

"Why did you keep him from killing me?"

"You did not fear death," Running Horse said. "That means your medicine is strong."

"Is Yellow Hawk a chief?"

"I don't know."

"How is it that you don't know if he is a chief or not?"

"He has led some of us on a new path. If this new

path is good, he will be a chief. If it is bad, he will not be a chief."

"The path is bad, Running Horse. Surely you can see that."

"It might be good," Running Horse said.

"I think it is not good. Why am I a prisoner?"

"You are a prisoner because you were not killed. Would you prefer death?"

"I would prefer to be free," she said. "You spoke to spare my life. Can you not speak to set me free?"

"Yellow Hawk will not set you free."

"But why would you want to keep me prisoner? I am of no value to anyone."

"I will speak for you, but I think it will do no good," Running Horse said.

"Thank you."

"The soldier who ran," Running Horse said. "Was he your man?"

"Yes."

"Why would you take as husband a man who is a coward?"

"I didn't know that he was a . . ." Sue started, but she didn't finish the sentence. "I don't know what you are talking about. Clay isn't a coward. He is a graduate of West Point, and he is an officer."

"He was chief of the others who were with you?" Running Horse asked.

"Yes."

"The other soldiers, those who were with you, they were not cowards. They fought well."

"And they all died."

"Your husband did not die. Your husband ran, because he is a coward."

"He was just afraid, that's all," Sue said. "You can't blame someone for being afraid."

"You were not afraid."

Brave Elk had taken part in the fight against the soldiers, and he was proud that he had fought well. But he was troubled that Yellow Hawk had taken the woman as prisoner. She was not a soldier. There would have been no nobility in killing her, nor was there in taking her prisoner. He was glad that Running Horse had prevented Yellow Hawk from killing her, but he didn't know how long Running Horse would be able to protect her.

He knew, now, that he had made a mistake in leaving the reservation to follow Yellow Hawk.

The Indians had whiskey and that night they drank the whiskey and beat the drums, and sang songs of battle and celebration.

In this circle, hear my song of battle.
Where there is courage,
There is cowardice.
Where there is good,
There must be evil.
If there is,
Then there is also, is-not.
If there is before,

There is after.
This land belongs to the Newe[2]
It does not belong to the white man.
Where there is life,
There must be death.
Where there is white snow,
There must be the red blood of the white man.
Where there is the silence of the night,
There is the music of the Newe.
Hear me in this circle I sing.

Sue wasn't sure how long she had been here, but she thought it might at least be two days. She had not been fed, but twice some women had come and untied her, then led her out so she could relieve herself. She considered running, but didn't for the simple reason that she had been in the same cramped position for so long, she knew she couldn't run.

The drums were still beating, and the Indians were still singing. Would they ever shut up? She could hear the singing, and though she had no idea what they were saying, there was a tonality and beat to it that was primeval and frightening. Then the flap of the tepee opened and someone came in. Because of the way she was lying, she couldn't see at first, but she could feel whoever it was standing there, looking down at her.

2. The People

"Please," she said. "If you are going to stand there and look at me, come around where I can see you."

To her surprise she heard the person moving then, and when she saw him, she gasped. It was the one who wanted to kill her, the one that she now knew was Yellow Hawk.

"Have you come to kill me?" Sue asked.

"No," Yellow Hawk said. "*Nimitawa ktlo.* You will be mine," he translated for her.

He knelt beside her and pulled her skirt up.

"Why this?" he asked, surprised to find that she had on bloomers beneath the dress.

Sue didn't answer. With everything in her power, she was trying to make herself unfeeling and unthinking.

"Are there more clothes under this?" he asked. "Why do white women wear so many clothes? Do they wish to stop their men?"

Sue closed her eyes, and bit her lip.

Yellow Hawk ripped open the bloomers, exposing her nakedness. Then he dropped his own trousers and breechclout, and got on his knees between her legs. Because her ankles were tied to ground stakes, her legs were spread wide and there was nothing she could do to prevent what happened next.

Long ago, Sue had learned to blot out all feeling when her husband exercised his conjugal rights, and she did so now.

Chapter Twenty-six

Brave Elk had seen Yellow Hawk go into the tepee, where he remained for several minutes. When Yellow Hawk came out, he stood there for just a moment as he adjusted his pants. Then, without looking around, he started toward the blazing campfire where the others continued with the drinking, drumming, singing, and dancing.

Brave Elk was afraid that Yellow Hawk had killed the white woman, so he went into the tepee to see. The skirt of the white woman's dress was pulled up to her waist. Yellow Hawk hadn't killed her, but it wasn't hard to figure out what he had done. The white woman's face was turned to one side and her eyes were tightly shut, though tears were sliding down her face. She was biting on her lower lip to keep from crying out.

Brave Elk said nothing to her, but bending over, he pulled her skirt back down to restore some modesty for her.

* * *

Sue had heard someone come back into the tepee after Yellow Hawk left, but she didn't open her eyes to see. She was sure it would be Yellow Hawk, either coming back to use her again, or to kill her. She still didn't open her eyes when she felt him readjust her skirt. She was sure he was just covering up his crime.

When Brave Elk stepped back outside the white woman's tepee, he looked around to make certain nobody had seen him. The celebration was still going on around the campfire and no one was paying attention to him. If he planned to leave this encampment, now would be the best time to do so.

Brave Elk went to the place where the horses were secured and finding his own horse, mounted and rode back to the Wind River Reservation.

Fort Laramie

On the next morning after he arrived at Fort Laramie on a horse that died from the effort it gave its rider, Lieutenant Clay Scott stepped into the regimental headquarters office. Sergeant Major Martell looked up from his desk.

"Good morning, Lieutenant. How are you feeling this morning, sir?" the Sergeant Major asked solicitously.

"Rested, thank you, Sergeant Major. But as I'm

sure you can understand, still much distressed over the death of my wife and the soldiers who were with me."

"Yes, sir, I'm sure you would be. What can I do for you, sir?"

"Colonel Gibbon requested that I write an after-action report and I have done so," Scott said, handing some papers to Martell. "Would you please give these to the commanding officer?

"Yes, sir, of course I will," Sergeant Major Martell replied. "Where will you be, sir, in case the colonel wants to speak with you?"

"I've already been detached from duty," Scott said. "So I shall probably spend some time over at the sutler's store until arrangements are made for me to continue my transfer to Fort Huachuca."

After Scott left, Sergeant Major Martell stepped into Colonel Gibbon's office and handed him the papers Scott had brought him.

"What is this?" Colonel Gibbon asked.

"Lieutenant Scott just dropped them off, sir," Sergeant Major Martell said. "It is his after-action report on what happened to him yesterday."

"Have you read it?"

"No, sir, I didn't figure it was my place to read it," Martell replied.

"All right, thank you, Sergeant Major."

Martell left the colonel's office, and Gibbon took his pipe from a holder on his desk, filled the bowl with tobacco and held a match to it. Not until the pipe was well lit did he pick up the papers and begin to read.

After-Action Report

On the 24th, instant, I was en route with my wife, a driver, and a four-man escort to Douglas so that I may catch the cars to my new assignment at Fort Huachuca, Arizona, when certain events transpired that are the subject of this report.

At a place some twelve miles distant from Fort Laramie, my escort detail and I were attacked by an overwhelming force of hostiles, numbering nearly fifty.

Sergeant Caviness, who was in charge of my escort, seemed exceptionally frightened by the overwhelming number of the attackers, and his fear immobilized him to the point that he was unable to issue coherent orders to his men. I do not fault him for this, as the odds against us appeared to be insurmountable.

I perceived, immediately, the degree of danger which faced the escort detail and my wife. Of course, I was in just as much danger, but at the moment the thought of personal danger was of no import to me. Even though I was the senior military person present, I was in transit; therefore the escort detail, properly, belonged to Sergeant Caviness. But as fear had him immobilized, I quickly became aware that I must assume command.

Because of my "officer en route" status, I was

unarmed, so I asked Sergeant Caviness for the loan of his handgun. He handed it to me, somewhat reluctantly, and I realized that he was not only immobilized for command, his fear was such that he could scarcely maintain any composure.

"Sergeant, you must get control of yourself," I ordered. "Remember, you must set an example for the men."

"Perhaps I should try and make an escape with your wife, and send back help," he replied.

I told him that such a move now was impossible, that we had but one recourse, and that was to fight.

The Indians, in classic fashion, formed a circle around us. As studied in military tactics classes at the Military Academy, I ordered the men to assume a hasty defensive position designed to provide a field of fire in all directions, and we took on the heathens. The fight lasted for several minutes, our fire taking effect upon their numbers. I personally killed five by pistol fire but attrition was also working its consequences on my small command until at last, only my wife and I were still alive, and I was out of ammunition. I called for Sue to get behind me, but before she could do so, one of the Indians struck her dead with a blow that crushed her skull.

Seeing my wife so brutalized had the effect of giving me exceptional strength, and, taking a knife from the belt of one the Indians I had killed,

I engaged the same savage who killed my wife. I am glad to report that I ended his life as well.

With that Indian dispatched and I weaponless, I was certain that my own demise was imminent. That was not to be the case however because the Indians, now realizing that they had paid dearly for their attack, departed from the field.

After the Indians left, I personally examined my wife, Sergeant Caviness, and each of the noble young soldiers who composed my escort, ascertaining that all were dead. Not knowing if the Indians' withdrawal was permanent or temporary, I took Sergeant Caviness's horse, and returned as quickly as possible to Fort Laramie.

I wish by means of this report to commend, albeit posthumously, Troopers Castlebury, Springer, Watson, and Dixon. With regard to Sergeant Caviness, while I cannot in good conscience include his name among those for commendation, neither do I condemn him, as it was fear, and not incompetence, which rendered an otherwise good noncommissioned officer, impotent.

Respectfully Submitted by Clayton Scott,
Second Lieutenant, Sixth U.S. Cavalry.

Colonel Gibbon held a formation of the entire regiment that same morning, and he called Lieutenant Scott out in front.

"I have submitted Lieutenant Scott's name for

the Medal of Honor," Colonel Gibbon announced. "This is how the citation will read." Clearing his throat, Colonel Gibbon put on his glasses, then raised the paper to read.

"'Second Lieutenant Clayton M. Scott was in transit with his wife when the small escort detail was attacked by a greatly superior force of hostile Indians. Quickly realizing that the noncommissioned officer in charge was inadequate to the task, Lieutenant Scott assumed command. He placed his small contingent of soldiers in defensive positions from which they fought the hostiles, inflicting heavy casualties, until all were killed but Lieutenant Scott. Not until the Indians had withdrawn did Lieutenant Scott, who had witnessed the brutal murder of his wife along with the death of every soldier in his command, leave the battlefield. For his command, intrepidity, and performance above the call of duty, Second Lieutenant Clayton M. Scott is recommended for the Medal of Honor. Colonel John A. Gibbon, Commanding.'"

Scott stood proudly as the citation was read. Then, Colonel Gibbon lowered the paper. "NCO's post!" he called.

The officers who were part of the formation left the formation and the first sergeants took charge of each of the troops. Command then passed to Sergeant Major Martel.

"First sergeants, dismiss your troops!" Martell called and a moment later, having been dismissed, the soldiers left the field to attend to their various duties.

Scott went to the officers' mess for breakfast. Duff was there, and so was Elmer. Lieutenants Pershing and Holbrook were there as well.

"I hope you gentlemen don't mind sharing the mess with me," Scott said. "But having checked out of my quarters, I have no other place to eat."

"That was a fine citation the colonel read," Holbrook said. "Too bad, though."

"Too bad? What's too bad about it?" Scott asked defensively. "Do you think I haven't earned the Medal of Honor? Why is it too bad?"

Holbrook and the others looked at Scott with curious expressions on their faces.

"Lieutenant, I meant it is too bad that your wife was killed in the action that has resulted in the citation," Holbrook said.

"Oh," Scott said. He pinched the bridge of his nose. "Yes," he said. "That was terrible."

"John, I know Scott was your classmate," Holbrook said when the two men were back in the supply room, resuming their work on the TO&E. "But there is something fishy about this. You mark my words, there is something damn fishy going on here. I mean he didn't seem at all concerned about what happened to his poor wife. I believe the rumors are true."

"What rumors?"

"Some of the wives have been suggesting that Scott was a wife beater."

"Oh, I didn't know that," Pershing said. "I don't hold with anyone who would hit a woman."

Holbrook got up from his desk, then walked over to the door and looked outside before he spoke again.

"Don't tell anyone I told you this, but it's more than just rumors," Holbrook said. "As you know, Mary is the daughter of the regimental surgeon, and he has had to treat Mrs. Scott more than once for bruises. She's tried to tell him things like, 'she tripped and fell,' or 'she ran into a door,' but he is absolutely certain that her injuries are consistent with someone who had been struck by a fist. And that someone could only be Clayton Scott."

Pershing tapped his pencil on the desk for a moment. "I can certainly see why you are suspicious of him."

"And to think that son of a bitch is going to get the Medal of Honor," Holbrook said.

"Maybe not," Pershing replied. "Give the system a chance. It might work out."

"Ha. If you think that, you have more faith in the army than I do."

"I have a feeling that the truth will come out, somehow. Let's don't pin the medal on Scott's tunic just yet."

"It's not his tunic I want to pin it on," Scott said. "I'd like to pin it right on his ass."

Pershing laughed, and then returned to the

work in front of him. "All right, follow me with this," he said as he began reading aloud. "'Field Heliograph consisting of following components: One, a signaling mirror; two, a white disc; three, a small-motion screw for vertical adjustment; four, a key for signaling on screen; five, a small motion screw on tripod for horizontal adjustment; six, the tripod; seven, the sighting bar; eight, the sighting bar clamp; nine, a screw for clamping the cross wire frame; ten, the crosswire frame; eleven, a sun mirror; twelve, a black disc; and thirteen, a screen.'"

Holbrook had said "check" after each item.

"All right," Holbrook said, "now how many do we authorize each regiment?"

"I think there should be one per troop," Pershing suggested.

"Plus one for regimental headquarters, so that makes five," Holbrook said. "And that means we need to go back and assign a signalman to regimental headquarters as well as each troop,"

"Ha!" Pershing said. "Jason, my boy, do you realize that with our very hands, we are making decisions that troop and regimental commanders will have to abide by."

"Yeah," Holbrook said with a smile. "Fun, isn't it?"

"You forget something though," Pershing said. "The day will come when we will be company and then regimental commanders."

"You, maybe," Holbrook saïd. "I don't think I'll ever even make captain."

"I'll remind you of that about twenty years from now, when we're both old, fat colonels," Pershing said.

Later that same day, a recovery team returned the bodies of Sergeant Caviness and the soldiers who were killed with him. They reported that they were unable to find Mrs. Scott's body, and the consensus was that the Indians had taken her body with them.

Chapter Twenty-seven

Wind River Reservation

Ska Luta had killed, skinned, and cleaned a rabbit, and was now spitting it over a fire. His wife, Sasha Quiet Stream, was rolling out dough for fry bread.

"Ska Luta," a voice called and, turning, Ska Luta saw Brave Elk.

"Brave Elk?" Ska Luta said. He prepared himself to fight, thinking perhaps that was why Brave Elk had called out to him.

Brave Elk held his right hand up, palm facing Ska Luta. "I come in peace," he said.

Ska Luta returned the gesture, "And I welcome you in peace." He pointed to the rabbit he had spitted over the fire.

"Eat with *shi aad* and me, Brave Elk," he said.

"You have taken a wife?"

"Yes."

Sasha Quiet Stream came up to stand, warily, beside Ska Luta.

"*Miyelo ca kola,* Sasha Quiet Stream," Brave Elk said.

"Then we welcome you as a friend," Sasha Quiet Stream answered. "My husband has asked you to eat with us. Will you honor us in this way?"

"I will," Brave Elk said as he watched Ska Luta and Sasha Quiet Stream continue with preparation of the meal.

"I thought you were with Yellow Hawk," Ska Luta said.

"No more."

Ska Luta knew that Brave Elk wanted to talk, so he waited for Brave Elk to speak.

"I left to follow Yellow Hawk. I thought this would be a path of honor. But I learned that it is a path of shame and now, I have brought dishonor on myself."

"No, Brave Elk," Ska Luta said. "You have left Yellow Hawk. And in doing so, you have left shame behind you. That is an honorable thing to do."

"There is more that I can do," Brave Elk said. "But I cannot do this alone. I will need someone to help me. Will you help me, Ska Luta?"

"Yes, I will help you." Ska Luta made the commitment without even asking what needed to be done.

Brave Elk smiled. "It is good that you will help."

"First, let us eat," Ska Luta said. "I think the food is ready."

During the meal, Brave Elk began to speak.

"With Yellow Hawk, I went to war against white

soldiers," Brave Elk said. "It was a good fight, and I was proud. But, with the soldiers was a *wasicun winyan.* I thought Yellow Hawk was going to kill the white woman, but he was stopped by Running Horse, Spotted Eagle, and Strong Bull.

"We took her back to the camp, and there, while the others beat the drums and danced and sang of victory, Yellow Hawk went into the tepee where the white woman was and he did a *Sicha.*"[3]

"Did the others not stop him?" Ska Luta asked.

"No. And I also did not stop him. But I think if the woman stays there, he will do it many times, and then he will kill her."

"That is bad," Ska Luta said.

"Will you help me?"

Ska Luta looked at Sasha Quiet Stream, and she put her hand on his arm. "Do what you must do, my husband. *Wakan tanan kici un.* May the Great Spirit go with you," she repeated in English.

Fort Laramie

The disbursement officer arrived from Cheyenne with the payroll, and with the money for Duff. In celebration, Duff threw a party for the entire post, utilizing the sutler's store to do so. Duff, Meagan, Colonel Gibbon, and his wife sat at a table in the back corner, watching the celebrants. A few minutes earlier, First Sergeant Cobb and Sergeant Major Martell had agreed to a match of Indian

3. Bad thing

wrestling, which was actually arm wrestling, and now the two sergeants were sitting across from each other at a table in the middle of the floor. Both had removed their jackets and rolled their sleeves up in preparation for the match. Sergeant Havercost was to be the referee to get the match started and, as backers for each gathered behind their champions, Havercost positioned their arms, and then had them clasp hands.

"Begin on the count of three," he said. "One, two, three!"

The participants started their struggle as their supporters cheered them on. They strained against each other, and the muscles on their arms popped out. First it appeared as if Cobb had the advantage as Martell's arm started toward the table, but Martell found the strength to bring his arm back up, then he went past the upright to force Cobb's arm down, but not all the way.

The two men struggled against each other for two minutes with neither being able to best the other.

"Gentlemen, shall I declare a draw?" Havercost asked.

Neither Cobb nor Martell replied immediately, though, after another moment Martell spoke. "What do you say, Top?"

"I say yes."

The two men ceased their struggle, then shook hands to the cheers of those who had watched.

Lieutenant Pershing came over to speak with Duff.

"Mr. MacCallister, I thank you for the party, sir."

"You are welcome," Duff said.

"And I've also come to tell you that we will be traveling together tomorrow."

"Oh?"

"Yes, sir. At least as far as the depot in Douglas. You'll be taking the train to Cheyenne, and I'll be taking the train to Assiniboine."

Duff smiled. "I'll be pleased to have your company, Lieutenant."

In another part of the room, Lieutenant Scott was holding court, telling and retelling the story of his great fight with the Indians.

"I'll tell you, boys," he said. "I didn't think I was going to make it out of there alive, and I still don't know how I did. There must have been fifty to a hundred Indians, screaming like fiends, pouring lead down onto us.

"'Sergeant, I am in transit,' I said to Sergeant Caviness after the attack started. 'This is your command.'

"'No, I, I don't know what to do,' Sergeant Caviness said. 'I beg of you, sir, take command.'

"So, what could I do but act as I had been trained? I immediately took charge and told the men to hold their fire until the savages were close enough that it would be impossible to miss.

"Ah, you would be proud of your fellow troopers. They fought well, and we killed many an Indian, prevailing until we ran out of ammunition. Yes, sir, it was a glorious fight." A huge smile was spread across Lieutenant Scott's face.

"But your wife was killed, wasn't she, Lieutenant?" one of the men asked.

The smile left Scott's face.

"Oh, uh, yes. And of course, the death of my wife, and those brave troopers, does add a poignancy to the fight. But it doesn't take away any of the glory. No, sir. Those brave young men deserve to be remembered for their glory."

"And yourself as well, Lieutenant," another soldier said. "You are the one getting the Medal of Honor."

"That is true, but the way I look at it, I will accept it, not for myself, but for those brave soldiers who gave their lives . . . in a way . . . so that I might live. That's why I feel an obligation to tell their story."

"Yes, sir. It's a shame about your wife, though."

"Yes, yes, it's a shame."

"I wonder why they didn't find her body."

Scott pinched the bridge of his nose. "Please, I don't want to think about it."

"Oh, I don't blame you, sir," the soldier said quickly. "I'm sorry I mentioned it."

The encampment of Yellow Hawk

As night fell over the encampment, it grew quiet. The rawhide bindings were beginning to restrict the blood circulation to her hands and Sue opened and closed her fingers several times, thinking perhaps that action would help pump the blood through. She pulled at the restrictions a couple of times, hoping to free herself, but each time she pulled, the bindings got tighter.

The flap of the tepee opened and someone came in. Because of the dark, and also the way she was lying, she couldn't see who it was, but she feared that it might be Yellow Hawk coming to claim her again.

"Please," she said. "If you are to defile me again, kill me first."

"Do not speak," a voice said in the darkness. "If the others hear, we will not be able to help you."

She had not heard this voice before. It wasn't the voice of Yellow Hawk, nor was it the voice of the Indian who had saved her life. This voice said they wanted to help her. Dare she believe that?

"Help me? You are going to help me?"

"Yes."

"Then please, take these bindings off. They are too tight, and they are restricting the blood flow."

She didn't realize until then that it wasn't one person, but two who had come into the tepee, because they squatted down on each side of her, and with their knives, cut through the rawhide thongs.

"Oh, thank you," Sue said. "Thank you very much."

For a moment it hurt more than it had earlier, because the blood started rushing back into her hands and feet. Sue sat up and began rubbing her wrists and ankles lightly.

"Do you think you can walk?" one of the two asked her.

"Walk? Walk where?" she asked a bit apprehensively.

"We are going to take you away from here. We are going to take you to your people."

"Are you telling me the truth?"

"Yes. When you can walk, we will go."

"I can walk," Sue said. She didn't know whether she could or not, but she intended to take the chance that was offered to her now, rather than wait until feeling came back into her hands and feet.

One of the two men, she now knew that both were Indians, lifted the flap of the tepee.

"Wait," he said. "I will look."

A second later, he called back in, saying the words quietly so that only Sue and the one who was with her could hear.

"Come now, there is no one to see."

When Sue started to walk, she realized that she had spoken too quickly about being able to walk, because her ankle gave way and she would have fallen had the Indian with her not grabbed her and held her up.

"I'm sorry," she said.

"Come."

Sue stepped outside with him and while it had been pitch dark inside the tepee, outside with the ambient light of the moon, she could see both of them. Both looked very young.

The coals of the night's campfire were glowing

a golden red in the dark. Because her arms and feet had been so tightly bound, she could hardly stand, let alone walk. But, despite the weakness of her ankles and feet, she made an effort to keep up with the two who had come to rescue her.

That is, if they had actually come to rescue her.

What if they were taking her from the camp for reasons of their own? Would she not be safer here, in the camp? There were women and children in the camp and she didn't think they would do anything to her in front of the women and children. And, there was also the Indian who had saved her. Surely, he would save her again if Yellow Hawk wanted to kill her.

But even as she was thinking this, she knew that any promise of safety by being in the camp was a false hope. Yellow Hawk had raped her, hadn't he? He had raped her right in the middle of the camp, and nobody did anything to stop it.

Of course, neither had she called out. But she had been very afraid that if she called out, he would have killed her. And, until these two had come to get her, she had been wishing that she had been killed.

She didn't know who these two were, or what they had in mind for her, but she believed that they were doing this for her own good. At least, she hoped they were, and with no other hope, she was determined to hang on to this.

"*Dho! Haho!*" someone shouted.

"We have been discovered," Ska Luta said.

"Take the woman and go!" Brave Elk said. "I will scatter their horses so they cannot follow."

"No, come with us," Ska Luta said.

"My friend, do not deny me this honor."

"*Yadalanh ohitika ozuye!*" Ska Luta said, putting his hand on Brave Elk's shoulder. He turned to Sue.

"Quickly, we must go."

"The horse has no saddle. I can't get on."

Ska Luta held his hand as a cup and when Sue stepped into it, he helped her up, and onto the horse. Then he leaped on another horse.

"Hold on to the horse, here!" he said, pointing to the mane.

Sue grabbed the horse's mane, and Ska took the horse's reins, then galloped away, pulling Sue's horse behind him. When they reached the top of a rise, Ska looked back and saw Brave Elk waving a blanket, scattering the horses. He also saw Brave Elk go down under a barrage of arrows.

Ska rode hard for several minutes until he knew that it was time to rest the horses. He stopped, held his hand up as a signal for Sue to remain mounted, then got down and put his ear to the ground. He listened for a moment. Then, with a smile, he stood up.

"They do not follow," he said.

"What did you say to your friend?" Sue asked.

"I said, 'Good-bye, brave warrior.'"

"He was brave," Sue said. "So are you, to rescue me like that. I am more thankful than I can say. Where do we go now?"

"We will rest here tonight," Ska Luta said. "When it is day, I will take you to the village and to the elders' council. They do not approve of Yellow Hawk, and they will send word to your people to come get you."

"Thank you again," Sue said.

"Rest. Tomorrow we must ride more."

Chapter Twenty-eight

Fort Laramie

The next morning, Colonel Gibbon invited Duff, Meagan, Holbrook, and the surgeon's daughter, Mary, as well as Pershing, and Holbrook's sister, Clara, and Major Allison and his wife, Julianne, for a going-away breakfast. He also invited Elmer, but Elmer said that he had made arrangements to take breakfast with Sergeant Havercost.

"Well, Mr. Holbrook, you and Lieutenant Pershing spent an entire month on the TO&E. What have you given us that it took you so long?" Colonel Gibbon asked.

"I probably could have done a faster job if I hadn't been burdened with John here," Holbrook said.

"Jason!" Clara said with a gasp. "What a thing for you to say!"

Holbrook smiled. "I said faster, not better," he

said with a laugh. "I figured, numbers are numbers, so what difference did it make what we put down? It was John who insisted that everything be correct."

Everyone knew, now, that Holbrook was teasing, and they all laughed.

"I think, Colonel, that the army, and especially the cavalry, will benefit from the TO&E we put together," Pershing said. "And don't let Jason tease you, he was very careful with the numbers, probably more so than I was."

"You have been a good guest to have, Lieutenant," Colonel Gibbon said. "I think the officers of the post will miss you when you return to Fort Assiniboine."

"Not just the officers," Holbrook said. "I think the ladies will miss him as well. Especially one lady," he added, looking pointedly at his sister.

"Jason!" Clara said, her face flushing in embarrassment.

"Mr. MacCallister, you will be missed as well," Colonel Gibbon said. "And I thank you very much for delivering the beef to us. This beef will be distributed throughout the army, but I'm happy to say that, thanks to the barbeque we had the other day, the Fifth Cavalry had the first taste of it."

"So, my dear," Kathleen said to Meagan. "It will be quite a change for you to be going back to your dress shop, won't it? I mean after such an adventurous thing as joining a cattle drive. Your dress shop will be sort of humdrum, won't it?"

"Oh, no," Meagan said. "I very much enjoy

designing and making dresses. In fact, as thanks for your hospitality, I intend to design and make an original dress for you, and for Mary, and Clara, and Julianne. And I will send them to you."

"Oh, how wonderful!" Mary said, clapping her hands.

"Lieutenant Pershing, I want you to know that I am sending an officer's evaluation report to your commanding officer at Fort Assiniboine, and in it I will be rating you as a most outstanding officer with a fine future in the United States Army. I know that you have contemplated leaving the army to teach school, but I do hope that you will remain in the service."

"More and more I am leaning in that direction, Colonel."

"Good, good."

"Colonel, do you think that Lieutenant Scott will actually get the Medal of Honor?" Holbrook asked.

"Why do you ask, Lieutenant? Do you think he should not?"

"I really can't say, sir. It's just that, if I understand it correctly, you have only his after-action report upon which to base the recommendation, is that right?"

"Think what you will of him, Lieutenant, he is an officer. And I am prone to accept an officer at his word. After all, if we do not have honesty and integrity in the officers' corps, what do we have?"

"Yes, sir. I suppose you are right, sir. It's just that, the way he has been acting, if you hadn't known it beforehand, there was absolutely nothing in his demeanor to suggest that his wife had just been killed. It was as if her getting killed was only a secondary event to his . . . bravery . . . under fire." Holbrook set the word "bravery" apart from the rest of the sentence to illustrate his point.

"Yes," Colonel Gibbon said. "I must confess that his behavior was most unusual. And to be honest with you, I have not yet forwarded the recommendation. I had already made the decision to hold it back for a while, just to sort of allow things to develop."

"Colonel, Mrs. Gibbon, 'tis most gracious ye have been, and ye've my thanks for the hospitality ye have shown to Meagan, m' men, and me. But the time has come for us to make our departure."

"I've assigned Sergeant Havercost to lead the escort detail," Colonel Gibbon said. "As a matter of fact, he volunteered for it. Sergeant Major Martell tells me that Sergeant Havercost and Mr. Gleason have become fast friends over the last few days."

"That's because they know each other from before," Duff said.

"Oh? Well, Sergeant Havercost has been in the army for almost thirty years. Perhaps their paths crossed when they served together at some point in the past."

Duff laughed. "Well, their paths did cross, but they weren't exactly serving together."

"What do you mean?"

Duff told the story of Elmer robbing Sergeant

Havercost when he was in charge of a money shipment. And though he didn't lie, he told the story in such a way as to suggest that it had been an authorized military mission during the war.

"Ha! Well, I'm glad that old enemies have been able to reconcile their differences. But, now that I think about it, Sergeant Terrell was, I believe, Captain Terrell in the Confederate army."

"Yes, sir," Holbrook said. "And Trooper McKay was a sergeant in the Confederate army."

"Well, now that we are united, again, I see no reason why men of good will couldn't serve together," Colonel Gibbon said. He stood then, as did the others. "I'll see you off."

There would be no wheeled vehicle this time. Duff and Meagan would be riding the same horses they had come up on, and Elmer would be riding Jimmy Sherman's horse. When they reached Douglas, they would make arrangements to ship the horses through on the train. Lieutenant John J. Pershing would be riding one of the horses belonging to the Fifth Cavalry Regiment, and Sergeant Havercost would bring it back.

When they went outside, Sergeant Havercost and three men were standing alongside their horses. Elmer was holding the reins to Jimmy Sherman's horse, Meagan's horse, and Sky. One of the troopers was holding an extra horse for Lieutenant Pershing.

"Ten hut!" Sergeant Havercost called to his men.

Then, as Colonel Gibbon and Lieutenant Pershing approached, Sergeant Havercost saluted.

"Sir, the escort detail is formed," he reported.

"Very good, Sergeant."

"Lieutenant Pershing, sir, your mount?" Sergeant Havercost said, extending his arm toward the extra horse one of the troopers was holding. Not until Pershing was mounted, did Sergeant Havercost give the command to the others.

"Prepare to mount! Mount!"

The soldiers mounted as one, and then Duff, Meagan, and Elmer mounted.

"Lieutenant Pershing, Mr. MacCallister, if you would, please, the four of you will ride in the middle. One of the troopers and me will ride in the front, and the other two troopers will ride behind."

"Aye, Sergeant, 'tis a foine plan," Duff replied.

"Good-bye, John!" a female voice called, and twisting in his saddle, Pershing saw Clara waving at him. He returned the wave, then turned back toward the front in time to return the salute of the guard at the gate.

With Ska Luta and Sue

Sue was exhausted and weak from hunger. The Indians who captured her had not fed her and this Indian, the one who rescued her, had no food with him. But the truth was, she was so tired she didn't know if she would be able to eat anyway. When the Indian told her they were going to rest for a while, she was glad. The Indian spread out a blanket for her, and she lay down under a tree and fell asleep.

Once, during the darkness, she woke up and, for a moment, didn't know where she was. She was immediately aware, however, that she wasn't tied down, and when she looked over at the Indian who had rescued her, she saw him sitting on the ground with his knees drawn up, and his head resting on his knees. Despite the fact that he was an Indian, and she had been captured by Indians, there was something comforting about seeing him there.

She went back to sleep.

She had no idea how long she had been sleeping when she was awakened by the smell of cooking meat and, at first, thought she must be dreaming. But when she woke up she could still smell the meat. Although it was growing lighter in the east, it was still dark. Despite the darkness, when she opened her eyes, she could see the Indian who had rescued her, front-lighted by the golden bubble of light that emanated from a small fire. The Indian was holding a stick over the fire, and skewered on the end of the stick was a bird. She had no idea what kind of bird it was, but the smell of it cooking actually made her salivate.

"Hello," she said.

The Indian looked up, then held up the stick. "I make food for you," he said.

"It smells delicious. What kind of bird is it?"

"It is *sheo,* what the white people call prairie chicken."

"Oh, yes! I have eaten prairie chicken before. It is quite delicious."

"What is your name?" the Indian asked.

"My name is Mrs. Sc—" Sue stopped in mid-sentence. To be truthful, she didn't know if she was a widow or not. She had no idea what had happened to Clay. But she did know that she had no intention of living with him anymore, so she changed her answer. "My name is Sue," she said.

The Indian pointed to himself. "I am called Ska Luta."

"Ska Luta? What does that mean?"

"That means 'red white,'" Ska Luta said. "My mother was Shoshone. My father was a white man."

"Well, they must be very proud of the fine man their son has become," Sue said with a pleasant smile."

"My mother is dead. I have never seen my father."

"Oh," Sue said. "Oh, that's too bad. I'm so very sorry. I'm also sorry for what happened to your friend."

"It was an honorable death for Brave Elk," Ska Luta said. "I think he was pleased."

"What a strange thing to say."

"I know that this is not something that a white person can understand," Ska Luta said.

Ska Luta pulled the bird away from the fire, then nodded.

"It is finished," he said. Finding a flat rock, he cleaned off the top of the rock, then lay the cooked bird on the rock and cut it into pieces. He picked up a choice piece and handed it to Sue.

"Eat," he said.

"Thank you." Sue blew on it to cool it, and then she took a bite. "Oh, my," she said. "I believe this is the most delicious thing I have ever tasted. Wait until I tell Sergeant Beck. He will be very jealous."

"Sergeant Beck?"

"He fancies himself quite the chef," Sue said. "But nothing he has cooked has ever tasted as good as this."

Ska Luta smiled. "My people have a saying: 'Hunger is the best cook.'"

Sue laughed. "We have a similar saying. 'Hunger is the best spice.'"

What was she doing? She was actually laughing, though she didn't know how that could be so, after everything she had been through for the last few days.

Sue ate all of the first piece and started to reach for another, and then she pulled back. "Where are my manners?" she said. She indicated that he should take a piece.

"No. You eat until you are filled. You need food. When your hunger is satisfied, I will eat."

"It is so good," Sue said. She ate two more pieces, then sat back. "My hunger is satisfied," she said with a smile, using his words.

Ska Luta nodded, then finished off the rest of the bird.

When the sun was a full disc above the horizon, Ska Luta picked up the blanket and draped it across the back of the horse Sue had been riding.

"I think, with the blanket, it will be easier for you to ride the horse," he said.

"Oh, yes, thank you. I'm sure it will be. I must confess that I wasn't looking forward to riding bareback again." Sue held up her finger. "But don't get me wrong," she said. "I'm so thankful that you got me away from Yellow Hawk that I would have grabbed on to the horse's tail and let him drag me."

Ska Luta laughed out loud. "Ho!" he said. "What a funny thing that would be to see, if you would hang on to the horse's tail and let him pull you."

"Well, Mr. Ska Luta, you are not only a fine man, but you have a sense of humor. I like a sense of humor."

As he had last night, Ska Luta helped Sue onto the horse, but today he handed her the reins.

"You can do this?" he asked, meaning could she ride.

"Yes, thank you," Sue said. One of the things that had bothered her a bit last night was the fact that she had not been given the reins. And though, as a practical matter, she could understand how it would be easier for her to keep up with Ska Luta if he led her horse, especially in the middle of the night, it also suggested that she wasn't really free.

Now, she knew that if she wanted to, she could probably run away from the Indian who was with her. But, why should she? He, and his friend, had rescued her from Yellow Hawk, and his friend had even died in the process.

They rode most of the morning, stopping a few times to rest, or in her case it was less a moment to rest than it was an opportunity to walk around a little to relieve the discomfort of extended bareback riding.

Then, mid-afternoon, Ska Luta held up his hand.

"Stop," he said.

"What is it?"

"Wait."

Sue sat astride her horse while Sky Luta rode on ahead until he disappeared behind some rocks and shrubbery. She thought he would come right back, immediately, but he didn't.

So she waited.

And she waited some more, waiting so long that she began to fear that he wasn't coming back.

That was strange, she thought. Earlier this morning, she had actually contemplated running away from him, now she was here, sitting bareback on a horse with absolutely no idea where she was, desperately wanting him to come back.

She thought about calling out loud to him but, even as she thought about it, she realized that that probably wouldn't be a very smart thing to do.

Finally, after what seemed an eternity, though so distorted was her concept of time due to her fear, it might have been only a few minutes, she saw Ska Luta returning.

"We cannot go that way," he said.

"Why not?"

"Yellow Hawk is there. And because of his victory over the soldiers, now he has many more warriors with him."

"Oh, Ska Luta, what will we do?"

"We will go this way," Ska Luta said, and as he indicated the way, she turned to follow him.

Chapter Twenty-nine

With Duff and the escort party

There had been some of the barbecued beef left, and the mess sergeant had provided the escort detail with freshly baked bread, jam, and butter. As a result, when the escort party stopped for lunch on the west side of Horse Shoe Creek, they had a picnic of sorts.

"Too bad we don't have a wee bit of the creature to wash it all down with," Elmer said.

"Och, Mr. Gleason, and would ye be for telling me, now, why ye'd want to spoil such a foine meal with liquor?" Meagan asked.

Elmer looked over at Duff with a smile on his face. "Duff, are you sure you didn't bring this woman over from Scotland, and you've just been keeping it a secret all this time? Damn me, if she don't sound exactly like you."

"Aye, 'tis been a bit of leg pulling the lass has been doing, that I'll grant you," Duff said.

It was mid-afternoon when one of the two soldiers at the rear of the escort party saw two riders coming toward them.

"Sergeant Havercost! Two riders comin' at a gallop!"

"Are they Injuns?"

"Looks like it!"

"Shoot 'em!" Sergeant Havercost ordered, and two of the soldiers raised their carbines to their shoulders.

"Wait!" Elmer shouted. "If there's just two of 'em and they're comin' toward us like that, they don't mean us no harm."

"Well, what are they doin' ridin' toward us like that?" Sergeant Havercost asked.

"I don't know, but if it was me, I'd wait and find out."

"I agree with Mr. Gleason, Sergeant," Elmer said. "I know this is your command, but I don't think you should shoot."

"All right, don't shoot, yet," Havercost said. "But keep an eye on 'em."

"Sarge, one of 'em is a woman," one of the troopers said, and no sooner had he reported it than Pershing recognized her.

"Sergeant, that's Mrs. Scott! That's Lieutenant Scott's wife."

"How can that be?" Havercost asked. "She's dead! Unless that's her ghost."

By now the two riders were close enough that everyone could see that the other rider was an Indian. The Indian held up his hand.

"Don't shoot, I am friend!" the Indian called.

"Sue, it is you!" Lieutenant Pershing called as the two riders pulled up.

"Thank God, I'm back with my own people," Sue said. Dismounting she moved quickly to Lieutenant Pershing and put her arms around him. Though he found the situation a bit awkward, Pershing realized that she needed this, and he embraced her, holding her for a long moment.

Finally, Sue backed away and looked at the others with a small smile.

"I swear, you all look as if you are seeing a ghost," she said.

"Well, Miz Scott, we all thought you was dead," Sergeant Havercost said. "Lieutenant Scott said that he seen a Injun crush in your head."

"Well, as you can see, I'm not dead," Sue said. She looked toward Ska Luta. "But I have him to thank for it."

"Are there more soldiers?" Ska Luta asked.

"Why do you want to know, Injun?" Sergeant Havercost asked.

"Because Yellow Hawk is coming, and he has many, many warriors with him."

"How many?"

"Maybe more warriors than there are bullets in all your guns," Ska Luta said.

"How the hell did he get so many warriors?" Elmer asked. "I thought that just a few left the reservation."

"That was true. But Yellow Hawk defeated the soldiers and now his name is spoken by all. Many young men who want to become warriors, and count coups, have gone with him."

"Sergeant Havercost, I suggest that we head back to the post," Lieutenant Pershing suggested.

"No, we can't," Sue said. "Not yet. The Indians are between us and Fort Laramie."

"Well, we can't stay here," Lieutenant Pershing said. "This position is untenable."

"I know a place," Ska Luta said. "It is beyond one more water where there is place like this." He made a swinging motion with his hand pointed toward the ground. "But has no water."

"You mean a dry gulch?" Sergeant Havercost asked.

"Yes, dry river. We should go there, quickly."

"Sarge, don't do it. If you ask me, I think the son of a bitch is tryin' to set us up," one of the soldiers said.

"No," Sue said, speaking up quickly. "He is telling the truth."

"Have you seen this here dry gulch, Miz Scott?" Sergeant Havercost asked.

"No, Sergeant. But Ska Luta and another young Indian rescued me. The other Indian lost his life doing it. If Ska Luta says that is the place to go, that is where we should go."

"Lieutenant?" Sergeant Havercost asked.

"By all means, Sergeant. I think we should do what Ska Luta suggests."

"What did you say the boy's name was?" Elmer asked.

"Ska Luta," Sue said.

Elmer stroked his chin and stared at the Indian for a long moment. "Yes, that's what I thought you said."

"Well, if we're goin' to go to this here dry gulch, I think we should go," Havercost said.

Lieutenant Pershing, Sergeant Havercost, Duff, Meagan, Elmer, Ska Luta, and Sue, and the four troopers all mounted. Then they rode away quickly.

On the field maps, the name of the stream they had stopped near was called Horse Shoe Creek. They rode at a rapid, but not killing pace, to the next stream, which on the map was called La Bonte Creek. Just beyond that creek, as the Indian had promised, was a dry gulch, about chest deep.

"Payne, you and Schulz take the horses into the tree line and secure them," Sergeant Havercost said. "Then come back!" he added.

Quickly, the horses were secured and all eleven

got down into the gulch in position to receive an Indian attack.

"Lieutenant, you ain't armed," Sergeant Havercost said. "Do you want my pistol, or my carbine?"

"I'll take your pistol," Pershing said.

"Miz Scott, you think you can shoot a gun?" Sergeant Havercost said.

"Yes."

"Payne, give the lieutenant's lady your handgun," Havercost ordered, and the soldier complied.

"I have my own pistol, and I can shoot," Meagan said.

"Yes, ma'am, I sort 'a figured you could," Sergeant Havercost said.

They were down in the dry gulch where they dug themselves in to create as secure an area as they could, under the circumstances.

"If they was chasin' you and Miz Scott, seems to me like they'd be here by now," Sergeant Havercost said.

"They are here," Ska Luta said. He pointed. "Look, there, on the ground at the top of the hill. They are watching us."

"I don't see nothin'," Sergeant Havercost said, looking toward the top of the hill. He carved off a bit of tobacco and put it in his mouth.

"They are low to the ground, like worms," Ska Luta said.

"The Injun's right, Sarge. I see the sons of bitches," Schulz said.

"Nissen, you go on down to the edge of the water, just this side, and keep a sharp eye. If you see the Injuns get mounted, come back here quick, and tell us," Havercost said.

"All right, Sarge."

"George, I wonder if you might share a chaw?" Elmer asked Sergeant Havercost.

Sergeant Havercost carved off a piece and handed it to Elmer, who stuck it in his mouth. Elmer had been studying Ska Luta ever since he learned his name. He was about to say something to the Indian when Nissen came running back.

"Get ready! Here they come! Injuns are comin'!" Nissen's call was shut off by the whistle and thud of an arrow. The arrow buried into his back, and Nissen spread out, face down on the ground before him. It was a shot of nearly one hundred yards, and when the bowman saw he was successful, he let out a victory cheer.

When all were mounted, Yellow Hawk held his rifle over his head, let out a loud yell, and then slapped his legs against the sides of his horse. His horse leaped forward, reaching full gallop in a couple of strides. The mounted warriors made a grand show of it, as they started down the ridge, then splashed through the stream that separated them from the entrenched group of whites. A shower of silver bubbles was kicked up as the horses entered the stream, and a fine rain was sustained for a few seconds by the churning action of the horses' hooves.

"Son of a bitch, look at 'em! Where'd they all come from?" Sergeant Havercost said.

The Indians didn't attack, but rode back and forth shouting, holding their weapons over their heads. One of them shouted, "*Zastee hohe anho!*"[4]

"Were there this many that attacked you and your escort team?" Pershing asked.

"No, there weren't nearly as many then as there are now."

"If you ask me, we should start prayin'. There are ten of us. Now nine, but there must be forty or fifty of them," Payne said. "What should we do?"

"The only thing we can do!" Havercost replied. "We'll fight them, but don't waste your ammunition. Wait until they come toward us and you are sure of your shot."

Ska Luta stood then and shouted out loud, holding his fist in the air, "*Hoka hay Hinzi Cetan, mieybo najin yunke-lo mila hanska!*"

"What the hell is that Injun tellin' 'em?" Schulz asked.

---

4. "Kill our enemies, count coups!"

"It's all right!" Elmer said quickly. "He just told Yellow Hawk that he would stand with, and die with, the soldiers."

"You speak their lingo?" Sergeant Havercost asked, surprised by the fact.

"Yeah," Elmer said. "I speak their lingo. The boy is on our side. We can trust him."

At that moment, one of the Indians raised his rifle and fired at them. They could see the white puff of smoke, followed an instant later by the whine of the bullet as it whizzed by. One of the cavalrymen fired back.

"Hold your fire, Payne! Don't shoot until you know you can't miss. We can't afford to waste ammunition."

Trooper Davis was the next to be hit. As it so happened, Duff was looking right at him when he went down. Duff heard the sound of the bullet hitting flesh, and he saw Trooper Davis holding his hand in front of him, looking, with surprise, at the blood that filled his palm. The blood came from a hole in Davis's chest.

"Davis!" Schulz shouted, moving to him quickly.

"Oh, shit," Davis said. He went down on one knee. "It don't look like I'm going to live long enough to collect that two dollars you owe me, Schultzie."

"Hang on, Davis! Hang on!" Schulz pleaded. But he knew that it was too late. Davis, like Nissen, was dead. Within less than a minute, two of the defenders were dead.

Now several Indians broke away from the others and galloped toward the defenders in the dry gulch.

"Start shooting!" Sergeant Havercost yelled, and the others were galvanized into activity by Havercost, keeping up a brisk fire against the Indians.

One Indian broke away from the group and started toward them. Elmer fired and the Indian went down.

For the next few minutes, it was quiet, and that gave Elmer the opportunity he had been looking for to talk to Ska Luta.

"Ska Luta. That means 'red white' don't it?" Elmer asked.

"Yes, sir."

"Does that mean you are a half-breed?"

"I . . . I don't think of myself as half white," Ska Luta replied. "I think of myself as all Shoshone."

"Yes, well, seein' as you was mostly raised by the Shoshone, I can see why. What part of you is white? Your mama, or your papa?"

"My father is white, but I have never seen him. And my mother was Indian, but she died as I was being born."

"Here they come again!" Sergeant Havercost shouted, his shout interrupting the conversation between Elmer and Ska Luta. "This time the whole bunch of 'em is comin' at once!"

The Indians came hard, galloping through the dust, shouting and whooping their war cries. They charged almost all the way up and fired from horseback, then withdrew.

Duff, Pershing, and Elmer took very careful aim, then fired. There were three Indians who went down, and three empty horses whirled and retreated, leaving their riders dead or dying on the ground behind them.

Over the next several minutes, the Indians attacked several more times, getting a little closer each time, before being driven away by deadly accurate gunfire.

"Why don't they come all the way?" Payne asked, nervously. "Seems to me like they're just playing with us, as many of them as there are."

"There are a lot more of them than us, that's true," Havercost said.

"If we can hold 'em off till dark, they'll go away. I've heard that Injuns don't like to fight at night," Schulz said. "Somethin' about the Great Spirit not bein' able to find 'em in the dark."

"Well, we don't like to fight at night, that is true. But that doesn't mean they will leave," Ska Luta said. "We could wake up in the morning and find them right on top of us."

"The boy is right," Elmer said. "If we are going to get rid of them, we're going to have to do it now, before it gets dark."

"How we going to do that?" Payne asked. "Run 'em down and club 'em?"

"Tell me that . . . and we'll both know," Elmer said.

Again the Indians attacked, and this time both Payne and Schulz went down. Sergeant Havercost was killed on the next charge and now, Lieutenant Pershing was the only soldier remaining, and the defenders had been cut down to only six: Pershing, Duff, Meagan, Elmer, Ska Luta, and Sue. Ten of the Indians had been killed, but opposing them were at least twenty-five more.

"I figure we've got about one, maybe two more charges, and that'll be it," Elmer said.

"If we could kill Yellow Hawk, the others would leave," Ska Luta said.

"Are you sure about that?" Lieutenant Pershing asked.

"Yes. Yellow Hawk has all the medicine. Without him, the others will return to the reservation."

"Which one is Yellow Hawk?" Duff asked.

"That one is Yellow Hawk," Sue said with a shudder. She pointed to an Indian that was sitting tall on his pony, holding a feathered lance, but keeping back behind the others.

"Are you sure?"

"The woman speaks the truth," Ska Luta said. "I will call him, and challenge him to come to the front. If I shame him, perhaps he will."

Ska Luta climbed up onto the edge of the dry gulch embankment.

"Hokahay, Hinzi Cetan, nimitawa ktelo, gusano!"

Ska Luta looked back at the others. "I told him that he is mine, and he is a worm."

At least three of the Indians fired, and Ska Luta fell back into the ravine with a hole in his chest, and a surprised look on his face.

"I thought Yellow Hawk would be man enough to come forth," he said in a tight, pain-filled voice. "I was wrong. I thought he was a man. But he is a coward."

Duff had seen such wounds before, and he knew that the wound was fatal.

"Ska Luta!" Sue called, kneeling on the ground beside him. She grabbed his hand and held it tightly.

Elmer knelt beside him as well, and he put his hand on Ska Luta's shoulder. *"Ska Luta Glee Jon, mita kuye ayasin cinks,"* Elmer said.

"Nituwe he?"

"Ate."

"Ate?" Ska Luta asked, his eyes opening wide.

"Ai."

Ska Luta grabbed Elmer's hand and squeezed it tightly.

"After all this time, that we should meet now," Ska Luta said.

"Hopo Naga Tanka," Elmer said. He repeated it in English. "Go with God."

"Ai, Hi disho."

Ska Luta took one last gasping breath, and then he died. Tears began flowing down Sue's cheeks, and Meagan moved over to embrace her. But it was when she looked up at Elmer, that Meagan got the biggest shock. There were tears welling in his eyes. For as long as she had known Elmer, she had never seen him exhibit such emotion.

Duff had been using a pistol, but now he walked over to Sergeant Havercost, and picked up the sergeant's carbine.

"If Ska Luta was right, we can end this, here and now," he said

"What are you going to do?" Lieutenant Pershing asked.

"I'm going to kill Yellow Hawk."

Pershing shook his head. "You can't do it from here."

"Watch me," Duff said.

"If that was a rifle, maybe," Pershing said. "But he's over five hundred yards away, and you're using a carbine. It doesn't have the range."

"We'll just have to do something about that," Duff said. He took two of the .45 caliber rounds, and pulled the bullet away from the cartridges in both. He loaded the cartridge, without the bullet, into the breach, then closed the breach. Next, he poured the powder from the second cartridge down the barrel. After that, he dropped the bullet down as well, ramming it home with a cleaning rod.

"Well, now," Pershing said. "I don't think I would have thought of that, but doubling the powder load might just give you enough range."

"If it doesn't blow the barrel apart," Elmer said.

"Aye, 'tis a possibility," Duff said. "I think 't would be best if ye dinnae stand close when I shoot."

"Duff, no!" Meagan said. "If the barrel explodes, you could be killed."

"Meagan, if I dinnae try, we could all be killed on the next charge of the heathens. 'Tis the only chance we have, I'm thinking."

"He's right, Miss Parker," Pershing said.

With the carbine double-loaded, Duff cut a "Y" shaped branch. Then he lay down and used the "Y" as a rest for the weapon. Estimating the range, he elevated the barrel, then pulled the trigger.

The sound of the shot was much louder than normal, and a huge cloud of smoke erupted from the end of the barrel.

Running Horse was next to Yellow Hawk, looking toward the dry gulch. He saw a puff of smoke, much larger than normal. Then he heard an angry buzz and the smack of a bullet hitting flesh. He heard Yellow Hawk grunt, and looking toward him, saw dark, crimson blood pouring from a very large hole in his chest. Yellow Hawk tumbled backwards from his horse.

"Yellow Hawk!" Running Horse called.

"What happened?" one of the other Indians asked.

"Yellow Hawk is killed!" Running Horse announced.

"Running Horse, what shall we do now?" Spotted Eagle asked.

Running Horse had not assumed the position of command, but it had been thrust upon him.

"Our way on the path of war is no more," Running Horse said. "We will return to the reservation.

When the handful of defenders saw the Indians leave, they breathed a sigh of relief.

"Come," Lieutenant Pershing said. "Let's get these brave men back to Fort Laramie for a decent burial."

When the party returned to the post, everyone turned out to see them and to celebrate the final defeat of Yellow Hawk, as well as Sue's return.

"Sue! Oh, my dear! How wonderful to see you! We thought you were dead!" Kathleen Gibbon said.

"Yes," Colonel Gibbon said. He turned to Lieutenant Scott who, significantly, was the only one who hadn't gone forth to welcome his wife's safe return. "Lieutenant, did you, or did you not put in your report that you had seen your wife bludgeoned to death by an Indian?"

"You told them, didn't you?" Scott shouted,

pointing an accusing finger toward Sue. "You told them I ran away and left my men to die!"

Sue shook her head. "I have said no such thing, Clay."

Scott suddenly realized what he had said, and sheepishly, he looked around to see all the officers, noncommissioned officers, and men. The eyes of everyone on the post were looking toward Scott with contempt.

"I—I left to get help." Scott tried to explain. "Tell them, Sue. Tell them I left to get help. Sweetheart, you know I wouldn't have just abandoned you and my command." His voice was weak and pleading.

"Captain Kirby," Colonel Gibbon said.

"Yes, sir?"

"Put this . . . officer . . . under arrest."

Colonel Gibbon set the word "officer" apart from the rest of the sentence, to show his disdain for Scott's commission.

"No! For God's sake, no!" Scott begged. "I had no choice, don't you see? There were too many of them. You tell them, Sue. You know I was leaving for help."

Sue looked at her husband with an expression that was a cross between pity and disgust, but she said nothing.

"Don't you see, Sue? When I first came back, they honored me as the sole survivor of the attack. I was going to get the Medal of Honor! Do you understand that? The Medal of Honor! Now, by coming back, you have ruined it. What white woman would want to come back, after being used by the Indians? You have ruined everything. What do you think this will do to my career?"

"Lieutenant Scott, you have no career," Colonel Gibbon said ominously.

Looking around, Meagan saw Elmer standing near Ska Luta's body, it being separated from the soldiers' bodies, preparatory to being taken to the Wind River Reservation. She walked over to stand beside him.

"Elmer, when you were talking to him, just before he died. What were you talking about?"

"I told him," Elmer said.

"You told him what?"

"I told him that he was my son."

Epilogue

Meuse-Argonne, France, October 4, 1918

The arrival of additional German troops had ended American hopes for a quick victory in the Argonne. While Montfaucon was taken, the advance proved slow and American forces were plagued by leadership and logistical issues. By October 1, the offensive had come to a halt. On October 4, Pershing ordered an assault all along the American line. This was met with ferocious resistance from the Germans with the advance measured in yards.

It was then that General John J. Pershing gave Sergeant Duff Tavish MacCallister, Jr. his orders. Bringing him back to the Château de Chaumont, Colonel George C. Marshall, who was General Pershing's chief of staff, spoke to him.

"I want to show you a couple of photographs," Marshall said.

"This is Colonel Fritz von Krueger." He put the first photograph on the table for Tavish to examine.

It was a picture of a man in jeans and a Stetson hat, leaning against the front of a Ford Model-T with his arms folded across his chest. He was wearing a holster and pistol. He looked like any of the men Tavish had known while growing up, and behind the car was a geographic feature that Tavish recognized instantly.

"That's Devil's Tower," Tavish said.

"Yes. Von Krueger has spent a lot of time in America, and he has a great fondness for the American West. He's met both Zane Grey and Owen Wister. And, before the war, he even had his own Western novel published. The title, I believe, was *Dead Man's Gun.*"

"What? No, I read that. It was written by someone named Ralph Cole," Tavish said.

Colonel Marshall chuckled. "You would be surprised at how many books you read that are written by people other than the name you see on the jacket cover. Cole is von Krueger's pen name. Here is a picture of him today."

This time the picture was of a man in a German uniform with the Pour le Mérite and oak leaf.

"Evidently the German command thinks highly of him. I see he is wearing the Blue Max," Tavish said, tapping the cross at von Krueger's neck.

"Yes," Colonel Marshall said. "I would say that he is my counterpart in that he is chief of staff to General Georg von der Marwitz, the German commander. But the difference is, if I get taken out, it will have little effect upon our army.

"But von Krueger is the mastermind behind Germany's defense. He is the one who was single-handedly responsible for our attack bogging down. It was von Krueger who directed six reserve divisions to shore up the German lines, and we believe he is drawing up plans for a counterattack that could set our timetable back by six months."

"I believe I see where this is leading," Tavish said. "You want me to shoot Colonel von Krueger."

"Yes. Will you have a problem with that? I'm not talking about your marksmanship. I mean, will you have a problem with specifically and purposely shooting one man, as opposed to shooting men in combat?"

Tavish looked up at General Pershing, who was standing a few feet away, leaning against the wall with his arms folded across his chest, not unlike the pose of von Krueger in the shadow of Devil's Tower.

Now, Tavish knew why General Pershing had told him the story of his father's shot to take out Yellow Hawk. The difference was the shot his father had taken probably saved his life, the life of his mother, Mr. Gleason, the wife of Lieutenant Scott and, pointedly, General Pershing's life. This shot, if Tavish took it, wouldn't save anyone's life. It would merely take the life of a man whose Western novel Tavish had read and enjoyed.

"Sergeant, will you have a problem with it?" Colonel Marshall repeated.

On the other hand, Tavish knew this campaign had already cost well over 20,000 American lives, and three times that many wounded. If he killed von Krueger, and it did change the battle, he could be saving thousands of lives, American and German.

Tavish nodded. "I'll do it," he said.

During the night, Tavish moved stealthily through his own lines, and up to Haudiomont, a small town in no-man's-land that was completely deserted because it had been gutted by artillery fire. All around him he could see the flashes of light and hear the sounds of heavy artillery fire as the men of both armies jerked lanyards to kill other men miles away, men they had never met, and who existed, not in their reality, but just in the artificial construct of war.

Tavish, with a scoped Springfield '03 bolt-action .30-caliber rifle in hand, began his walk to the town, his eyes sweeping back and forth checking for shadows within shadows. He moved down rue de Traversiu and across place de le Freie, in between destroyed buildings, heading to a nearby church. Most of the church had been destroyed by cannonading, but an earlier observation plane had brought back information that the towering steeple still stood.

In addition to the scoped rifle, Tavish had a powerful pair of goggles, and he knew where to find his target.

* * *

The next morning, just as the sun was half a disc above the battle-denuded eastern horizon, a soft, easy light spread across the land. The thunder of artillery was temporarily stilled, with the only sound coming from frogs and insects, which were oblivious to the death struggle of men.

Tavish checked the tactical map and saw the small house that was being used by Colonel von Krueger. Then, using his binoculars, he located it.

"Sergeant, the house is eight hundred and fifty yards from your position in the steeple tower," the briefing officer told him.

That was more than half again the distance of the shot his father had made against Yellow Hawk. But his father was using a carbine, and had to boost the powder to get the range. Tavish was shooting a rifle with an effective range of one thousand yards, and it was scoped.

"Piece of cake," he said, quietly.

Tavish watched the house through his binoculars. Then he saw his target come outside and stand on the front porch. Von Krueger was holding a cup of coffee in his left hand, while his right hand was on one of the porch posts.

Putting the binoculars down, Tavish picked up his piece and sighted through the scope. The face he saw was that of the man in the pictures. This was his man. And though he was in uniform, for just a moment, Tavish saw him, not as a German officer, but as the man standing by the Model-T Ford before Devil's Tower. He could have been a younger Elmer Gleason, or Falcon MacCallister, or Smoke or Matt Jensen, Western heroes he had known in his life. He could even be his own father.

And for a moment, Tavish couldn't pull the trigger.

"*If we can take him out, Sergeant, we can save from ten to fifteen thousand lives, American, French, and German,*" Colonel Marshall told him.

Tavish pulled the trigger. The rifle kicked back against his shoulder, but when he looked back through the scope he saw von Kruger with both hands at his neck, a surprised expression on his face, and blood oozing through his fingers. He watched until von Krueger fell. Then he climbed down from the tower, offered a quick prayer of contrition before the destroyed altar, then left the church and made his way back to his own lines before he was discovered.

From the *Chugwater News:*

CURTAIN ROLLS DOWN
On Most Stupendous
Tragedy of History

WASHINGTON, NOV. 11—President Wilson issued a formal proclamation at 10 o'clock this morning announcing that the armistice with Germany had been signed. The proclamation follows:

"My Fellow Countrymen: The armistice was signed this morning. Everything for which America fought has been accomplished. It will be our fortunate duty to assist by example, by sober friendly council and by material aid in the establishment of just democracy throughout the world.—Woodrow Wilson."

The greatest war in history ended this morning at 6 o'clock, Washington time (4 o'clock, Chugwater time) after 1,567 days of horror, during which virtually the whole civilized world has been convulsed.

Announcement of the tremendous event was made at the State Department at the Capitol at 2:45 o'clock this morning and in a few seconds was flashed throughout the continent by the telegraph wires of the Associated Press.

The terse announcement of the State Department did not tell anything of the scene at Marshal Foch's headquarters at the time the armistice was signed. It was stated, however, that at 5 o'clock Paris time the signatures of Germany's delegates were affixed to the document which blasted forever the dreams which embroiled the world in a struggle which has cost, at the very lowest estimate, 10,000,000 lives.

Although it is not known exactly what role Chugwater resident Duff Tavish MacCallister, Jr. played in the final act, he was singled out by General John J. Pershing for "particularly meritorious service."

Young MacCallister's father, local rancher Duff MacCallister, has promised a city-wide party to welcome Tavish home from the war, when that happy day arrives.

A Little Bit of William W. Johnstone
by J. A. Johnstone

William W. Johnstone was born in southern Missouri, the youngest of four children. He was raised with strong moral and family values by his minister father, and tutored by his schoolteacher mother. Despite this, he quit school at age fifteen.

"I have the highest respect for education," he says, "but such is the folly of youth, and wanting to see the world beyond the four walls and the blackboard." True to this vow, Bill attempted to enlist in the French Foreign Legion ("I saw Gary Cooper in *Beau Geste* when I was a kid and I thought the French Foreign Legion would be fun") but was rejected, thankfully, for being underage. Instead, he joined a traveling carnival and did all kinds of odd jobs. It was listening to the veteran carny folk, some of whom had been on the circuit since the late 1800s, telling amazing tales about their experiences which planted the storytelling seed in Bill's imagination.

"They were honest people, despite the bad reputation traveling carny shows had back then," Bill remembers. "Of course, there were exceptions. There was one guy named Picky, who got that name because he was a master pickpocket. He could steal a man's socks right off his feet without him knowing. Believe me, Picky got us chased out of more than a few towns."

After a few months of this grueling existence, Bill returned home and finished high school. Next came stints as a deputy sheriff in the Tallulah, Louisiana, Sheriff's Department, followed by a hitch in the U.S. Army. Then he began a career in radio broadcasting at KTLD in Tallulah that would last sixteen years. It was here that he fine-tuned his storytelling skills. He turned to writing in 1970, but it wouldn't be until 1979 that his first novel, *The Devil's Kiss,* was published. Thus began the full-time writing career of William W. Johnstone. He wrote horror (*The Uninvited*), thrillers (*The Last of the Dog Team*), even a romance novel or two. Then, in February 1983, *Out of the Ashes* was published. Searching for his missing family in the aftermath of a post-apocalyptic America, rebel mercenary and patriot Ben Raines is united with the civilians of the resistance forces and moves to the forefront of a revolution for the nation's future.

Out of the Ashes was a smash. The series would continue for the next twenty years, winning Bill three generations of fans all over the world. The series was often imitated but never duplicated. "We all tried to copy *The Ashes* series," said one publishing executive, "but Bill's uncanny ability, both then and now, to predict in which direction the political winds were blowing, brought a dead-on timeliness to the table no one else could capture." *The Ashes* series would end its run with more than thirty-four books and twenty million copies in print, making it one of the most successful men's action series in American book publishing. (*The Ashes* series also, Bill notes with a touch of pride, got him on the FBI's Watch List for its less than flattering portrayal of spineless politicians and the growing power of big government over our lives, among other things. "In that respect," says collaborator J. A. Johnstone, "Bill was years ahead of his time.")

Always steps ahead of the political curve, Bill's recent thrillers, written with J. A. Johnstone, include *Vengeance is Mine, Invasion USA, Border War, Jackknife, Remember the Alamo, Home Invasion, Phoenix Rising, The Blood of Patriots, The Bleeding Edge,* and the upcoming *Suicide Mission.*

It is with the Western, though, that Bill found his greatest success and propelled him onto both the *USA Today* and *New York Times* bestseller lists.

Bill's western series, co-authored by J. A. Johnstone, include *The Mountain Man, Matt Jensen the Last Mountain Man, Preacher, The Family Jensen, Luke Jensen Bounty Hunter, Eagles, MacCallister* (an *Eagles* spin-off), *Sidewinders, The Brothers O'Brien, Sixkiller,*

Blood Bond, The Last Gunfighter, and the upcoming new series *Flintlock* and *The Trail West.* Coming in May 2013 is the hardcover western *Butch Cassidy, The Lost Years.*

"The Western," Bill says, "is one of the few true art forms that is one hundred percent American. I liken the Western as America's version of England's Arthurian legends, like the Knights of the Round Table or Robin Hood and his Merry Men. Starting with the 1902 publication of *The Virginian* by Owen Wister, and followed by the greats like Zane Grey, Max Brand, Ernest Haycox, and of course Louis L'Amour, the Western has helped to shape the cultural landscape of America.

"I'm no goggle-eyed college academic, so when my fans ask me why the Western is as popular now as it was a century ago, I don't offer a 200-page thesis. Instead, I can only offer this: The Western is honest. In this great country, which is suffering under the yoke of political correctness, the Western harks back to an era when justice was sure and swift. Steal a man's horse, rustle his cattle, rob a bank, a stagecoach, or a train, you were hunted down and fitted with a hangman's noose. One size fit all.

"Sure, we westerners are prone to a little embellishment and exaggeration and, I admit it, occasionally play a little fast and loose with the facts. But we do so for a very good reason—to enhance the enjoyment of readers.

"It was Owen Wister, in *The Virginian,* who first

coined the phrase *'When you call me that, smile.'* Legend has it that Wister actually heard those words spoken by a deputy sheriff in Medicine Bow, Wyoming, when another poker player called him a son-of-a-bitch.

"Did it really happen, or is it one of those myths that have passed down from one generation to the next? I honestly don't know. But there's a line in one of my favorite Westerns of all time, *The Man Who Shot Liberty Valance*, where the newspaper editor tells the young reporter, 'When the truth becomes legend, print the legend.'

"These are the words I live by."

TURN THE PAGE FOR AN EXCITING PREVIEW!

The Jensen clan is William W. Johnstone's epic creation—God-fearing pioneers, bound by blood, on an untamed and beautiful land. Once more, Preacher, Smoke, and Matt are reunited in a clash of cultures and a brutal all-out fight for justice. . . .

HELL TO PAY

Smoke Jensen and his adopted son, Matt, are cooling their heels in Colorado when they are called to the Dakotas. Preacher, the legendary mountain man, is in the midst of a vicious struggle. Someone has kidnapped a proud Indian chief's daughter and grandchild. When the kidnapping turns to murder, and Preacher vanishes after clashing with a ruthless Union colonel turned railroad king. Matt sets out to infiltrate the colonel's gang of killers. Smoke seeks out the only honest citizens in the crooked town of Hammerhead. It will take brave men to blow Hammerhead wide open and force the colonel and his gunmen on a hard ride into a killing ground.

And the Family Jensen will make sure there is hell to pay. . . .

THE FAMILY JENSEN
HARD RIDE TO HELL
by William W. Johnstone
with J. A. Johnstone

Coming in May 2013 wherever Pinnacle Books are sold.

Chapter One

The two men stood facing each other. One was red, the other white, but both were tall and lean, and the stiff, wary stance in which they held themselves belied their advanced years. They were both ready for trouble, and they didn't care who knew it.

Both wore buckskins, as well, and their faces were lined and leathery from long decades spent out in the weather. Silver and white streaked their hair.

The white man had a gun belt strapped around his waist, with a holstered Colt revolver riding on each hip. His thumbs were hooked in the belt close to each holster, and you could tell by looking at him that he was ready to hook and draw. Given the necessity, his hands would flash to the well-worn walnut butts of those guns with blinding speed, especially for a man of his age.

He wasn't the only one with a menacing attitude. The Indian had his hand near the tomahawk that was thrust behind the sash at his waist. To anyone watching, it would appear that both of these men were ready to try to kill each other.

Then a grin suddenly stretched across the whiskery face of the white man, and he said, "Two Bears, you old red heathen."

"Preacher, you pale-faced scoundrel," Two Bears replied. He smiled, too, and stepped forward. The two men clasped each other in a rough embrace and slapped each other on the back.

The large group of warriors standing nearby visibly relaxed at this display of affection between the two men. For the most part, the Assiniboine had been friendly with the white men for many, many years. But even so, it wasn't that common for a white man to come riding boldly into their village as the one called Preacher had done.

Some of the men smiled now, because they had known all along what was coming. The legendary mountain man Preacher, who was famous—or in some cases infamous—from one end of the frontier to the other, had been friends with their chief Two Bears for more than three decades, and he had visited the village on occasion in the past.

The two men hadn't always been so cordial with each other. They had started out as rivals for the affections of the beautiful Assiniboine woman Raven's Wing. For Two Bears, that rivalry had escalated to the point of bitter hostility.

All that had been put aside when it became necessary for them to join forces to rescue Raven's Wing from a group of brutal kidnappers and gun-runners.* Since that long-ago time when they were forced to become allies, they had gradually become friends as well.

Preacher stepped back and rested his hands on Two Bears's shoulders.

"I hear that Raven's Wing has passed," he said solemnly.

"Yes, last winter," Two Bears replied with an equally grave nod. "It was her time. She left this world peacefully, with a smile on her face."

"That's good to hear," Preacher said. "I never knew a finer lady."

"I miss her. Every time the sun rises or sets, every time the wind blows, every time I hear a wolf howl or see a bird soaring through the sky, I long to be with her again. But when the day is done and we are to be together again, we will be. This I know in my heart. Until then . . ." Two Bears smiled again. "Until then I can still see her in the fine strong sons she bore me, and the daughters who have given me grandchildren." He nodded toward a young woman standing nearby, who stood with an infant in her arms. "You remember my youngest daughter, Wildflower?"

"I do," Preacher said, "although the last time I saw her, I reckon she wasn't much bigger'n that sprout with her."

"My grandson," Two Bears said proudly. "Little Hawk."

---

*See the novel *Preacher's Fury*

Preacher took off his battered, floppy-brimmed felt hat and nodded politely to the woman.

"Wildflower," he said. "It's good to see you again." He looked at the boy. "And howdy to you, too, Little Hawk."

The baby didn't respond to Preacher, of course, but he watched the mountain man with huge, dark eyes.

"He has not seen that many white men in his life," Two Bears said. "You look strange, even to one so young."

Preacher snorted and said, "If it wasn't for this beard of mine, I'd look just about as much like an Injun as any of you do."

Two Bears half-turned and motioned to the one of the lodges.

"Come. We will go to my lodge and smoke a pipe and talk. I would know what brings you to our village, Preacher."

"Horse, the same as usual," Preacher said as he jerked a thumb over his shoulder toward the big gray stallion that stood with his reins dangling. A large, wolflike cur sat on his haunches next to the stallion.

"How many horses called Horse and dogs called Dog have you had in your life, Preacher?" Two Bears asked with amusement sparkling in his eyes.

"Too many to count, I reckon," Preacher replied. "But I figure if a name works just fine once, there ain't no reason it won't work again."

"How do you keep finding them?"

"It ain't so much me findin' them as it is them findin' me. Somehow they just show up. I'd call it fate, if I believed in such a thing."

"You do not believe in fate?"

"I believe in hot lead and cold steel," Preacher said. "Anything beyond that's just a guess."

Preacher didn't have any goal in visiting the Assiniboine village other than visiting an old friend. He had been drifting around the frontier for more than fifty years now, most of the time without any plan other than seeing what was on the far side of the hill.

When he had first set out from his folks' farm as a boy, the West had been a huge, relatively empty place, populated only by scattered bands of Indians and a handful of white fur trappers. At that time less than ten years had gone by since Lewis and Clark returned from their epic, history-changing journey up the Missouri River to the Pacific.

During the decades since then, Preacher had seen the West's population grow tremendously. Rail lines crisscrossed the country, and there were cities, towns, and settlements almost everywhere. Civilization had come to the frontier.

Much of the time, Preacher wasn't a hundred percent sure if that was a good thing or not.

But there was no taking it back, no returning things to the way they used to be, and besides, if not for the great westward expansion that had fundamentally changed the face of the nation, he never would have met the two fine young men he had come to consider his sons: Smoke and Matt Jensen.

It had been a while since Preacher had seen Smoke and Matt. He assumed that Smoke was down in Colorado, on his ranch called the Sugarloaf near the town of Big Rock. Once wrongly branded an outlaw, Smoke Jensen was perhaps the fastest man with a gun to ever walk the West. Most of the time he didn't go looking for trouble, but it seemed to find him anyway, despite all his best intentions to live a peaceful life on his ranch with his beautiful, spirited wife, Sally.

There was no telling where Matt was. He could be anywhere from the Rio Grande to the Canadian border. He and Smoke weren't brothers by blood. The bond between them was actually deeper than that. Matt had been born Matt Cavanaugh, but he had taken the name Jensen as a young man to honor Smoke, who had helped out an orphaned boy and molded him into a fine man.

Since Matt had set out on his own, he had been a drifter, scouting for the army, working as a stagecoach guard, pinning on a badge a few times as a lawman. . . . As long as it kept him on the move and held a promise of possible adventure, that was all it took to keep Matt interested in a job, at least for a while. But he never stayed in one place for very long, and at this point in his life he had no interest in putting down roots, as Smoke had done.

Because of that, Matt actually had more in common with Preacher than Smoke did, but all three of them were close. The problem was, whenever they got together trouble seemed to follow, and it usually wasn't long before the air had the smell of gun smoke in it.

Right now the only smoke in Two Bears's lodge came from the small fire in the center of it and the pipe that Preacher and the Assiniboine chief passed back and forth. The two men were silent, their friendship not needing words all the time.

Two women were in the lodge as well, preparing a meal. They were Two Bears's wives, the former wives of his brothers he had taken in when the women were widowed, as a good brother was expected to do. The smells coming from the pot they had on the fire were mighty appetizing, Preacher thought. The stew was bound to be good.

A swift rataplan of hoofbeats came from outside and made both Preacher and Two Bears raise their heads. Neither man seemed alarmed. As seasoned veterans of the frontier, they had too much experience for that. But they also knew that whenever someone was moving fast, there was a chance it was because of trouble.

The sudden babble of voices that followed the abrupt halt of the hoofbeats seemed to indicate the same thing.

"You want to go see what that's about?" Preacher asked Two Bears, inclining his head toward the lodge's entrance.

Two Bears took another unhurried puff on the pipe in his hands before he set it aside.

"If my people wish to see me, they know where I am to be found," he said.

Preacher couldn't argue with that. But the sounds had gotten his curiosity stirred up, so he was glad when someone thrust aside the buffalo hide flap over the lodge's entrance. A broad-shouldered, powerful-looking warrior strode into the lodge, then stopped short at the sight of a white man sitting there cross-legged beside the fire with the chief.

"Two Bears, I must speak with you," the newcomer said.

"This is Standing Rock," Two Bears said to Preacher. "He is married to my daughter Wildflower."

That would make him the father of the little fella Preacher had seen with Wildflower earlier. He nodded and said, "Howdy, Standing Rock."

The warrior just looked annoyed, like he wasn't interested in introductions right now. He looked at the chief and began, "Two Bears—"

"Is there trouble?"

"Blue Bull has disappeared."

Chapter Two

Blue Bull, it turned out, wasn't a bull at all, not that Preacher really thought he was. That was the name of one of the Assiniboine warriors who belonged to this band, and he and Standing Rock were good friends.

They had been out hunting in the hills west of the village and had split up when Blue Bull decided to follow the tracks of a small antelope herd, while Standing Rock took another path. They had agreed to meet back at the spot where Blue Bull had taken up the antelope trail.

When Standing Rock returned there later, he saw no sign of Blue Bull. A couple of hours passed, and Blue Bull still didn't show up. Growing worried that something might have happened to his friend, Standing Rock went to look for him.

This part of the country was peaceful for the most part, but a man alone who ran into a mountain lion or a bear might be in for trouble. Also, ravines cut across the landscape in places, and if a pony shied at the wrong time, its rider could be tossed off and fall into one of those deep, rugged gullies.

"You were unable to find him?" Two Bears asked when his son-in-law paused in the story.

"The antelope tracks led into a narrow canyon, and so did Blue Bull's," Standing Rock replied. "The ground was rocky, and I lost the trail."

The young warrior wore a surly expression. Preacher figured that he didn't like admitting failure. Standing Rock was a proud man. You could tell that just by looking at him.

But he was genuinely worried about his friend, too. He proved that by saying, "I came back to get more men, so we can search for him. He may be hurt."

Two Bears nodded and got to his feet.

"Gather a dozen men," he ordered crisply. "We will ride in search of Blue Bull while there is still light."

Preacher stood up, too, and said, "I'll come with you."

"This is a matter for the Assiniboine," Standing Rock said, his voice stiff with dislike. Preacher didn't understand it, but the young fella definitely hadn't taken a shine to him. Just the opposite, in fact.

"Preacher is a friend to the Assiniboine and has been for more years than you have been walking this earth, Standing Rock," Two Bears snapped. "I would not ask him to involve himself in our trouble, but if he wishes to, I will not deny him."

"I just want to lend a hand if I can," Preacher said as he looked at Standing Rock. He didn't really care if the young man liked him or not. His friendship for Two Bears and for Two Bears's people was the only thing that really mattered to him here.

Standing Rock didn't say anything else. He just stared back coldly at Preacher for a second, then turned and left the lodge to gather the search party as Two Bears had told him to.

The chief looked at Preacher and said, "The hot blood of young men sometimes overpowers what should be the coolness of their thoughts."

"That's fine with me, old friend. Like I said, I just want to help."

As they left the lodge, Preacher pointed to the big cur, who had come with him to the village and went on, "Dog there is about as good a tracker as you're ever gonna find. When we get to the spot where Standin' Rock lost the trail, if you've got something that belonged to Blue Bull we can give Dog the scent and he's liable to lead us right to him."

Two Bears nodded.

"I will speak to Blue Bull's wife and make sure we take something of his with us."

Several of the warriors were getting ready to ride. That didn't take much preparation, considering that all they had to do was throw blankets over their ponies' backs and rig rope halters. Preacher had planned to spend a few days in the

Assiniboine village, but he hadn't unsaddled Horse yet so the stallion was ready to go as well.

The news of Blue Bull's disappearance had gotten around the village. A lot of people were standing nearby with worried looks on their faces as the members of the search party mounted up. Two Bears went over to talk to one of the women, who hurried off to a lodge and came back with a buckskin shirt. She was Blue Bull's wife, Preacher figured, and the garment belonged to the missing warrior.

Two Bears swung up onto his pony with the lithe ease of a man considerably younger than he really was. He gave a curt nod, and the search party set out from the village with the chief, Standing Rock, and Preacher in the lead.

Standing Rock pointed out the route for them, and they lost no time in riding into the hills where the two warriors had been hunting. Preacher glanced at the sky and saw that they had about three hours of daylight left. He hoped that would be enough time to find Blue Bull.

Of course, it was possible that nothing bad had happened to Blue Bull at all, Preacher reflected. The warrior could have gotten carried away in pursuit of the antelope and lost track of the time. They might even run into him on his way back to the village. If that happened, Preacher would be glad that everything had turned out well.

Something was stirring in his guts, though, some

instinctive warning that told him they might not be so lucky. Over the years, Preacher had learned to trust those hunches. At this point, he wasn't going to say anything to Two Bears, Standing Rock, or the other Assiniboine, but he had a bad feeling about this search for Blue Bull.

Standing Rock pointed out the tracks of the antelope herd when the search party reached them.

"You can see they lead higher into the hills," he said. "Blue Bull followed them while I went to the north. He wanted to bring one of the antelope back to the village."

"Why did you not go with him?" Two Bears asked. "Why did you go north?"

Standing Rock looked sullen again as he replied, "I know a valley up there where the antelope like to graze. I thought they might circle back to it."

Two Bears just nodded, but Preacher knew that his old friend was just as aware as he was of what had really happened here. Standing Rock had thought he could beat Blue Bull to the antelope by going a different way. Such rivalry was not uncommon among friends.

"Did you see the antelope?" Two Bears asked.

Standing Rock shook his head.

"No. My thought proved to be wrong."

Two Bears's silence in response was as meaningful and damning as anything he could have said. Standing Rock angrily jerked his pony into motion and trotted away, following the same path as the antelope had earlier.

Preacher, Two Bears, and the rest of the search party went the same way at a slower pace. Quietly, Two Bears said, "If anything happened to Blue Bull, Standing Rock will believe that it was his fault for not going with his friend."

"He wants to impress you, don't he?" Preacher said. "Must not be easy, bein' married to the chief's daughter."

"He is a good warrior, but he does not always know that."

Preacher nodded in understanding. He had always possessed confidence in himself and his abilities, and he had learned not to second-guess the decisions he made. But he had seen doubts consume other men from the inside until there was nothing left of them but empty shells.

Eventually, Standing Rock settled down a little and slowed enough for the rest of the search party to catch up to him. The antelope herd had followed a twisting path into the hills, and so had Blue Bull as he trailed them. Preacher had no trouble picking out the unshod hoofprints of the warrior's pony.

The slopes became steeper, the landscape more rugged. In the distance, the snow-capped peaks of the Rocky Mountains loomed, starkly beautiful in the light from the lowering sun. They were dozens of miles away, even though they looked almost close enough to reach out and touch. Preacher knew that Blue Bull's trail wouldn't lead that far.

The tracks brought them to a long, jagged ridge that was split by a canyon cutting through it. Standing Rock reined his pony to a halt and pointed to the opening.

"That is where Blue Bull went," he said. "The tracks vanished on the rocks inside the canyon."

"Did you follow it to the other end?" Two Bears asked.

"I did. But the tracks of Blue Bull's pony did not come out."

"A man cannot go into a place and not come out of it, one way or another."

Standing Rock looked a little offended at Two Bears for pointing that out, thought Preacher, but he wasn't going to say anything. For one thing, Two Bears was the chief, and for another, he was Standing Rock's father-in-law.

"Let's have a look," Preacher suggested. "We can give Dog a whiff of Blue Bull's shirt. He ought to be able to tell us where the fella went."

The big cur had bounded along happily beside Preacher and Horse during the search. He still had the exuberance of youth, dashing off several times to chase after small animals.

They rode on to the canyon entrance, where they stopped to peer at the ground. The surface had already gotten quite rocky, so the tracks weren't as easy to see as they had been. But Preacher noticed something immediately.

"Some of those antelope tracks are headed back out of the canyon," he said to Two Bears. "The critters went in there, then turned around and came out. They were in a hurry, too. Something must've spooked 'em."

Standing Rock said, "There are many antelope in these hills. Perhaps the tracks going the other direction were made at another time."

Preacher swung down from the saddle and knelt to take a closer look at the hoofprints. After a moment of study, he shook his head.

"They look the same to me," he said. "I think they were all made today, comin' and goin'."

He knew that wasn't going to make Standing Rock like him any better, but he was going to tell things the way he saw them to Two Bears. He had always been honest with his old friend and saw no need to change that policy now.

"What about the tracks of Blue Bull's pony?" Two Bears asked.

"He went on into the canyon," Preacher said. "Can't see that he came back out, so I agree with Standin' Rock on that. The way it looks to me, Blue Bull followed those antelope here and rode up in time to see 'em come boltin' back out. He was curious and wanted to see what stampeded 'em like that. So he rode in to find out."

"It must have been a bear," Standing Rock said. "Blue Bull would not have been so foolish."

"Blue Bull has always been curious," Two Bears said. "I can imagine him doing as Preacher has said." He looked at the mountain man. "As you would say, old friend, there is one way to find out."

"Yep," Preacher agreed. "Let Dog have Blue Bull's scent. If there's anybody who can lead us right to him, it's that big, shaggy varmint."

Chapter Three

Two Bears took out the shirt Blue Bull's wife had given him from the pouch where he had put it and handed it to Preacher. Preacher called Dog to him, knelt beside the big cur, and let Dog get a good whiff of the shirt.

"Find the fella who wore this," Preacher said. "Find him!"

Dog ran into the canyon, pausing about fifty yards in to look back at Preacher, and then resuming the hunt.

Preacher swung up onto Horse's back and nodded to Two Bears.

"He's got the scent. All we have to do is follow him."

They rode into the canyon, moving fairly rapidly to keep up with Dog. Now that they were relying on Dog's sense of smell rather than trying to follow tracks, they could set a slightly faster pace.

The canyon was about fifty yards wide, with

rocky walls that were too steep for a horse to climb, although a man might be able to. Although there were places, Preacher noted, where the walls had collapsed partially and horses might be able to pick their way up and down as long as they were careful.

Preacher frowned slightly as he spotted a shiny place on a flat rock. The mark was small, barely noticeable. Preacher knew that the most likely explanation for it was that a shod hoof had nicked the rock in the fairly recent past. Blue Bull, like the rest of the Assiniboine, would have been riding an unshod pony when he came through here.

So another rider, most likely a white man, had been in the canyon recently. Preacher couldn't be sure it was today, but the evidence pointed in that direction. The antelope herd had started through the canyon, only to encounter a man on horseback. That had startled the animals into bolting back the way they had come from.

Then, Blue Bull's curiosity aroused by the behavior of the antelope, the Assiniboine warrior had ridden into the canyon as well, and . . .

Preacher couldn't finish that thought. He had no way of knowing what had happened then. Blue Bull could have run into the same hombre. There might have even been more than one man riding through the canyon.

This was Indian land, maybe not by treaty but by tradition, and the ranchers in the area had always respected that because of the long history of peace between the whites and the Assiniboine. They had never stopped white men from crossing their hunting grounds, as long as everyone treated each other with respect. It was possible some cattle had strayed up here from one of the ranches, and cowboys from that spread had come to look for the missing stock.

However, that bad feeling still lurked in Preacher's gut. It grew even stronger when he saw Dog veer toward a cluster of rocks at the base of one of those caved-in places along the canyon's left-hand wall. There was no hesitation about the big cur's movements. He went straight to the rocks and started nosing around and pawing at them.

"Your animal has lost the scent," Standing Rock said. "There is nothing there."

"We better take a closer look," Preacher said. He glanced over at Two Bears, who nodded. The chief's face was set in grim lines, and Preacher knew that his old friend had a bad feeling about this situation, too.

The search party rode over to the side of the canyon. Nothing was visible except a pile of loose, broken rocks, some of them pretty big, but the way Dog continued to paw at the stones told Preacher most of what he needed to know.

"Move those rocks," Two Bears ordered.

"But—" Standing Rock began. He fell silent when Two Bears gave him a hard look. Scowling, Standing Rock dismounted. He went to the rocks and started lifting them and tossing them aside.

Several other warriors got down from their ponies and moved to help him.

They hadn't been working for very long before Standing Rock suddenly let out a startled exclamation and stepped back sharply as if he had just uncovered a rattlesnake.

Preacher leaned forward in the saddle to peer into the jumble of stone. He had a pretty good idea it wasn't a snake that Standing Rock had come across.

It was a foot.

Visible from the ankle down, the foot had a moccasin on it. The rest of the leg to which it was attached was hidden under the rocks.

The other warriors had recoiled from the grim discovery as well. Curtly, Two Bears ordered them to get back to moving the rocks. They did so with obvious reluctance.

Everybody knew what they were going to find. It didn't take long to uncover the rest of the body. It belonged to a young Assiniboine warrior. The rockslide that had covered him up had done quite a bit of damage to his features, but he was still recognizable. Standing Rock said in a voice choked with emotion, "It is Blue Bull."

"He must have been standing here when those rocks fell on him and killed him," one of the other men said.

"Why did he not get out of the way?" another man wanted to know.

"There must not have been time," Standing Rock said. "My . . . my friend . . ."

Deep creases appeared in Preacher's forehead as the mountain man frowned. He said to Two Bears, "Somethin' ain't right here. You mind if I take a closer look?"

"Go ahead," the chief said with a nod.

Preacher dismounted and approached the dead man. Standing Rock turned to face him. The warrior's stubborn expression made it clear he didn't want Preacher disturbing his friend's body. Like all the other tribes, the Assiniboine had their own rituals and customs for dealing with death.

"Standing Rock," Two Bears said. "Step aside."

"I won't do anything to dishonor Blue Bull," Preacher said to Standing Rock. "It's just that I don't think this is what it seems to be. Look at how he's layin' on his back with his head toward the wall and his feet toward the middle of the canyon."

"That means nothing," Standing Rock snapped.

"I think it does," Preacher said. "Let's say he came over here and was standin' facin' the wall for some reason. When those rocks came down on top of him, likely they would've knocked him facedown. If he heard the rocks start to fall and turned to try to run, not only would he be facedown, his head would be pointed toward the middle of the canyon."

"You cannot be sure about these things," Standing Rock insisted.

"Maybe not, but I think there's a pretty good

chance I'm right. What it really looks like is that somebody dragged Blue Bull over here, and then climbed up the canyon wall to start the rockslide that covered up his body."

Two Bears said, "He would have had to be unconscious or dead for that to happen."

Preacher nodded.

"Yep, more than likely. Maybe we can tell, if you let me take a good look at the body."

"He was my friend," Standing Rock said. "Stand back. I will do it."

"Sure," Preacher said. He moved one step back, but that was as far as he went. He wanted to be able to see whatever Standing Rock found.

Standing Rock knelt beside his dead friend and looked him over from head to toe.

"There are no injuries except the ones the rocks made when they fell on him," Standing Rock announced.

"Turn him over," Preacher suggested.

Standing Rock sent a hostile glance at the mountain man, but he did as Preacher said and gently took hold of Blue Bull's shoulders. Carefully, he rolled the body onto its left side.

A sharp breath hissed between Standing Rock's clenched teeth. Preacher saw what had prompted the young warrior's reaction.

A bloodstain had spread on the back of Blue Bull's shirt, just to the left of the middle of his back. In the middle of that bloodstain was a small tear in the buckskin.

"A knife did that," Preacher said. "Somebody stabbed him in the back, probably out in the middle of the canyon, and then tried to hide the body."

Two Bears said, "That would mean . . ."

"Yep," Preacher said. "This was no accident. Blue Bull was murdered."

The big man paced back and forth angrily. Despite his size, his movements had a certain dangerous, catlike quality to them. His hat was thumbed back over his blocky, rough-hewn face.

"Let me get this straight," he said. "You didn't have any choice but to kill the Indian."

"That's right, Randall," replied one of the men facing him. "He seen us. He might've gone back to his village and warned the rest of those redskins that we're up here in the hills."

The eyes of the man called Randall narrowed as he stared coldly at the two men he had sent out as scouts.

"There are several big spreads bordering the Indian land," he said. "And Two Bears doesn't mind if the punchers who ride for those ranches cut across the Assiniboine hunting grounds. You *know* that, damn it! We all do. So what in hell made you think that running into a lone warrior was going to cause a problem?"

The two men, whose names were Page and Dwyer, shuffled their feet uncomfortably. They didn't like being in dutch with the hard-bitten ramrod of this gun-hung bunch that waited in the hills for nightfall.

Thirty men, along with their horses, stood around in whatever shade they could find, watching as Randall confronted the scouts. The others were every bit as rough and menacing-looking as their leader.

Page had spoken up earlier. Now Dwyer said, "You weren't there, Randall. You didn't see how spooked that redskin acted. He knew somethin' was up, I tell you. Page and me did the only thing we could."

"And we covered his body up good and proper," Page added. "Nobody'll ever find him."

Randall said, "You seem mighty sure about that. You know that as soon as the rest of his people miss him, they'll come looking for him."

"They won't find him," Page insisted.

Randall wanted to say something else. He wanted to cuss the two fools up one way and down the other. Instead, he just jerked his head in a curt nod and said, "You'd better hope they don't. Finding one of their own warriors stabbed in the back is likely to spook them a lot more than running across a couple of riders would have."

Earlier, when the two men had come back from scouting the approaches to the Assiniboine village, they had brought an Indian pony with them, trailing from a rope lead held by Dwyer. When Randall had demanded to know where the animal came from, they had hemmed and hawed around for a minute and tried to say they found it, but it hadn't taken long for his cold stare to get the truth out of them.

They had run into a warrior in a canyon that cut through a ridge several miles from the Assiniboine village. The Indian kept asking questions, the scouts claimed, so Dwyer had distracted him while Page got behind him and put a knife in his back. Then they had dragged him over to the side of the canyon and caved in part of the wall on him. Chances were they were right about nobody finding the body, at least not in time to have any effect on the mission that had brought Randall and his men to this part of the territory.

With the matter settled for the time being, unsatisfactory though it might be, Randall turned and stalked away to give himself a chance to control his anger. He looked up at the sky.

In a couple of more hours, it would be dark.

And once night had fallen, he and his men could ride down out of these hills and do what they had been sent here to do. That thought put a faint smile on Randall's rugged face.

The prospect of killing always did.

THE EAGLES SERIES BY
WILLIAM W. JOHNSTONE

__**Eyes of Eagles**
0-7860-1364-8 **$5.99**US/**$7.99**CAN

__**Dreams of Eagles**
0-7860-6086-6 **$5.99**US/**$7.99**CAN

__**Talons of Eagles**
0-7860-0249-2 **$5.99**US/**$6.99**CAN

__**Scream of Eagles**
0-7860-0447-9 **$5.99**US/**$7.50**CAN

__**Rage of Eagles**
0-7860-0507-6 **$5.99**US/**$7.99**CAN

__**Song of Eagles**
0-7860-1012-6 **$5.99**US/**$7.99**CAN

__**Cry of Eagles**
0-7860-1024-X **$5.99**US/**$7.99**CAN

__**Blood of Eagles**
0-7860-1106-8 **$5.99**US/**$7.99**CAN

Available Wherever Books Are Sold!

Visit our website at **www.kensingtonbooks.com**